Their eyes met. He d... a ... double take, as if he were surprised to see her. As if he *recognized* her.

She jolted back behind the partition.

He couldn't have recognized her. Delphinia had never met him before. He was not the kind of man to whom one would forget being introduced. She'd never seen him from afar, either. A Greek god with a scar on one eyebrow and a tattoo on one arm could not walk around the campus unnoticed.

But had he seen *her* before? She'd been reading by a window earlier. Perhaps he'd noticed her. Her cheeks felt warm at the thought.

Romeo and Juliet continued their scene. Delphinia let it restore some order to her mind. She knew the lines, the play, the students. She knew herself and her role in life. She was who she was, the brainy girl who loved books. She wasn't the kind to catch a passionate man's attention, not like Juliet. She wasn't anything like the alluring heroine in her paperback novel.

She cleared her throat. She sat up straighter...and peeked around the partition.

He was still looking at her. That handsome face, that strong physique, all that calm confidence was zeroed in on her.

He'd *noticed* her.

MASTERSON, TEXAS:
Where you come to learn about love!

Dear Reader,

"Opposites attract" is a truism we've all heard. But in a romantic relationship, what if only one of the two people knew they were opposites? That's the reality for the couple in this book. Our heroine believes she is madly in love with a man who is just like her. Most important, they are both book lovers. When they're together, the physical chemistry is mutual, too—and hard to resist!

The hero, however, is certain they are polar opposites. She's got a PhD in English; he never graduated from high school. She's the fourth generation of a family whose history is full of college presidents; he hasn't seen his mother since he was a teenager. Most important, she is a respected professor at the university, and he is a convicted felon. He's served his time, but the record will stay with him for life.

So, which person has the correct perception? Is the heroine right, and they are perfect for each other? Or is the hero correct that if he loves her, then he won't burden her with a man whose past always comes back to drag him down?

You'll have to read the book for the answer, but I can give you a big hint: the author sincerely believes that true love conquers all.

I'd love to hear what you think. You can find me on Facebook easily, or you can contact me through my website, www.carocarson.com. I look forward to hearing from you.

Cheers,

Caro Carson

The Bartender's Secret

Caro Carson

HARLEQUIN
SPECIAL
EDITION

HARLEQUIN® SPECIAL EDITION™

ISBN-13: 978-1-335-89439-7

The Bartender's Secret

Recycling programs for this product may not exist in your area.

This edition published by arrangement with Harlequin Books S.A.

For questions and comments about the quality of this book, please contact us at CustomerService@Harlequin.com.

Harlequin Enterprises ULC
22 Adelaide St. West, 40th Floor
Toronto, Ontario M5H 4E3, Canada
www.Harlequin.com

Printed in U.S.A.

Despite a no-nonsense background as a West Point graduate, army officer and Fortune 100 sales executive, **Caro Carson** has always treasured the happily-ever-after of a good romance novel. As a RITA® Award–winning Harlequin author, Caro is delighted to be living her own happily-ever-after with her husband and two children in Florida, a location that has saved the coaster-loving theme-park fanatic a fortune on plane tickets.

Books by Caro Carson

Harlequin Special Edition

American Heroes

The Lieutenants' Online Love
The Captains' Vegas Vows
The Majors' Holiday Hideaway
The Colonels' Texas Promise

Texas Rescue

Not Just a Cowboy
A Texas Rescue Christmas
Following Doctor's Orders
Her Texas Rescue Doctor
A Cowboy's Wish Upon a Star
How to Train a Cowboy

Montana Mavericks: What Happened at the Wedding?

The Maverick's Holiday Masquerade

The Doctors MacDowell

Doctor, Soldier, Daddy
The Doctor's Former Fiancée

The Bachelor Doctor's Bride

Visit the Author Profile page at Harlequin.com for more titles.

This book about an English professor must be dedicated to the teachers and professors who brightened my school years with their love of books. Thank you, Mrs. Feintuch and Mrs. Hughes, for introducing me to *Romeo and Juliet* and *Othello* in high school. I could not have written this book without you! And to my professors at West Point, especially Colonel Freeman, Colonel Stromberg and Colonel Hoy, thank you for every great book that opened a new window to the world beyond our rockbound highland home.

Chapter One

The first time he saw her, she was reading a book.

Connor McClaine's customers often read books in his pub. The Tipsy Musketeer was located roughly twenty yards from the edge of Masterson University's campus, so it wasn't unusual to serve a hand-drawn Guinness to a student who was studying Socrates or sociology.

This reader was...different.

In the quiet of the Tuesday afternoon lull, Connor took his time polishing the pub's antique brass taps as the woman turned another page. There was an intriguing grace to the motion of her index finger, a simple touch of light pressure on the paper, a slide to the left to reveal two more pages full of black type.

She fell still once more. Only her eyes moved as she

devoured the fresh lines. Her hand didn't waver as she held the book with its pages tilted toward the window. The Texas sunshine was constant, golden, steadily illuminating the deep brown of her hair, the dark wood of his pub's floor. The ivory pages of her book reflected the light up to her throat, so the picture she made had the kind of otherworldly illumination one saw in paintings. She made a beautiful picture.

Traditionally, Irish pubs were dark shelters from a harsher outside world, and the Tipsy Musketeer, despite being located in Central Texas, was as traditional as an Irish pub could be. For relief from the often desertlike heat, the Victorian-era building's heavy shutters had kept out the sunlight for over 130 years. But its proprietor now was Connor McClaine, and he'd once been forced to live for precisely 180 days in a building with no windows, so the Tipsy Musketeer's green shutters were now fastened open—permanently.

Their shade was no longer necessary. The building might be historic, but its air-conditioning units were modern and efficient. It had taken most of the past ten years, virtually his entire adult life, but Connor had brought this building to a place where he was assured there would always be windows and light and breathable air. He had everything he needed, as long as everything stayed as it was—his pub, his life, unchanging.

The reading woman stayed just as she was. Unchanging. A work of art.

Connor moved from the brass taps to the mahogany bar, polishing as he drank in the shades of whiskey in her hair. One hundred shades of brown—that was how many different colors Rembrandt had used to paint a woman's hair. Connor had read that in an art history book he'd found on the wrong shelf of a prison library. He'd wanted to see a Rembrandt in real life ever since.

Here she was.

With one graceful fingertip, she turned the page, read another line.

She laughed, a single squeak of surprise.

Connor stopped in mid-stroke, startled that a work of art had made a sound. She continued coming to life, setting the book down, resting her elbow on the table, her chin on her hand. Her smile lingered over something she'd read, a humorous twist she'd hadn't expected. Connor had a burning desire to know...

To know...

Not her, of course. He already knew women like her—educated, peaceful, lovely. Women who lived calm lives. Women who'd never been denied windows and daylight. Women who were out of his league, fortunately for them.

He didn't begrudge them their lovely lives. They'd done nothing to hurt him, after all, and the world would be a grim place if everyone had to come from the same darkness he had. There was only one common denominator between Connor and this woman: he could read whatever she read. He could share that one piece of a lovelier, lighter life.

What was she reading?

She was in his establishment. He could step out from behind the bar, walk over to that table and ask her if she needed anything. He'd see the book cover. He'd know something about her. If he read that same book later, he'd know a lot more about her. He'd try to guess exactly which page, which paragraph had made her laugh out loud.

Her smile faded. With one finger, she pushed the book a few inches away from herself.

Ah, he knew more about her already. He understood that feeling. A book could carry him away to another place, putting him in a different mood—a better place, a better mood. But always, the book would end, and life would resume. Depending on how bad life was at the moment, the return to reality could feel like a hangover, the price one paid for a brief escape. When books had let him escape a windowless prison, the hangover had been vicious.

Connor turned away from the picture-perfect woman and pitched his polishing cloth in the laundry bin with last night's bar towels. She was not a painting for him to analyze. She wasn't here for his viewing pleasure. But her hair was whiskey and her throat was lovely, and he could ask her that most basic question of bartenders everywhere: *What's your pleasure?*

He wanted to know.

He rested his forearms on the bar and waited, savoring the moment as he watched his living Rembrandt, imagining he understood how she felt. She'd glance his way any second now. *What's your pleasure?*

"Connor, save me." A different woman stuck her head in his line of sight, a teenager who read books only when required to by her teachers. For the ten years he'd known her, Bridget Murphy had read only school assignments, and for ten years, Connor had been pushing her to do her schoolwork. She'd been nine when the previous owner, Mr. Murphy, had hired Connor, who'd been a miserable nineteen. Bridget had always gotten in the way when Connor had been learning the ropes, but she was the niece of Mr. Murphy. Connor had always figured she had more of a right to be at Murphy's Tipsy Musketeer than he did. In any case, Connor would never say a bad word against a Murphy.

"Just shoot me," she said.

"Tempting, but I can't do both. Shoot you or save you? You have to decide."

Bridget plopped herself onto a barstool, the one directly between himself and the intriguing woman, blocking his view. That was Bridget. She would have made a perfect pest of a little sister, had Connor had a family. With a dramatic groan, she plunked her red head on the bar.

He spoke to the top of her head. "A word of advice. When you turn *twenty-one*, two years from now, and you can legally drink, be sure to avoid cheap booze at wild college parties, or else you'll get a hangover that feels exactly the way you're feeling right now."

"Devil take ye and yer best dog," she muttered into the burnished wood, in a fine approximation of her great-uncle's Irish brogue. "If you're so sure this is a hangover, you could make me one of your hangover cures."

With Bridget's head out of his way, Connor could see the woman again. She was entirely back in this world now, tucking her book into a cloth book bag. Any second, she'd look at him.

What's your pleasure?

"Pretty please?" Bridget popped her head up, blocking his view again.

Connor came just that close to growling in annoyance.

"What? What I'd do?"

"Nothing." Connor began making a hangover cure, glancing toward the woman in the window as he did. She'd stood and was heading toward the restrooms, book bag on her shoulder. Her chiffon skirt swished around her knees with each step. Connor scooped ice into a glass and watched as her hair turned from glowing mahogany to nearly ebony as she moved out of the sunlight.

"Who was that?" Bridget asked.

"Who?"

"That woman whose butt you're checking out instead of saving me."

Connor poured tomato juice into the glass and shrugged. "A customer. I'm not checking out her butt." *I'm checking out the swing of her hair.*

Bridget turned around to check out the now empty table. "Yeah?"

And her legs.

"Your customer doesn't have a drink or anything."

"I haven't asked her what she wants yet. She's been reading."

Bridget rolled her eyes as only a college drama major

could. "People can drink and read at the same time. You could've interrupted her. She might have appreciated it."

"She was reading intently, the way your professors want you to." He added three dashes of Tabasco to the glass.

"Intently? You were watching her read *intently*? That's so weird."

And a fourth dash.

"You were watching her walk away pretty intently, too."

"I said she was reading intently. I wasn't watching her intently as she read. Syntax, Bridget. It matters."

"Syntax, Bridget," she repeated, in an admittedly fine approximation of his patronizing tone. "You should be an English teacher, not a bar owner. You'd meet more women who read *intently,* instead of the kind that get drunk and try to jump your bones. How does a bookworm proposition you? 'Hey, hottie. Let's get naked and talk about literature.' Does size matter when it comes to books?"

Connor tossed Bridget a lemon wedge. "Suck on that."

"Hey—"

"It's good for you. Vitamin C." He squeezed two more lemon wedges into the glass, gave it a stir, then slid it across the bar with just enough force that it stopped in front of Bridget.

She glared at it. "You forgot the vodka."

"That's for alcohol-induced hangovers. Since you're underage, I know you weren't drinking alcohol last night, so you don't need it this afternoon."

"Uncle Murphy says you need the hair of the dog that bit you."

"I'm not losing my liquor license by serving vodka to a college sophomore. Drink your juice."

The woman who'd been reading walked back into the main pub area. She'd look his way any second now, maybe even stop at the bar to get a drink to carry back to her table.

What's your pl—

"Hey, boss." This time a young man stuck his head in Connor's way, speaking with all the energy and volume of a college student who was *not* hungover. "Everyone's on their way. A few texted they'd be late, but they're still coming."

Kristopher Newell was a junior at Masterson and one of Connor's bartenders. The state of Texas didn't require bartenders to be twenty-one—employees could serve alcohol at eighteen, as long as they didn't drink any—but Connor required it. Kristopher had bused tables for a full semester, an eternity for a college student, until he'd turned twenty-one and Connor had let him move behind the bar. Like Mr. Murphy before him, Connor appreciated good employees and took care of them. No revolving door here, even in a college town. Not until they graduated and moved on to the rest of their lives, diplomas in their hands.

"How'd your test go?" Connor asked. Taking care of his employees meant being sure they had their priorities straight.

Kristopher's buoyancy dropped a notch. "Pretty well.

Not as well as I'd hoped. But hey, if I ace this Shakespeare thing, it'll balance out."

There was a small stage in one corner of the pub, used by countless musicians since before Connor had been born. This afternoon, it would be used by students to rehearse a theater course assignment. Connor had offered it up, because it was one way he could ensure Kristopher and Bridget actually practiced for their Shakespeare project. The pub was usually empty between the lunch crowd and happy hour on a Tuesday in March, anyway.

But not this Tuesday. The woman by the window had come here to read. Maybe Miss Rembrandt had hoped the pub would be an oasis away from the students who thronged every other business on Athos Avenue. Generally, it was; the Tipsy Musketeer checked IDs. It was common knowledge around campus that this pub would serve the bread but not the beer to those under twenty-one, so the Musketeer drew an older clientele: the professors rather than the students, the coaches rather than the athletes, the university president rather than the fraternity president.

She didn't strike him as a college student. She was young, but not nineteen. *Ms.* Rembrandt, then. College students could be any age, but Masterson University was a traditional campus, with a football stadium and red-bricked dormitories. Most Musketeers were kids who entered straight from high school and graduated four years later at an outdoor cap-and-gown affair. It was very likely this woman had come into the pub seeking a student-free zone.

She stopped at the same table and pulled her book out once more. When Connor took her drink order, he'd warn her that a dozen college kids were about to arrive and start emoting in sixteenth-century English.

If you're brave enough to stay, your drink is on the house. What's your pleasure?

"I've got this." Kristopher jogged over to Ms. Rembrandt. "What can I get you?"

Great. Connor had hired the most conscientious, eager twenty-one-year-old in town. Kristopher wasn't even on the clock until five.

Kristopher's enthusiastic *What can I get you?* was less evocative of an earlier time period than *What's your pleasure?* which Connor had picked up from Mr. Murphy, along with the man's string of Irish curses that all began with "the devil." Mr. Murphy had a long and creative list of things he wanted the devil to do.

Connor had every excuse to gaze at Ms. Rembrandt now, because he was waiting for Kristopher to turn and relay her drink order. Any second now. If Kris stopped monopolizing the woman's attention.

She had an energy about her. Her navy sweater and that light blue skirt were not as sedate as she'd probably intended them to be. When she reached back to the table and slid her book behind herself, her sweater hugged her curves.

Her smile was more than polite; it was genuine. Then she laughed, a bright sound that filled the space between them. He saw the light in her face, *heard* bright light in her voice. Connor sucked in a breath. He wanted to know...

To know…

He didn't want to know what book she'd read. He wanted to know *her*. He wanted to know where she was from, what she was doing, where she was going.

He could make small talk as easily as he made cocktails. He could find out all about her.

It would lead to nothing.

This pub was a fantasy world. An Irish pub needed a publican, an owner who treated everyone as if they'd arrived as welcome guests to his own home. It was the role Connor had taken over from Mr. Murphy when he'd bought the business.

It was a role he never stopped playing, even after the pub was closed. If he accepted the invitation of a woman who'd lingered until quitting time, he knew she expected him to be the same man in her bed as the man she'd flirted with among the mirrors and mahogany. It was better for him to be that man, best to keep the fantasy intact.

The real him wouldn't be so welcomed by women, nor so successful in business. Connor kept his secrets. Nothing exotic or intriguing, merely that he was an ex-con, a common dropout who'd gotten caught riding in a stolen car at nineteen. Joyriding was a felony in Texas. He'd stood in handcuffs before a judge and pled guilty.

That felony conviction still affected his life. It always would. He hadn't been able to get a driver's license for almost two years. He hadn't been able to take over for Mr. Murphy until enough years had passed that the government would allow him to apply for a liquor license. He'd had to publish his intent to get the license in the newspaper twice, to give the public time to object to a convicted felon operating a bar in their town.

Nobody had objected. Connor doubted many had read the single sentence in the local newspaper. That was best for business. Nothing about his past suited the image he needed to maintain as the proprietor of the Tipsy Musketeer.

Nothing about the real him would be interesting to a woman who looked like a Rembrandt and smiled like the girl next door. He could get to know her, but the most that might come of it was a warm night in her bed as her charming bartender.

Bridget polished off her juice, gave Connor one more dirty look, in case he wasn't aware how she felt about its lack of vodka, and headed toward the stage. The main door was close to it, and the cluster of guys who walked in were unmistakably students, thinking nothing of hollering *Yo, Kristopher* across the room.

Connor kept an eye on Ms. Rembrandt to see how she'd react to the student invasion. The second Kristopher looked toward his friends, she groped around the table behind herself until she grabbed her book and stuffed it into her bag. She asked Kristopher something. He gestured toward the door, and she headed for the exit.

That was it. She was leaving.

Connor tapped a stainless-steel keg with the toe of his boot. It sounded like there was next to nothing left in it. He ducked beneath the bar to disconnect the line to the empty keg. He heard the door open and close, more raucous students coming in as she went out. Customers came and went all the time. It didn't matter.

But it felt like it did.

Connor pulled out the keg, then tilted it on its edge to roll it out from behind the long bar, stopping under the ornate iron chandelier that had been converted from candles to kerosene to gas to electricity. It still amazed him that he lived here now, surrounded by beauty that had lasted more than a century. When he finished a book, the hangover was no longer terrible, because Connor didn't dread returning to this world.

But Ms. Rembrandt had not enjoyed returning to hers. She'd smiled at Kristopher. She'd laughed—God, that bright laugh—but Connor had seen that moment of sadness. He should have talked to her. He was a bartender, after all. Hangover cures were part of the repertoire.

Doesn't matter. It wouldn't have led to anything, anyway.

No, but he could have discovered the title of the book with the blue cover, the one she'd stuffed into her bag like she'd stolen it. He would have known her, then, in his own way.

Devil take it to hell and back. Twice.

Connor hefted the keg to chest height and headed for the storeroom, leaving his fantasy of a beautiful world behind.

Chapter Two

The first time she saw him, he was carrying a keg.

Why Delphinia found this so fascinating, she couldn't say, although it was a fairly rare occurrence in her life to see a man hefting a stainless-steel keg—in fact, she'd never seen a man heft a keg anywhere, ever.

The sight stopped her dead in her tracks. The keg wasn't light; the muscles in the man's arms bulged in hard curves as he lifted it high against his chest. As he walked away from her, the strong flex of his back and shoulder muscles were apparent beneath the snug, black T-shirt he wore. Snug jeans, too. She watched him until he disappeared around a corner.

He did not look like most men she knew. She was a professor, and in her corner of academia, the male professors were studious and svelte. The students she taught tended to be, too. Not many jocks took upper-level elective courses in literature. But that man? His body looked like the kind of bare male torso one saw on a titillating cover designed to sell a racy paperback.

Kind of like the one she'd just stuffed into her bag.

"Here's your ice water, Dr. Dee. You're sure you don't want a lemon slice in it?"

Delphinia forced her attention back to Kristopher, the student she was here to help. "I'm certain, thank you. Plain is good."

She hoped he hadn't seen her checking out the bartender's body. At least she was certain he hadn't seen her novel. She'd gotten that off the table and back into her bag without anyone seeing her do it.

She shouldn't have to hide any book, but her parents were going to be horrified when she got the courage to tell them she'd begun teaching Shakespeare to drama students on the side. If her parents heard that Dr. Delphinia Ray, their progeny and prodigy, had been caught reading a mass-market paperback at a bar this afternoon, they'd probably disown her.

"It's not three yet, but a lot of us are here already." Kristopher looked around. "Bridget's here somewhere. I saw her when I came in."

Bridget received a special mention, did she? In the middle of the fall semester, Delphinia had taken over a Shakespeare course at Bryan Community College in the town just west of Masterson, when the regular teacher had gone on maternity leave. Two nights a week, as Delphinia had guided everyone through *A Midsummer's Night Dream*, she'd noticed how often Kristopher and Bridget snuck glances at one another during class, how they abruptly looked away when they happened to catch one another staring, how Kristopher nearly blushed, how Bridget struggled to look unaffected instead of giddy.

Delphinia knew living, breathing romance when she saw it—no matter what her parents believed about her. The boy was smitten.

"Bridget and I could start *Romeo and Juliet* now, instead of waiting for everyone else." Kristopher turned toward the empty bar. "Where'd she go?"

I don't know. I was watching the man in the tight black T.

"She probably went to freshen up," Delphinia said, but Kristopher turned toward the restrooms, cupped his hands around his mouth and belted out, "Bridget!" He sounded like a drill sergeant, not a lover.

Bridget walked in, waiting until she was close to Kris before cupping her hands around her mouth and yelling at him as loudly as he'd yelled across the pub. "What is your malfunction?"

Delphinia cringed.

"Sorry, Dr. Dee. I didn't recognize you from behind earlier, or I would have said *hi*. Hi."

"All done with the drink you nursed along for ten minutes?" Kristopher asked Bridget. "Some of us can't lounge around after an all-night party."

Delphinia looked between the two of them with a sinking heart. Her parents were right: she had no radar. Her parents didn't use slang like *radar*, though. Their daughter had *no ability whatsoever to gauge roman-*

tic attraction when it didn't occur between the covers of a book.

They meant that affectionately. Her parents enjoyed teasing her because she'd been oblivious to the attentions of an eligible, suitable, new professor at the start of the school year. She'd met him at the annual dinner for new faculty members. Vincent Talbot, JD, PhD, had been new to the College of Law. She, Delphinia Ray, PhD, was not new, so she'd thought nothing of it when the seating chart placed them side by side. That was how it was always done, every year: a new professor was seated next to someone who was already part of the Masterson University faculty.

It wasn't until she and her parents had returned to their home that she'd been informed that Vincent Talbot was markedly interested in her. He'd requested to sit beside her, in fact. Her parents knew this, because her father and mother were Dr. Archibald Ray and Dr. Rhea Acanthus-Ray, respectively, the dean of Masterson University's College of Liberal Arts and the chair of the Department of English, also respectively.

In addition to being a professor, Vincent Talbot was a lawyer. Tall and well-groomed, too. Most suitable, her parents had agreed. Hadn't Delphinia found Vincent charming?

Not really. He'd been determined to make her agree that the banquet's red wine was too fruity. She'd pretended that her ninth sip had revealed the truth of his position, so he'd stop. *Yes, notes of blueberry. I do see what you mean.*

She hadn't caught him sneaking glances her way

during the dinner. He'd never blushed. She'd never felt giddy. Shouldn't a romance begin like that?

Judging from her parents' amusement, no. Love in real life was not as dramatic and exciting as it was in the literary worlds she inhabited. Shakespeare was her favorite. Everything was colorful and passionate in Shakespeare's plays, from the courtships to the sword fights. She loved teaching them.

Too bad she wasn't allowed to.

Mother did not care for Shakespeare. The plays had been written for the common man. Four hundred years later, they were still common, easily reworked into movies, even comic books. The revered complexity of Hamlet could be reduced to a Disney-drawn lion cub. That said it all, in Mother's opinion.

Therefore, EN313 Victorian Prose and Essays was Delphinia's assigned course. She spent her days lecturing on the Victorian-era men who'd believed the world needed to know their personal opinions about the superiority of industry over agriculture, as well as the men who'd written lengthy rebuttals that championed shepherds over steelworkers. She spent her nights propped up in her bed, grading student essays about the essayists. Was it any wonder the youngest Dr. Ray hadn't recognized that the new Dr. Talbot found her fascinating?

Or that she'd been so wrong about the two students who were bickering before her right this second?

Delphinia interrupted. "Which scene from *Romeo and Juliet* did you select?"

Kristopher heaved a sigh and rolled his eyes. "She

wants to do the balcony scene, because she's dying to use the balcony."

"It's because I am an actress, so I want to perform one of the most famous scenes ever written," Bridget said through clenched teeth. "It's not because the balcony is cool."

Delphinia looked up. The balcony was actually very cool. A second-story loft ran the length of one wall. The wood railing would make a great balcony from which Juliet could confess her love to Romeo, below. His passion would enable Romeo to scale the wall of his enemy's home to reach his lover for the kiss that would seal their fate.

Delphinia gauged the balcony's height. Realistically, it would require passion plus a significant amount of upper-body strength. *Oh, our Delphinia, always so pragmatic.*

Her gaze drifted from the balcony to the corner around which the bartender in the black T-shirt had disappeared. Shakespeare had written Romeo as a physical role, requiring the character to dance at a masquerade, to scale garden walls, to break up street brawls. Passion required more than pretty words. It should inspire a man to use his body, to take action, to carry a keg—

A keg. What was *wrong* with her?

"Where do you want to go?" Kristopher asked.

"What do you mean?" Delphinia didn't want to go peek around that corner. Really.

"The booths face the stage, but they're about as comfortable as sitting in a church pew."

Directly across from the stage were three partitioned

seating areas. Delphinia stepped closer and ran her hand down the dark wood of a carved post. "Gorgeous. I wonder when this place was built. It's clearly Victorian, but—"

"1889," Bridget said. "I know that because my uncle owned this place for decades."

"It's also written on the sign," Kristopher said, giving Bridget a smirk before calling everyone over. "This is the Dr. Dee I told you about. She taught Shakespeare at BCC last semester. If you haven't taken Intro to Shakespeare yet, take it at BCC instead of MU. It's much, much easier."

"Because she does such a good job explaining what's going on in the plays. Not because she's an easy teacher." Bridget smacked Kristopher on the arm. "You dweeb."

Delphinia would have been more amused, but she was too anxious that one of the other students might recognize that Dr. Dee from BCC was also Dr. Ray from Masterson U.

"I just meant you're the best, Dr. Dee. It's nice of you to help us out."

She'd identified herself as Dr. D. Ray on the first papers she'd graded at the community college. Kristopher had picked up on the Dr. D and left off the Ray, and the nickname had stuck. Conveniently.

Delphinia couldn't resist sitting in one of the vintage booths. Kristopher's church pew was actually one long bench, perhaps fifteen feet long, divided into three alcoves by wood partitions. Unlike a modern cubicle, the walls were tall enough that, even standing, no one would see over them, unless they were on the MU basketball team. Two extra chairs and a small table fit in each section. She chose the center alcove and sat down with relief.

So far, so good. None of the students had recognized her, and she was sheltered here from anyone who might walk by and look in the picture windows.

Cowards die many times before their deaths.

Could a more dramatic Shakespeare quote pop into her head? She would tell her parents that she was moonlighting at BCC if it were relevant. It wasn't, not yet. If she applied to teach Masterson's Shakespeare electives, then a discussion of her experience at the community college would be cogent.

Not if. *When.* She would apply. Someday.

Her parents had assumed her absences from the house every Tuesday and Thursday evening were standing dinner dates with Vincent. She hadn't corrected them. They believed she was adding passion to her life, and she was…to her professional life.

She rejected the premise that her personal life was hopeless. She hadn't always been so inept when it came to dating. High school had been lonely, of course, because she'd been the youngest person in every class, but she'd finished it in three years. Once she was far from home, at her beloved alma mater in New England, she'd made the shocking discovery that there were a lot of people who liked her. She'd felt so normal—and she'd dated boys without needing anyone to point out their interest in her at all.

But at nineteen, she'd graduated with her bachelor's

degree, and her parents had insisted that she return to Masterson for her master's degree and PhD. There'd been no more dormitory taco parties, no book clubs, no time to date while she completed her thesis at a record pace. Centuries-old literary figures had been her main companions during her twenties.

She was twenty-nine now. She'd begin her thirties with Professor Vincent Talbot by her side. He was perfect for her. She would feel a spark of passion for him at some point. She would.

She ran one finger over a detailed rosette carved into the back of the bench. How many passionate stories could that rose tell? How many declarations of love had been made right here on this bench?

Her story wouldn't be one of them, even if—no, when—she and Vincent took their relationship to the next level, because Vincent would never take her to a pub. He preferred the cocktail hours her parents hosted at their home for visiting professors, guest lecturers and the occasional politician. Delphinia had been attending such soirees since the fifth grade, when her parents had expected her to greet the guest of honor politely and then excuse herself to go read in her bedroom. Silently.

Now, twenty years later, she greeted the guests of honor politely and then stood next to Vincent for the entire evening. Silently.

Her gaze drifted to the corner where the man in the black T-shirt had disappeared.

"O, Romeo, Romeo. Wherefore art thou Romeo?"

Bridget's plea came floating down from the balcony. On the stage, Kristopher threw up his hands in disgust. "Not yet. I say my lines first."

Not yet, not yet.

Someday.

Chapter Three

Connor carried the empty keg toward the storeroom, down the hall that marked the end of the original building and the start of the addition Mr. Murphy had added in the 1980s, but Connor's thoughts stayed with the woman who'd preferred her book to her real life.

She's gone. So are her problems.

Mr. Murphy had looked very serious—as serious as a man who looked like a wizened leprechaun could look—when he'd warned Connor that he'd burn out if he couldn't let other people's sadness roll off his back.

You poured them a pint, they poured out their problems to you, and that's the end of it. You made them feel better for a moment. That is what a pub can do, but that is all a pub can do. Don't be taking everyone's sad tales out of this pub with you. Leave them here when the workday is through.

Easier said than done, some nights—and this afternoon.

Connor set down the keg and unlocked the door to the storage room. The floor was cement. The lighting was fluorescent. There were no windows.

Mr. Murphy had guessed, as he'd guessed so many things about Connor, that this room was a constant reminder of the one place where Connor never wanted to be again.

But you control the doors here, lad. And what do we lock within them? The ale we sell to keep this roof over our heads. To a true businessman like myself, this room is more beautiful than the ones we show our guests. It will be the same for you one day, or my father never called me Seamus Murphy.

The day Mr. Murphy had sold the Tipsy Musketeer to Connor, they'd conducted a formal walk-through with the real estate attorney. It was in this room that Mr. Murphy had passed him the keys to the kingdom. It hadn't been accidental, Connor was certain.

Connor kicked a wedge under the door to keep it open. Mr. Murphy couldn't be right about everything: Connor still hated this room.

After he rolled a full keg into the hallway, he dislodged the doorstop with his heel. A heavy-duty dolly waited in its usual place by the door. His employees used it to move kegs, but Connor did not. A full keg weighed 150 pounds, but if Connor couldn't carry a 150-pound steel barrel into the bar, then he couldn't escort a 200-pound troublemaker out of the bar, either, before anyone might have a cause to call the police. Now and then, *escort* might be a euphemism for *lift him to his toes by his shirt collar and make him scurry along,* but never, in all ten years that he'd been here, had Connor thrown a punch.

He never would. Texas law would normally be on the side of a property owner who defended himself in a fight, but as a felon, Connor wasn't willing to bet an assault charge would go easily for him. Many a lawyer had sat at the bar to celebrate the dismissal of a client's case, but the client had still waited in jail before that dismissal. That was not going to happen to Connor. Not again.

Connor dead-lifted the heavy keg and returned to the bar where he'd spend the rest of his day—and probably the rest of all his days—making sure everyone else enjoyed the trouble-free world he created for them in the Tipsy Musketeer.

He hoped *everyone* would include the woman with her secret sadness and the blue book she hid. If she came back, he would talk to her, and maybe she would stay a little while, absorb some of the safe and friendly atmosphere, then leave her sadness here. It was what a good pub could do for a person.

It was all Connor could do for her.

If she came back.

Someday.

"But soft! What light through yonder window breaks?"

Delphinia listened to Romeo's lines. Kristopher said them breathlessly, a young man so ready for the most exciting thing to happen in his life. Romeo knew he should rein in his passion for the woman he'd been instantly attracted to, but that didn't mean he could.

"I am too bold." Every action was driven by a burning lust.

The bartender walked back into the bar, carrying another keg.

Delphinia tried not to stare, but that man was impossible to *not* see. This keg was clearly heavier, because his muscles weren't just flexed; they were working. Hard.

Still, the man moved with confidence, as if he lugged kegs around all the time and knew exactly where he was going and what he was doing and how much he could handle.

Delphinia perched on the edge of the bench so she could see farther past the partition. His path took him out of her line of sight.

She leaned forward a little bit more. He walked behind the bar and set the barrel down, then he straightened, facing away from her, stretching the muscles in his back and shaking out his arms. He began to turn toward the stage.

She sat back quickly.

Kristopher forgot his next line. Delphinia would have prompted him, but she'd lost track of what was going on, too.

Bridget shouted Kristopher's line from the balcony. "'Her vestal livery is but sick and green,' you dweeb."

Kristopher picked up his part once more. The next few lines about Juliet's eyeballs leaving her head to

shine in the sky had always struck Delphinia as a ridiculous way for a young man to express lust. Even
Shakespeare couldn't be right all the time.

She leaned forward again, just far enough to peek
at the rest of the pub. The bartender was watching the
play with his full attention—more than she was giving
it—his hands braced against the rich wood of the bar.
The short sleeve stretched snugly around the circum-
ference of his biceps. His body was perfect.

Perfection. That was it—that was why she was so
fascinated. He was the embodiment of a Victorian ob-
session, the subject of many an essay: *The Greek Ideal*.
Perfect male beauty.

During the Victorian era, the classical statues had
been unearthed for the first time. The essayists had
concluded that the sculptors must have been working
from imagination, because the bodies of the Greek gods
were perfect in statue after statue. Along with six-pack
abs, every chiseled muscle was proportional, with an
ideal mathematical ratio between neck and shoulders,
thighs and calves.

The bodies of the Greek gods were so strong that
when they hurled a trident or wrestled a lion, their beautiful muscles were flexed and defined, but never straining. *That* was why Delphinia hadn't been able to stop
staring as he'd carried that keg. It was a feat that required strength, but he had the body to do it without
straining his muscles to the breaking point.

The statues also had an ideal facial expression: calm,
almost bored, even when depicted in battle. For purely
academic reasons, Delphinia let her gaze rise from the

bartender's biceps to his shoulder to his face. His expression was even, revealing no strong emotions. Not a warrior, not a lover. Just an aloof god, capable of taming whatever needed taming, should he feel like it.

He was truly the Greek Ideal, except for a scar that noticeably nicked his right eyebrow. Perhaps he'd been in a bike accident or a car crash at some point in his life. She liked the scar; it revealed him to be merely mortal.

He shifted to more of a resting position, leaning forward to set his forearms on the bar. The motion made the sleeve of his T-shirt rise up, revealing part of a tattoo, a curve of black ink.

Fascinating. Tattoos were not Victorian. They weren't common in academia, either. Delphinia didn't know anyone with a tattoo. Not her father. Certainly not Vincent.

"Start over," Bridget ordered from above.

Kristopher began again. "But soft! What light through yonder window breaks?"

Delphinia forced her attention to the stage. Once more, Romeo failed to rein in his bold desire. Again, he rhapsodized about celestial eyeballs.

Delphinia's favorite line was coming up, one so good that it made her forgive the eyeballs-in-heaven stuff that came immediately before it. Juliet would rest her chin in her hand, and Romeo would wish he were a glove on her hand, just so he could touch the bare skin of her cheek. What must it feel like to love someone so much, you would become something so humble if it allowed you the most innocent brush with their skin?

With a black curve of ink on their tan skin?

Delphinia had never touched someone's tattoo. Was there a different feel to the skin? If her eyes were closed and she brushed her hand down the bartender's arm, would she be able to tell when her fingertips brushed over ink?

"See how she leans her cheek upon her hand."

She leaned forward to peek at the bartender's tattoo, but her gaze caught on his mouth, the perfect, masculine curve of his lips, because he was reciting the lines, murmuring the words under his breath. Did he even know he was doing it? But, oh, he knew the words, all the words, her favorite words spoken by a strong, beautiful man.

"Oh, that I were a glove upon that hand, that I might touch that cheek."

Their eyes met. He did a little double take, as if he were surprised to see her. As if he *recognized* her.

She jolted back behind the partition.

He couldn't have recognized her. Delphinia had never met him before. He was not the kind of man to whom one would forget being introduced. She'd never seen him from afar, either. A Greek god with a scar on one eyebrow and a tattoo on one arm could not walk around the campus unnoticed.

But had he seen *her* before? She'd been reading by a window earlier. Perhaps he'd noticed her. Her cheeks felt warm at the thought. She took a sip of ice water. Or a gulp.

Romeo and Juliet continued their scene. Delphinia let it restore some order to her mind. She knew the lines, the play, the students. She knew herself and her role in life. She was the professor who read, semester after semester, the essays of long-dead men. She was the woman who stood beside a law professor, unnoticed, and agreed he was her perfect match. She was Professor Delphinia Acanthia Beatrix Ray.

"O! Be some other name," Juliet pleaded.

Such a futile, adolescent wish.

Delphinia set down her glass and plopped her cloth book bag onto her lap. The hard edges of her course's textbook and the softer edge of her paperback novel rested on her thighs. She was who she was, the brainy girl who loved books. She wasn't the kind to catch a passionate man's attention, not like Juliet. She wasn't anything like the alluring heroine in her paperback novel, either.

Therefore, she'd imagined that double take from the bartender. It was the only sensible conclusion. Her mistake.

She cleared her throat. She sat up straighter…and peeked around the partition.

He was still looking at her. That handsome face, that strong physique, all that calm confidence were zeroed in on her.

He *noticed* her.

Excitement swept through her, an effervescence that left her light-headed.

From above, Juliet called down to her Romeo. "It is too rash, too unadvised, too sudden. Too like the lightning…"

Delphinia ignored Juliet's dire warning. She might feel somewhat giddy, but this couldn't be the start of an epic romance. She already had a suitable suitor, and that bartender surely had women falling for him daily. Hourly.

But he'd noticed her.

She was flattered. They were at a safe distance, and she'd be going home directly after this, so she ventured a smile. *It was nice of you to notice me.*

Then she sat back. Lust and angst were over. Juliet came down the stairs. Romeo didn't even notice her as she stalked past him.

Delphinia could never stalk past Vincent. She'd see him tonight, in fact, because he'd invited himself to be her plus-one at her parents' soiree. She hadn't planned on attending, but Vincent would want her to justify herself if she said so. *I don't feel like it* was a very weak argument in a lawyer's eyes. It was easier just to attend.

A new student took the stage. "This selection is from *The Tragedy of Othello*."

Ah, an entire play about obliterating romance. Delphinia reached for her glass once more, but it was empty. No matter; it wasn't as if she were in any danger of overheating.

For any reason.

Chapter Four

She was still here.

Ms. Rembrandt must be a student, after all. She was right in the mix of the drama kids who were using Connor's stage. It made sense now, the way Kristopher had first run over to her and then talked to her too long. They were in the same class.

She'd never left. The entire time Connor had been in the storeroom, she'd been hanging out with her fellow drama majors. The whole time he'd wondered what great sadness she held deep inside, she'd been chatting with Bridget and Kristopher and the rest.

He'd misread her book hangover. Her life was not worse than her book. Her book could have been sadder than anything she could imagine in her real life. That had to be it.

And yet—

The picture of her by the window was burned into his brain. She'd been deeply unhappy after closing her book.

Mr. Murphy would chide him for having an overactive imagination. He would surely tell Connor not to forget to take his nose out of his books and look at the real world now and then.

Connor was looking now.

She was looking back. After a long moment, she smiled. Then she sat back, out of sight.

That wasn't a *come and get me* smile. She wasn't flirting. He'd been pursued often enough—it was routine, a part of his world as a bartender—to know when a woman was trying to get him interested. Rembrandt wasn't.

Connor pushed himself away from the bar. This was the hour he usually took for himself. The bar was ready for the evening rush. Kristopher would handle any stray customers who might wander in early, so Connor should head upstairs. His home, like all the publicans before him, was the entire third floor of this building. He'd shower and shave, eat something for dinner, read another chapter or three of the book he was in the middle of.

Or, he could stay here and watch more Shakespeare. It was the same as reading a book, practically, like having one read aloud.

Romeo and Juliet were through. Kristopher and Bridget were sitting on opposite sides of the room, pretending each other didn't exist. After some murmuring among the students, a young man took the stage, clutched his heart and hung his head.

Connor felt just as disappointed. He'd hoped to see Rembrandt's performance. He'd read all of Shakespeare's plays. He wanted to know which one suited her taste, her style, her interest.

"He holds his soul light. He dies upon his motion." The forlorn young man on the stage dropped to his knees, pleading now to the heavens. "Silence that dreadful bell."

Wait—Connor knew this bit. It was from *Othello*. This scene was a bar fight, which was probably why it had stuck in Connor's head. Too much alcohol had been drunk for too long, and the army's military officers were fighting among themselves.

Not in this student's version. He recited Othello's lines as if he were mourning a long-lost love. So much for flipped tables, spilled beer and treachery.

The other students were listening attentively, nodding sagely. Ms. Rembrandt had left her partitioned area to stand closer to the stage, frowning in concentration. Connor crossed his arms over his chest and watched the dead-wrong interpretation.

With a wail of despair, the student finished his soliloquy on his knees, looking down to address an imaginary lover who was apparently dying. "On thy love, I charge thee."

Connor rubbed his jaw, using his hand to cover his mouth a bit so he wouldn't laugh out loud.

He heard a squeak. He knew that sound: Rembrandt's squeak of amusement when she'd turned the page of her book. She bit her lip and turned away from the stage, struggling not to laugh.

Their eyes met again. They were the only two who were getting the joke. He grinned at her—and then the boy on the stage let out a final groan and collapsed in a heap.

It was too much. She lost her struggle, and her laugh escaped as a few bright notes before she swallowed the rest. She sobered up before turning back to the stage. "Stop. Let's stop here for a second."

So, she was a woman who took charge, was she? Connor felt all kinds of interest stirring in all kinds of places as he watched her step up on the stage. She was color in motion, that dark hair, that pastel skirt. If Connor could paint, he would paint her.

"I'm afraid if you do it that way," she said, "the professor will know you didn't read the play. Do you know what Othello's job is?"

Her fellow student got to his feet. "He's a military guy."

"Yes, but not just any military guy. He's the top commander. Even though he's not from Venice, even though it's the sixteenth century and Othello is not the same race as those under his command, he's so brilliant that he's been entrusted with the safety of the whole country. He even married one of the noblemen's daughters without her father's permission. Anyone else would have been jailed, but he got promoted. That's how much of a badass he is."

All of the students chuckled. Connor smiled as he rubbed his jaw. He'd thought it odd that a quiet reader would choose drama as her major, but now he could see how naturally she addressed an audience.

"But he says all these mushy lines about souls," the drama dude said. "He can't stand the ringing of a bell."

"The bell is the fire alarm, that's all. Othello has shown up because... What is happening?"

The clueless guy looked at his friends for help. Connor looked at the back of Bridget's head.

Come on, Bridget. You should know this. I made you read it in high school.

"It's a bar fight," Bridget called from her seat.

Yes.

"Yes," Rembrandt said, clapping her hands together with enthusiasm. "And who is fighting? His highest-ranking officers. Othello has to break it up because he's the only person who outranks them. He was in bed with his new bride when the alarm went off. So, when he shows up at the bar, he's not mushy and weepy. He's...?"

She waited. Connor waited, too, arms crossed. No way was he going upstairs.

"He's annoyed?" the clueless dude ventured.

Rembrandt deflated a little at the tepid answer, but she didn't give up. "He wasn't having much of a honeymoon if he was only annoyed. The guy was having sex with his hot young wife, the one he married without permission."

The student laughed, but he looked away nervously. The others were snickering. They were all the age where they were close to obsessed with sex, but not mature enough to talk about it as anything but a dirty joke.

Connor wouldn't want to be that young again. Nine-teen had sucked. Thirty was okay.

"So, there's sexual frustration on top of the officers-behaving-badly thing. Shakespeare is piling it on to make everything more dramatic. Forget fistfights. This is a sword fight. Deadly weapons. If it happened now, it would be like arriving at a bar and finding your own officers pointing guns at each other, right?"

Connor couldn't paint her. It wouldn't do justice to her energy and enthusiasm. She was the furthest thing possible from a still life by a window.

"When he says the next guy who moves doesn't value his soul, he's yelling 'freeze.' If anyone moves a muscle, he'll finish him off personally." She held her hands up like she was the Incredible Hulk or something, and re-peated "Finish him" in the ominous tone of the *Mortal Kombat* video game.

Everybody laughed, and Rembrandt headed back to her seat in a swirl of blue. She glanced Connor's way. He gave her a salute, a touch of his fingers to his forehead. She smiled as she ducked behind the wood partition.

Something crazy stirred in his chest. There went a woman of color and motion, a woman who read books intently and addressed a group comfortably and made everyone laugh while she made Shakespeare come alive.

Damn.

Connor might have fallen a little bit in love with her in the last two minutes.

Kristopher got out of his chair, very Joe Cool, hands in his jean pockets. "I told y'all she was great." He went to join her behind the wood partition.

Damn again.

Kristopher couldn't be dating Rembrandt. He was not even close to being right for a woman like her, yet he'd just bragged about her as if he'd brought her here because he'd wanted to show her off to his buddies.

Rembrandt and Kristopher? Completely wrong.

But...

They were students of the same subject. Kristopher was twenty-one, a more reliable young man than most, which was why Connor had hired him. She was probably older than Kristopher, but Connor doubted she was more than twenty-five. It wasn't so outrageous of a possibility.

Bridget got out of her chair as the next person took the stage. She came back to the bar to reclaim her barstool. Grouchy, peevish—was she just hungover, or was she upset that the guy she had a crush on was getting cozy with someone else?

Connor walked down the bar to her seat. "How's the hangover?"

"I'm not happy."

Yes, but why? Do you have a reason to be jealous?

Because if she did, then Connor had a reason to be jealous, too.

That was as crazy a thought as he'd ever had. He threw open the lid to the ice bin and put an angry scoop in a water glass.

There was nothing to be jealous about. He was a bartender. Ms. Rembrandt was a college student. She'd take her degree and move on to bigger things soon enough, just like Kristopher would. Just like they all did.

He set the water glass in front of Bridget with a hard thunk. "Keep drinking."

In those first few tumultuous years in this bar, while Connor had struggled to change his mind-set from useless dropout to reliable employee, he'd learned that no matter how passionately a girl obsessed over him at the beginning, he'd become no more than part of her college experience in the end. She'd don her cap and gown and leave Masterson, same as the one before her, same as the one after her.

Once he'd started fielding flirtations with his eyes wide open, he'd enjoyed dating women as they came and went. At some point, he'd started preferring the worldliness of a woman having a fling at forty, but in the end, the older women's emotions followed the same pattern as the coeds'. Once flirting turned to sex, women wanted the bartender in their bed to be somebody he was not.

They'd claim they never wanted him to leave, because they'd fallen in love with him. Connor appreciated that they were sincere in the moment. He also knew their feelings would burn themselves out in a couple of months, and they'd be on their way, whether they were twenty-one or forty-one. It was easy for Connor to let go, because he never held on in the first place.

If Rembrandt was the object of Kristopher's affection, what did it matter to Connor? Connor was already part of too many women's fond memories of Masterson University.

He didn't want Bridget to be heartbroken, though. "What aren't you happy about?"

"Can't a girl just have a headache?" She plunked her head on the bar again.

Connor dug out a bottle of aspirin from under the bar. He shook the bottle by her ear gently, like it was a baby's rattle, before he set it down by her head.

He checked his watch. Kristopher should have clocked in already. Connor needed to get some dinner and change his clothes. The rehearsals had wrapped up, yet Kristopher was still sitting cozy behind a wood partition with Rembrandt, not that it mattered.

It never mattered.

But Connor didn't like it, and Connor was the boss of this fantasy world. He walked out from behind his bar, crossed under his chandelier and went to check on his employee.

"Now everybody wants to sign up for your class next semester," Kristopher said.

Delphinia laughed at that. "They'll all forget during spring break. If they don't, you should warn them away. EN313? Not a fun class."

"But you're a fun teacher. You're great."

"Victorian prose is not a great subject. Don't tell anyone I said that, except for everyone you like who is considering choosing it as their literature elective. If it's someone you don't like, go ahead and let them be suckers."

She'd expected Kristopher to laugh. Instead, he leaned in to speak seriously. "Then you'd end up with a lecture hall full of people I hate. I could never do that to someone like you."

That felt distinctly and uncomfortably like a romantic overture. Her radar couldn't be that broken.

"I've given a lot of lectures in a lot of lecture halls filled with all kinds of people at this point in my career. I lectured for years as a PhD candidate, and I've been on the faculty for three *more* years since then." Was she being too obvious, emphasizing the difference in their ages? She was twenty-nine. He couldn't be more than twenty-one.

"I'm sure glad I took Shakespeare at BCC." Kristopher smiled at her. "I wouldn't have known what I was missing."

Had she imagined it, or had Kristopher pitched his voice lower to murmur that last sentence to her, as if he were trying to sound seductive?

She pulled her book bag into her lap and felt the familiar shape of the paperback novel. Its leading man could murmur anything to the heroine and make her melt into a puddle of sexual arousal. If Kristopher was trying to be like that, he was failing. Sexual charisma wasn't something a man could *try* to sound like he had.

The heroes in the paperbacks she'd read so far all seemed to have been born with it—and she'd read quite a few this year. The first one she'd started at the end of that awful first week of school, the same week her parents had laughed over her ignorance of Vincent's intentions at the faculty dinner. That Friday, she'd taped the reading list for EN313 to the door of her classroom and had felt no excitement, no anticipation, no passion for her work or her life. Nothing.

Alone in her classroom, she'd brooded until she could

brood no more. She'd picked up her phone and accepted a date with Vincent. Next, she'd replied to an email from the BCC professor who needed someone to cover her Shakespeare course. Perhaps most radically of all, Delphinia had put herself on the waiting list for one of the studio apartments that were available on campus for junior faculty, a place that would be her own.

Her classroom was in Hughes Hall, home of the English department, where one bookcase in the lobby was a take-one, leave-one place for students to swap books. As Delphinia had left that evening, heart pounding from the three changes she'd put in motion, she'd passed the bookcase. A paperback lying face up had stopped her dead in her tracks.

The book cover had depicted a woman wearing red lingerie and a man wearing no shirt at all. The focus was on their torsos—their heads weren't even on the cover—but all Delphinia had seen were hands, her hand gripping his biceps, his hand spanning her rib cage, wrinkling the red silk.

Delphinia had stuffed the paperback into her book bag. That would be her fourth change: she'd read a modern, popular book to get in touch with passion in *this* century. That first romance novel had led to another. And another. And another dozen.

The military officers, the billionaires, the cowboys: she'd loved them all, but they'd added to her worries. When she'd met Vincent, it had been bad enough that she hadn't been blindsided by the instant attraction Juliet had felt for Romeo. Now, Delphinia worried that no sexual awareness had sizzled along her skin, either, not as it had for the heroine of the paperback she had hidden in her bag.

Its hero was more than an alpha male or a lone wolf. He was a shape-shifter. Literally, he could become a wolf. So far, the hero had found his human mate, resisted her charms, then lost that battle in a rather spectacular kiss. Delphinia had read that scene as she'd waited by the window today, and she'd known there was nothing like that in her life. Nothing at all.

Maybe sexual sizzles were a paranormal thing that one felt when they met a destined mate. Maybe Delphinia was the silliest of girls to expect sizzles in actual humans.

Kristopher leaned his elbow on the back of the bench as he angled himself to face her fully. *No sizzle.*

He tilted his head charmingly to rest his cheek upon his hand—*oh, no. Not that.*

"I don't remember how I got to calling you Dr. Dee last semester. I know it's not your name. Now that the class is over, what should I call you?"

She clenched the book bag in her lap so tightly, the spine of the paperback indented her inner thigh. "You may call me Dr. Ray or Professor Ray."

Kristopher blinked. He leaned closer to say something, but he was silenced by another man's voice.

"Kristopher."

Kristopher jerked in surprise. Delphinia turned, too. There, framed in the open side of the alcove, stood the man with the chiseled body, the Greek Ideal with the nicked eyebrow, the man who had given her a casual salute after her impromptu class on *Othello.*

"A word with you?" The phrase might have been a question, but the man said it like a military officer's command.

Kristopher scrambled to his feet and checked his smartwatch. "Am I late? Yeah, you need to get out of here. My uniform's in my car. Let me go grab it, and I'll be dressed. Two minutes, I swear."

The man made a dismissive gesture, a billionaire's magnanimous wave. "Take fifteen." He hesitated briefly. "If you're done here."

Delphinia realized what he really meant was *if you're done with her*, because he looked at her, sweeping his gaze over her whole body, head to toe and back up again. Not one iota of their earlier shared amusement was evident in his expression. He was calm, impassive—and so very *large*, standing in the opening to the alcove. But the way he raked his gaze down her body—

There were alpha males in the real world, after all.

"Yeah, we're done. Sorry." Kristopher sidled past the man, leaving with nothing for Delphinia but an apologetic smile. "Thanks again for coming."

The man turned away, too, breaking the tension she'd imagined stretching between them. The relief that an awkward conversation with a student had ended was real enough. Delphinia huffed out her breath in gratitude.

The man turned back to her and studied her face— not her body—for a second. Had she looked too obviously relieved when Kristopher left? Had her sigh been too loud?

"I enjoyed your explanation of Othello's bar fight."

The bass in his voice was gentle, not commanding when he spoke to her, more like a cowboy taming a horse.

"Thank you."

"You're welcome to stay as long as you like." His gaze dropped to her stomach, her thighs, to places so very intimate. "This is a good place to enjoy a book."

He was looking at the book bag in her lap, not at her *thighs*. She was an idiot. "I like it in here. You've got nice, um, alcoves."

"The old word is a 'snug.' They were built to let women drink in a space where they wouldn't be bothered."

"Nobody's bothering me." *Duh. He can see that.*

He smiled briefly, then walked away.

She watched him leave the snug. Those jeans were still snug.

Stop staring.

This was a nice place to read; she should read. She took her paperback out of her bag and smoothed her hand over the blue cover with its solo, shirtless male model. She glanced at the bartender, comparing perfection to perfection.

Shake it off.

There'd been a scene where the hero had shaken the water off himself after being submerged in a moonlit lake. He'd been in human form, but he'd shaken himself as a wolf would. It had been the heroine's first clue that he was no ordinary man.

The bartender stopped at the table where she'd been reading earlier. He looked out the window for a moment, a silhouette against the last of the late afternoon sun, a man who was trapped on the inside, looking out. A lone wolf or, more simply, a lonely man.

You're still staring. This sudden attraction was fanciful, fueled by fiction and utterly ridiculous. She opened her book, but she couldn't focus on the black type.

If that man was a lone wolf, then Delphinia would have to be the meekest, most domesticated puppy. She was her parents' academic lapdog, at any rate. She knew what they wanted and how to please them, and she did so for a pat on the head. She'd never dare to adventure near an alpha male who looked at her as if he were a ravenous wolf. He could eat her in one bite.

She closed her book in defeat and ran her hand over the bench's carved rosette. Even the tamest lapdog had a little bit of an inner wolf, didn't it? Hers was getting restless again, as it had at the start of the school year, when she'd been brooding alone in her classroom. She'd made changes then.

She was cowering alone in a snug now. Something had to change.

Delphinia took out her phone. There was an email she hadn't answered for a week, but now she knew what she wanted to say. She hit Reply and began typing to the head of the English department—not her mother. The one at BCC.

I'm sorry to hear that your professor must have surgery. Yes, I will be able to teach Shakespeare II in his place when classes resume after spring break. Thank you for the offer.

She jabbed the send button. There. She'd answered the call of the wild.

Now what?

She stared at the stage.

At the balcony.

O, that I might touch that cheek.

Now, she wanted to stop resisting this pull she felt toward the bartender. It wasn't every day that she ran into a man with the physique of a Greek god and the words of Shakespeare on his lips. He'd noticed her. He'd saluted her. When he'd come closer, that alpha aura had practically been a tangible force. It attracted her as if he were iron and she were a magnet.

Nothing would come of it. He wasn't her type, and she couldn't possibly be his, but she wanted to see what it felt like to be near the kind of man she fell in love with in paperbacks. Besides, it would never be easier to approach a lone wolf without being in any danger of getting eaten. He was a bartender. She only had to walk up to the bar, set her glass down and talk.

He was leaving soon, once Kristopher returned. Delphinia took her lip gloss and a travel-sized hairbrush out of her bag, hurrying before her time ran out. *Look out, world*—Dr. Dee was going to let her inner wolf free for fifteen whole minutes.

Then she'd scamper back to her safe little doghouse on the second floor of her parents' home, because she possessed all the inner wolf of a puppy.

Arf, arf.

Chapter Five

Rembrandt walked up to Connor's bar.

This could be trouble.

There were twenty barstools. Bridget was at seat fifteen, head still down, trying to sleep. Connor had a feeling Rembrandt wasn't coming to check on Bridget.

He was right. She took a seat on the barstool directly across from where he happened to be standing, seat seven. She took a breath, and without any other preamble, she said, "You know your Shakespeare."

"It's entertaining enough." He placed a coaster in front of her, a cardboard square with a Celtic love knot printed on it.

"Enough for what?"

She wanted to strike up a conversation with him, did

she? Her hair was fluffed, her lips were shiny. Connor knew the signs. She'd come to flirt.

This was definitely trouble.

Connor couldn't make small talk with a woman who looked like a painting and laughed like sunlight and nailed an impersonation of a video game, not if she was just killing time with him while she waited for Kristopher to return.

"I like it enough to suffer through Bridget and Kristopher's performances, even when I have to listen to them cooing like a couple of lovebirds to each other on my stage." In his peripheral vision, he saw Bridget pick up her head. He spoke to Rembrandt. "Doesn't bother me. Does it bother you?"

Bridget rolled her eyes and flounced away without a goodbye. If Rembrandt was her rival for Kristopher, Bridget wasn't putting up a fight.

Connor watched Rembrandt watching Bridget leaving the field of battle, as it were. Rembrandt looked sad instead of victorious.

No romantic rivalry there, then. Connor felt victorious instead of sad.

Bridget tried to slam the door behind herself, but the door had a damper that prevented anyone from closing it too quickly.

Rembrandt sighed as she turned back to him. "Never have a Romeo and Juliet hated each other so much."

"Hate? Is that what's going on there?"

"You don't think they hate each other?"

Connor picked up a clean dishtowel and polished the water spots off a wineglass. "Love and hate can look a lot alike at their age." Maybe he was laying it on a bit thick by pointing out Kristopher's relative youth.

"Can you keep a secret?" she asked.

"I'm a bartender."

"The two of them were in my class last semester, and the whole time, I kept thinking what a cute couple they'd make. I hope you're right. I hope they don't really hate each other."

Connor turned his back to hang up the wineglass. Jubilation wasn't an emotion he often dealt with, but jubilant he felt. She did not return Kristopher's obvious interest in her, not at all. It shouldn't have mattered, but it did.

He wiped the smile off his face and turned toward her again. "We'll see. The course of true love never did run smooth."

"So quick, bright things come to confusion."

He stopped polishing.

"Sorry." She seemed embarrassed. "You said that line about the course of true love, so I was adding another line that from that scene. *A Midsummer's Night Dream*, act one, scene one."

"That's an impressive bar trick. Most girls just try to tie a cherry stem into a knot with their tongue."

She sighed wistfully. "My roommate in New England could do that. I gave up trying, but I have to warn you, if we have a contest to see who can slip in the most Shakespeare lines, I'll win."

"I have no doubt."

She narrowed her eyes at him in a calculating way.

"And not because you'd let me win in some misbegotten notion that the customer is always right."

Connor only smiled. His Rembrandt was here, right here at his bar, empty glass in hand. *What's your pleasure?*

A different question came out. "What's your name?"

"You'll never guess it." She was being playful.

He draped the dishtowel over his shoulder and braced his hands on the bar, giving her his full attention, but something else had caught hers. Her gaze had dropped to his arm. His left arm, the one with the tattoo. He didn't need to check whether or not his sleeve had ridden up and revealed some ink. It obviously had. Women loved it. Rembrandt was most definitely a woman.

Quickly, she looked him in the eye again. Her blush added a warm touch of pink to the picture she made. "I'll give you one guess, though."

"Rembrandt."

Her second of surprise was followed by that bright laugh. "That sounds like the name an art history professor would give to his puppy. Rembrandt. Kind of cute *for a dog*."

"There went my one guess. I guess you're going to have to tell me now."

Her smile dimmed. "It's Delphinia. I know, I know. If you knew my parents, you wouldn't be surprised. They are exactly the kind of people who would give a baby the four-syllable name of a somewhat-persnickety flower. The flower is delphinium, by the way. Not Delphinia."

"What's in a name?" Connor asked, since he'd just gotten a refresher this afternoon on the lines from

Romeo and Juliet. "That which we call a delphinium by any other word would smell as sweet."

Her smile returned, brighter. "It doesn't have quite the same ring to it, does it? My parents could have given me a more normal flower name, like Rose. A rose by any other name would smell as sweet. That's catchy. Might last a century or four."

"Sure, but why should you envy a common name? Rose. Lily. Daisy is really a roadside weed. None of them sound as sweet."

She pinkened so perfectly. He leaned in a little closer, so he could murmur his question quietly. "So, my one and only Delphinia, what's your pleasure?"

Her breath left her in a soft rush, and then, silence. She looked at him, and he looked at her. Suddenly, he wasn't breathing, either. In the little space between them, something sparked to life, burning up all the oxygen they weren't breathing. He felt it on his skin, energy just waiting to happen, static ready to spark if they touched.

He wanted her.

"Oh," she said, in the way a woman might say *oh* when she was touched just right while making love. *Oh.*

He wanted to bury his fingers in that whiskey-brown hair. He wanted to taste the lips that she'd glossed just for him. Lust, yes—but in this space between them, the lust coalesced into something so intense, so tight, it left room for another feeling to rush in. He didn't know what it was, exactly, but he knew with certainty that he wanted this woman, this one woman, and the devil could take everything else.

The pub's door opened, people came in. Connor couldn't stop looking at Delphinia, not when she couldn't stop looking at him, either, but he eased back as Kristopher jogged behind the bar toward him.

Kristopher gave him a single slap on the shoulder, like he was tagging someone for a relay race. "I'm back. Made it in ten. You can go."

Delphinia looked down at her glass. The spell was broken.

Connor took a breath. The bar was still here. The new customers were sitting down. It was jarring to realize that nothing had actually happened. A man and a woman had looked at one another for a few heartbeats. That was all.

But his throat felt too tight to speak. He nodded an acknowledgment that he'd heard Kristopher, and he indicated the new customers with a jerk of his chin.

Kristopher bounded over to them. "What can I get y'all?"

Connor stayed by Delphinia. He held up her glass and found his voice. "What's your pleasure?"

"I was having ice water."

He got her a clean glass and filled it with ice, feeling more normal with each familiar move. They'd shared one of those *Are you thinking what I'm thinking?* moments. Nothing too exotic about that. They'd done it earlier from across the room, when the weepy Othello had made them want to laugh.

He topped the ice off with water and set it on the coaster. "Water's a necessity. The question was, what's your pleasure?"

She shifted in her chair and tossed her hair back a bit, and he knew she was trying to shake off that weird moment of silence between them, too. She looked everywhere except at him. He understood.

Her gaze settled on the mirrored shelves behind him, moving across the long row of whiskey bottles the same way it had moved across the lines on the pages of her book.

"I don't really know what the proper drink is at an Irish pub," she said.

"It's anything you want it to be. There's no law that says you must have a Guinness."

"Is there such a thing as whiskey for beginners? A trainer whiskey?"

She was cute and beautiful at the same time. The very fact that she existed made him want to smile, so he did. "How about a bourbon and Coke?"

She smiled, too. They could look at one another again now. "That sounds like something I can handle. It sounds more dignified than 'trainer whiskey,' too."

"Over twenty-one?" He didn't need to check her ID, although it was tempting, if only to find out where she lived.

"Twenty-nine," she said.

His age, or nearly. He wouldn't have guessed. She didn't look as old as he did. Then again, he'd quit school, he'd fought, he'd starved. He was glad she didn't look as battle-hardened as he did, but it was a sobering reminder of how unalike their lives were. She would take her degree and move on. That was right; she should.

Connor mixed her drink as more customers came

in. Because of the large university, there were always strangers, but the town of Masterson itself was small, so there were regulars he knew by name. Ernie, one of the city councilmen, took a seat and nodded at Connor.

Connor set Delphinia's drink in front of her and moved on like a normal bartender would, no matter how little he wanted to. He started building a Guinness for the city councilman without waiting for him to order it.

Connor had been pressuring Ernie and the rest of the council for the better part of a year to fund a safer crosswalk at the intersection between the campus and the Tipsy Musketeer. Too many students jaywalked to get to one of the student-friendly storefronts on the block: a coffee shop, a bookstore, a Mexican cantina. Connor had even paid to have preliminary sketches made for a pedestrian bridge that could span Athos Avenue and let the college kids come and go as they pleased, since they obviously had no patience to wait for the traffic lights and never would.

One student had been hit last year. Connor couldn't forget the image of her lying on the pavement, legs twisted in a way legs could not twist. According to the college newspaper, it had taken a year of surgeries, but she'd returned to campus. No one had been hit so far this year, but there'd been too many near misses. Connor heard the screech of tires outside his windows each time, and each time he ran outside to help. It was a relief to see a driver and pedestrian yelling at one another, instead of another student's life derailed by a year of pain, or worse. Connor wanted them all to get their diplomas and go on to bigger things.

Like Delphinia would.

As he and the councilman talked municipal budgets for a few minutes, impatience ate at him. He was doing what he needed to be doing, but a beautiful Rembrandt had never walked into his bar before today, and there was no guarantee she'd ever return. If this was the only time he'd be able to talk to her, then he wanted to talk to her.

He glanced her way. Kristopher was standing in his place.

"So, we'll talk before the next meeting," Ernie said. "I'll bring Joe around. We need to get him in on this. Joe Manzetti. You know him?"

"Sure. I'd be happy to talk to Joe any time." *Any time but now.* Connor headed back down the length of the bar.

Delphinia was looking at her phone, not at Kristopher. The sadness was back, a new anxiety along with it. Connor could see it from two paces away.

"I'm sorry, I've got to leave," she said to Kristopher. "How much do I owe you?"

Kristopher turned to the touchscreen of the register as he asked Connor to confirm what the drink had been. "Seat seven is a bourbon and Coke?"

Connor waved him off the register. "On the house."

"There you go," Kristopher said to her, like he'd just done her a favor. He casually leaned on the bar, giving Delphinia the same suggestive smile he'd given to other college coeds. "You were great this afternoon. I really enjoyed myself."

"I did, too." She was distracted, somber, as she turned off her phone and slipped it into her bag.

Kristopher tried harder, adding a wink to his smile. "We should do it again."

Connor had been here during the rehearsals. He knew exactly what Kristopher was talking about, but the sexual innuendo of *enjoying* Delphinia in the afternoon screwed with Connor's head.

She wasn't his. He knew that. He did.

It didn't matter. There was no way Connor would ever be able to stand by while another man painted that picture, no matter how irrational this possessive instinct was. He gave Kristopher an almost-friendly push in the direction of some other customers.

Delphinia stepped down from her barstool, anxiety and urgency evident in every move. Connor's first impression by the window had been correct: something in her world made her very unhappy.

She was so rushed, he expected her to turn and go without so much as a wave, but she reached toward him and set her palm on the mahogany, as if she were putting her hand on his arm. "Thank you for the drink, but I forgot myself. I forgot something I'm supposed to do."

Back to her sad life she had to go, but she'd been happy here for an afternoon. That was what a good pub could do for a person. It was all a good pub could do.

"It was nice to meet you, Rembrandt. Come back any time you need to take a break from the world."

Come back again, so I can look at you and lose my mind. Please.

She dragged her palm over the polished wood as

she backed away, then she turned and made a beeline for the door.

Kristopher returned to enter an order on the touchscreen. "She's great, isn't she?"

Connor grunted an agreement around the churning craziness in his chest.

An unfamiliar woman sat at seat seven and smiled at him. "White wine, please. Something sweet."

Connor was getting a bottle of Riesling out of the wine cooler under the register when Kristopher said, "You can see why she's my favorite professor."

Connor stopped with his hand wrapped around the neck of the bottle. "Professor?"

"Yeah, she's the Dr. Dee I had last semester. Bridget and I talked about her, remember?"

"That was Dr. Dee? She's... She's young." He kept his voice down and his back to the customers as he uncorked the wine.

"Tell me about it. When she walked into class last semester, I wasn't the only guy singing 'Hot for Teacher' in my head." Kristopher started singing the chorus under his breath.

"Your professor," Connor repeated through clenched teeth.

Kristopher looked confused. "What?"

"You were making a move on your *professor* this afternoon?"

Kristopher didn't deny it. He turned away, but Connor turned him right back with a hand on his shoulder. They might look to the public like coworkers reviewing an order on a touchscreen, but Connor wanted to pick him up by the scruff of the neck and shake some sense into him. "What is wrong with you? Do you know how much trouble she'd be in if she slept with one of her students? She'd be fired."

"I wasn't trying to *sleep* with—well, I mean, I wouldn't turn it down—but I wanted to see if we got along, you know? Outside of class. She's not my professor this semester."

"She's not interested," Connor said.

"How do you know?"

"Because I have eyes." He really was losing his mind. He felt driven to protect a woman who was not his to protect. "You know what she *is* now? She's in danger of having her reputation trashed, her professional reputation. You acted like she was your friend all afternoon, your buddy, not your professor. You helped yourself to her personal space, sitting in the snug with her, and you made it look exactly the way you wanted it to look to the other guys."

"Okay, okay. No harm done. Nothing happened."

"It's not what you're doing, it's what it looks like you're doing. That's the way the world works. You better learn that, quick, before somebody gets hurt." Connor let go of him.

Another one of his employees joined them at the register, a server named Gina. "Hi, guys. Is something wrong with the touchscreen? I need to clock in."

"Go ahead." Connor stepped back, hoping he seemed normal when he felt anything but.

Gina looked at his T-shirt. "Aren't you going to change? Kris and I can handle this."

The staff uniforms were a bit upscale, a nod to the elegant brass and glass of the place, but nothing too formal. It was a pub, after all. She and Kristopher were wearing black button-downs and pin-striped black slacks. Connor was still in jeans and a T-shirt.

"I'm going up now."

After Gina moved away, a more contrite Kristopher spoke under his breath to Connor. "Don't worry. I'll tell the guys she stone-cold blocked me. She did, too, right before you walked up. Gave me the choice to call her either 'professor' or 'doctor.' Harsh, right?"

Connor clung to his last shred of patience. "No, you won't say anything to your friends except how useful it was to have her there to tutor all of you. That's it. Tutoring. School. Grades. Not a whiff of anything else gets connected to her. Are we clear?"

Connor was barely aware of leaving the bar, yet he was already pounding up the back stairs to the third floor before he saw any color but red.

Kristopher needed to grow up and stop thinking of sex as a sport and every woman he met as fair game on his playing field. Someone needed to teach him how the world worked, how the game was played. You didn't try to charm a married woman into your bed, for one. You didn't try to seduce coworkers. You didn't take advantage of a girl who thought she was in love with you— Connor stumbled on that step.

How many women had told him they loved him? He didn't try to make them fall in love with him; they just did, once sex became part of the relationship. He kissed them without answering and let them believe they loved him for as many weeks or months as they wanted to, until the day they inevitably changed their minds and moved on.

But he couldn't remember having a woman say she loved him before they started sleeping together. He wouldn't have slept with her, in that case. He wouldn't have taken advantage of her feelings.

He stomped up the rest of the stairs. This wasn't about him. This was about Kristopher. *You don't try to seduce a woman if it would violate a school ethics code and get her fired.* Kristopher needed to learn that basic rule before somebody got hurt—specifically, Rembrandt.

A professor.

Damn it, damn it, damn it. Not a student teacher, either, not a PhD candidate, but a full doctor. She held a position of trust in the community. She was *somebody*.

She was way out of his league—but he'd known that from the first moment he'd laid eyes on her, hadn't he? Like an idiot, he'd let her flirt with him, anyway. He'd flirted back like an even greater idiot. They'd shared that electric, time-stopping moment—so now, he wanted a woman who was out of his reach.

He hit the third-floor landing and stalked through his apartment to the iron ladder that led to the roof. She was so damned young to be a full professor, even at a community college. She must be some kind of genius, the kind who graduate from high school early and zoom through their college educations before they're legal to drink. An actual genius.

Of course she was.

He walked out to the roof, went straight for the punching bag he kept there and started pummeling it.

Of course. Of course. Out. Of. His. League.

He stopped, eventually. The heavy bag swung from its chain, slowing, coming to a rest. Connor swiped his forearm over his wet forehead and caught sight of his constant reminder: the small purple tattoo near his inner elbow, badly drawn by another prisoner using the cell block's one contraband needle, a souvenir tattoo Connor had been given the night before being released. Ink was hard to come by on the inside, but the cell block had deemed him worthy. Most inmates on his block got a going-away gift of black eyes and kidney punches, so Connor had held out his arm as if he didn't mind having his body altered permanently by criminals.

He threw more body shots at the heavy bag, but his hands needed to be taped up. He flipped open the lid of the storage bench to grab the tape, although it was too late. The skin over his knuckles was already scraped from the canvas. Stupid of him. It would make him look like a thug who'd been in a fistfight when he handed a customer a drink in a fancy glass.

He *was* a thug. He just refused to fight in public and let the world see that he was. He'd set up the makeshift gym where no one could see him, on the roof over the 1980s addition in the rear of the building, out of sight of the street. As he wound a strip of cloth around his stinging hand, he walked to the street-front edge. Central Texas was so flat, Connor could see the central green of Masterson University to the north. The lawn was always manicured, the fountain in its center always a shimmering circle of blue, even in the hot Texas summertime.

He looked down an alley to the east, to the grittier side of town, warehouses and construction offices, the sheriff's office with its holding cells. To the west, he could see the rest of the historic downtown, all the way to the end of the picturesque original streets of Masterson. It was easy to pinpoint where the building code changed, because the logos of the gas stations at that distant intersection were brightly, jarringly colored after a mile of mellow brick and stucco. College kids didn't dart into traffic to run from one gas station to the other.

Past the horizon, the road ran through miles of ranchland, then into the town of Bryan, where Kristopher and Bridget had driven together two nights a week to learn Shakespeare at the community college from Dr. Dee.

Connor turned in a slow circle as he secured the hand wrap at his wrist. Somewhere out there, to the east or the west or maybe only one street away, a woman named Delphinia was very sad.

Don't be taking everyone's sad tales with you out of the pub, lad.

He walked back to the bag and started hitting.

If she walked back into his bar one day, he would make her a bourbon and Coke and leave her to her own business, just as he would with any other customer.

He hit hard. Harder. Since he liked the way she looked, he might admire her from a distance, but anything more between them would be absurd.

She was a woman with a doctorate. He had taken the GED test and gotten a piece of paper that said his education was equivalent to a high school diploma. Worse, he'd done that behind bars, years after he should have graduated from a real high school. The only reason he'd gotten the GED was because the study sessions took him out of the prison's common area for two hours, five days out of seven. He'd just wanted two hours a day where he didn't have to be ready to use his fists without a second's warning.

His fists and wrists were hurting now. He moved to the softer speed bag, but he got the rhythm going too easily. It did nothing to distract him from his thoughts.

A genius professor and a bartending felon weren't even close to being equals. She liked him, though. She'd come to talk to him after the rehearsal, when she could have left. He'd watched as her gaze had dropped to his tattoo—yeah, there was some high-voltage sex just over the horizon, if they headed in that direction. He knew it in his bones. He'd felt it on his skin.

He couldn't let it happen. She might love it—she might, like others, believe she was in love with him when the sex was good—but it would only end badly for her. A convicted felon was never an asset. His presence would cause raised eyebrows in her world. People would question her judgment. He would be a social albatross around her neck, dragging her down professionally. It wouldn't be long before that dragged her down personally, too.

He'd told her she was welcome to come back any time, but it would be best if she never did.

He would be her biggest mistake.

Connor stopped punching. The teardrop-shaped bag swung to a stop.

It had been a good afternoon, nothing more. Nothing less. He'd always wanted to see a Rembrandt, and now he had. She'd been reading a book that had surprised a laugh out of her.

He'd wanted to read the same book she read. That had been enough for him at the beginning, a harmless connection. He could make it be enough now—but he didn't know the book's title. If she never came back, then he'd never know.

It shouldn't matter.

But it felt like it did.

Chapter Six

Delphinia nearly, but not quite, ran up the walk toward her front door.

It would be unseemly for any of the Drs. Ray to be seen racing across the campus on foot, no matter how late she was—and she was quite late. Not only had Vincent called her to ask her to account for herself, but her parents had, too.

The brick walk was longer than it needed to be, because it took a serpentine path from the road to the house. The house itself was significant, one of four Greek Revival homes that had been built in the 1920s for the deans of the four colleges that made up Masterson University. Tourists stopped their cars on the street to photograph the home and read the tasteful roadside plaque which announced that Dumas House was on the National Register of Historic Places.

The other three homes were Aramis, Athos and Porthos, named after the Three Musketeers. This house really should have been named D'Artagnan after the fourth musketeer, but Delphinia assumed no dignified dean wanted their house associated with a hot-headed young man of ignoble birth, even if D'Artagnan was the hero of the story. Instead, the house had been named Dumas after the author of the Musketeer books. Her parents found this quite satisfactory.

Dumas House had eight thousand square feet of living space, with an attached portico to one side and a detached garage behind, which had held horse carriages when motorcars were still unreliable curiosities.

The first floor was used to host college events, from large receptions in the ballroom to soirees in the library or music room. The caterers had a checklist to follow in the kitchen, so they'd leave it as they'd found it, but Delphinia's things still went missing. Last week, it had been a quart of milk and a whimsical whisk with a lighthouse for its handle. The whisk was a mass-produced souvenir, so the dollar amount of the theft could not justify wasting the campus police's time. Her parents did not fuss over insignificant things like a souvenir from New England.

Her father had become the dean while she'd been at her college in New England, so she hadn't grown up in Dumas House. When she'd moved back to Texas after finishing her bachelor's degree, she'd chosen the bedroom that had French doors leading out to the roof of the portico, which was flat and had a low iron railing all around. Delphinia had thought it would be lovely to sit out there and read. She hadn't known that she'd be photographed by tourists if she tried to.

Regardless, given Dumas House's size and location, it would be nonsensical for her to live anywhere else, as her parents had stated. They were correct, although Delphinia had never felt at home here. She had not earned this house. Her father had.

She balked as she neared the front steps. She was windblown and breathless, not fit to greet this evening's guests, if any should be lingering in the foyer. She changed direction and cut across the grass to the portico entrance.

She slowed her steps. It was time to compose herself. This was it, the end of her adventure. She'd gone to a pub. She'd immersed herself in Shakespeare instead of Victorian essays. She'd dared to talk to a man who looked like a keg-carrying Greek god, just to satisfy her curiosity about what it was like to spend time talking to an alpha male.

It was arousing, that's what it was.

She wished she'd never spoken to him. That little detour had taken her down a dead end. Now she had to get back to the main road, metaphorically, but she felt so disoriented. Not giddy. There was a difference.

Delphinia stood before the portico's double doors and took a steadying breath. Seven months had passed since she'd put herself on the waiting list for the junior faculty apartments. She was nearly next in line. She could do this for a little while longer.

With a turn of the doorknob, she entered her parents' world.

The coast was clear. She'd cross the foyer, tiptoe up the grand staircase to her bedroom, freshen up, then join the alumni cocktail event that Vincent had insisted she invite him to.

She was on the second step of the staircase when she realized the foyer wasn't completely empty. Vincent was standing by the front door, looking outside through the leaded glass. He was silhouetted by the last of the daylight, alone. Just like the bartender.

He dropped his gaze to the floor. His shoulders drooped. If he wasn't a dashing lone wolf, he was still a faithful guard dog, keeping vigil by the door. She would give him more credit from now on. He might seem remote at times, even cold, but this was evidence of how much he cared for her.

She turned and leaned over the banister, intending to call his name, when Vincent kicked the front door. "Where is that *bitch*?"

She froze, shocked. He'd said it so rapidly under his breath, she might not have heard it right. She must not have heard it right. But he'd kicked that door, undeniably.

In the next second, she realized a part of her wasn't really shocked at all. She'd had an uneasy feeling about him from the start, but he'd never done anything violent or even discourteous to confirm her nonspecific uneasiness.

He kicked the door again in another burst of violence, startling a gasp out of her.

He whirled toward her and for one second, she saw his eyes go wide and his face go white. It was gone so fast, she might have imagined it.

"There you are!" He rushed over, and she braced herself for who-knew-what, but he only stopped by the staircase to grasp her hands and lift them off the banister to kiss her fingers, her knuckles, the back of her hands. She was only two steps above him, but it had the disconcerting effect of looking down on the man as if he were down on one knee to propose.

"I have been worried sick," he said, sounding heated, not cold. "You're an hour late."

"I'm—I'm sorry." She tugged her hands back, but he kept a firm grip.

"Where were you?" He looked so concerned, yet she'd heard him call her a bitch. Hadn't she?

"I was tutoring. I forgot about the reception."

"You forgot."

"Yes." She tugged her hands hard enough that he couldn't pretend she wasn't trying to get loose. When he let go, she put her hands behind her back, but that made her feel unstable on the steps, so she rested one hand on the banister, higher than the top of Vincent's head, so he couldn't grab it easily.

This was ridiculous. She was in her house. There were probably forty people only a room away. She shouldn't be feeling so unsafe, so she raised her chin and asked, "Why did you kick the door?"

But he spoke at the same time. "You're lying. I drove to Hughes Hall myself, looking for you. You were not there. No tutoring was taking place."

"I didn't say I was tutoring in Hughes Hall. I was tutoring elsewhere. Now, if you'll excuse me, I don't feel well. I'm going to retire for the evening."

She saw a flash of anger in his eyes, before he dropped his forehead into his hand. "I'm making such a mess of this, aren't I? I've been so worried for a full hour. When I couldn't find you at Hughes Hall, all kinds of terrible scenarios went through my mind."

She felt like she was in *The Twilight Zone*. He'd violently kicked the door, but now he looked so devastated. "Masterson is a very safe campus—"

"I know, I know." He sighed and shook his head, then looked up at her a little flirtatiously, but like a sad puppy dog, too. "I know, but you are a very pretty girl, Miss Delphinia Ray. If a girl were going to be stolen away, a thief couldn't find anyone prettier than you."

She wasn't a girl. She was nearly thirty. *You may call me Dr. Ray or Professor Ray.*

Vincent put his hands in the pockets of his slacks. "I let my imagination run wild. It's not hard to do when you're a lawyer. I've seen too much in courtrooms. It's one reason I decided to teach instead of do. Forgive me?"

Maybe she was the one who'd let her imagination run wild. *I saw a flash of anger in his eyes* sounded like a line from a novel. She was too susceptible to fiction, too easily carried away by stories. She'd sat on a barstool and talked to a bartender, and she'd fooled herself that she'd felt some kind of special, sizzling connection. The fact was that he had a great body, and she'd simply been aroused.

Once, she and her girlfriends in New England had lied about their ages to see an all-male review. There must have been hundreds of women in the audience, and every single one had been aroused to some degree, laughing and flipping their hair and tucking cash into men's thongs. Incredibly fit men had a predictable, primitive effect on the female brain. It wasn't magic or romance or love. It was science.

She needed to be practical. The fact was, a kick to a door took one impulsive second. She had to weigh that against the fact that Vincent had been consistently polite, even solicitous, for months and months.

"Nothing to forgive." She managed a smile and started up the stairs. "Just give me a few minutes to freshen up."

He took his hand out of his pocket immediately and looked at his watch. "How many minutes? I want to meet Joe Manzetti. He's the CEO of one of the biggest construction companies in Texas."

"Ten minutes?" She waited for the magnanimous billionaire's wave. *Take fifteen.* Or for the patient cowboy's answer. *Take as long as it takes.*

"Make it five. He was one of the first ones here. He might leave any minute."

"Why don't you go on in, then? I'll find you."

"Because I need you to introduce me."

"I don't know him very well. He's only been here a couple of times, and you could—"

"Delphinia Ray. I cannot walk in there without you by my side. When your parents noticed you weren't here, I rather publicly volunteered to drive over to

Hughes Hall to get you. If I walk into that reception now, empty-handed, I'll look like an ass whose date couldn't be bothered to show up for him. An ass who then went chasing around campus after her but couldn't find her. Don't do that to me."

Delphinia felt tired. It was easier just to go along. "I'll be as quick as I can."

"Hurry."

She'd only made it halfway up when he called after her. "Don't wear that black dress again. I want people to talk to me, not be distracted by you."

"All right." She'd never thought of herself as the kind of femme fatale whose appearance could make men forget what they were doing. Vincent was being absurd, but it was a compliment. She couldn't object to a compliment.

Hours and hours later, when she was lying in her bed and staring at the dark, she realized Vincent had never answered her question. Why had he kicked the door?

He must not have heard her, because he'd spoken at the same time. Spoken *over* her.

Unlike the bartender, the man to whom she'd only been physically, predictably attracted. *It's only science.*

He wasn't her type. Vincent was her type. Vincent had always been her type.

She kept staring at the dark.

There was a science behind human arousal, but the bartender had not been flexing bared muscles like in *Magic Mike* when she'd felt that special sizzle. He'd been making her laugh with Shakespearean wordplay.

Maybe her usual type had been wrong all along.

Chapter Seven

"There's no problem in the world that isn't best faced once a man has a dram of whiskey in his hand and a friend who'll lend an ear. Mark my words as true, or my father never called me Seamus Murphy."

Connor handed Mr. Murphy one of the rocks glasses that had come from the pub and sat down in an armchair. *"Slainte."*

They both raised their glasses, but neither of them took a drink. They held the whiskey up to the light for a moment to admire the color. Connor was not Irish, but Mr. Murphy was, and he'd taught Connor that long and poetic toasts were part of drinking with an Irishman. Connor rarely waxed poetic, but his mentor was looking at him with one gray eyebrow raised expectantly.

Connor held his glass a little higher. "Grateful we are

for the one hundred shades of brown in this aged Irish whiskey, in an old masterpiece's strokes of paint…and in a young woman's hair on a sunny day."

After a beat of silence, they lowered their glasses and took the first sip.

"Saints above, lad. You're going to be an Irishman yet. That near brought a tear to my eye." Since that statement was practically a toast in itself, they both took another sip.

They didn't try to drink whiskey like a couple of synchronized swimmers. It just came naturally when Connor drank with the man who'd taught him to slow down and appreciate a proper drink—the man who'd taught him to slow down and learn everything else worth knowing. The things Connor had learned on his own, like how to break a man's nose or break into a man's car, led to life in a cell. Mr. Murphy's lessons led to life in a building that had stood for 130 years and a business that had been operating inside it for just as long.

Connor sat back and put his boots up on a newspaper-strewn side table and eyed Mr. Murphy over the rim of his glass. This would have been a perfect afternoon, two gentlemen at leisure, enjoying the good Lord's finest gift to man—according to Mr. Murphy—if only Mr. Murphy weren't enjoying his whiskey as he sat up in a stark white hospital bed.

Connor toasted again silently. *Grateful we are not to be in the ICU.*

This was an assisted living facility, and he was in Mr. Murphy's studio apartment, which had a kitchenette, a small living area, a huge bathroom wide enough for a wheelchair to navigate, and a bed. Connor had moved Mr. Murphy's sturdy oak bed from the pub's apartment to this place, but a few months ago, the old man had fallen and broken his pelvis. He'd needed a wheelchair for the first time in his life. Pneumonia had set in, and the facility staff had put the oak bed in storage and brought in this hospital bed.

Mr. Murphy kept his whiskey in one hand and used his other to press the buttons on the bed rail. "I have to confess, I'm in no hurry to get rid of this bed. That wheelchair is another tale entirely. I walked for ten minutes the other day without so much as a cane. I did have a fair and fine physical therapist beside me, so I have to take care not to get better too fast, or I'll lose the pleasure of her company, but I'll be back on my feet, you'll see."

"I'm glad to hear it."

Mr. Murphy pushed a button and elevated his feet. "Ah, that's nice. I'm keeping the bed. Now we're all situated, so why don't you tell me what you came here to tell me? I expect you on Mondays, when the Musketeer is closed. Friday is payday, don't you know? You should be getting the pub in order. Folks will be wanting to end their work week with a pint."

"I do know." Connor's heart broke a little every time the old man thought he was telling Connor something he'd never mentioned before. "I haven't forgotten what you taught me."

"Then you won't be having time to stay all day, for surely I taught you that you need to be at the pub when the pub needs you to be there. Let's get down to it. What is bothering you, lad?"

I miss a woman I barely know.

Connor sipped his whiskey. "There was another close call outside the pub last night. Those screeching tires get to me every time."

"That's sorry news. You've been doing all you can. The picture of that bridge is a thing of beauty."

Connor nodded. The architecture student he'd hired to render a pedestrian bridge had been very talented. Connor had hoped the city council would move to allocate funds for that solution once they'd had it envisioned for them. So far, they hadn't.

"You can only do so much from the outside," Mr. Murphy said. "You need to be on the inside. You need to sit on the city council yourself, and sure that is."

"Me?" Connor had to laugh. "Run for office?"

"You. Run for office."

"I can't."

"Humpf." Mr. Murphy tipped his glass to him. "There's nobody in this town who hasn't heard a good word about you. You care about this city and you've made it your home for a full ten years now. You can run for the city council, and what's more to the point, you can win."

It touched Connor's heart that this man thought so highly of him. It broke his heart that Mr. Murphy had forgotten why Connor could not be a city councilman. He didn't want to have to tell him all over again.

"You've got what it takes, lad. The ladies do love you. I don't need to be telling you that which you know, but I'm not at all sure you know that men think highly of you. So do the women who have better things to do than chase you to bed. You know how to keep your temper, and you know how to stop trouble before it starts. You don't blabber on about yourself, and you don't let fools waste your time. You're a strong man, and others see that. They'll vote for you. They'll want you on their side, taking care of business without showing off. It's what you do best."

Connor had to set his whiskey down. This was high praise, and it churned up too many emotions when those emotions hadn't settled back down since Rembrandt had walked into his bar. Two of those emotions were now pity and sorrow, because Mr. Murphy had forgotten where Connor came from as surely as he'd forgotten that Connor already knew Fridays were paydays.

"I'm humbled, Mr. Murphy. I respect your opinion, but there are real obstacles."

"Set them up, then. Set them up, so I can knock them all down."

Connor hated that he had to do this. It was the second time this week that the weight of his shortcomings was crushing. "I didn't finish high school. That wouldn't look good if an opponent plastered it all over any town during a campaign, but especially not in a college town. Two of the current council members have an MBA. One has a doctorate. I didn't finish eleventh grade."

Delphinia had her PhD, and if he ran, she'd get a lovely campaign brochure in the mail from his opponent that would emphasize Connor's lack of the most basic qualifications.

"High school would matter indeed, if anyone considered electing a seventeen-year-old. They'll be voting for the man you are now, for a thirty-year-old, self-made man."

"Self-made? I had help." He and Mr. Murphy weren't given to hugs and such, but Connor set his hand over Mr. Murphy's on the bed rail. His larger hand covered the older man's hand and his wrist, as well. The skin felt too loose over the bones, too frail. Connor fought back the fear, because Mr. Murphy's hand was also warm and no longer gray with illness. Connor squeezed gently and let go. "I had the best of help."

"You worked hard for every scrap of every good thing you've got, so don't be starting with the sentimentality." Which meant, of course, Mr. Murphy was feeling sentimental himself. "You're smart and you have your head on straight, and that's more than most people can say to the good Lord. The city needs you."

Connor took his boots off the newspapers and sat forward, giving himself a minute to roll his whiskey glass between his hands before he broke the heart of the man who thought so highly of him at the moment. "I appreciate your faith, but believe me when I say I can't run. Legally, I cannot be a candidate for elected office. I think you forgot—I think you've overlooked the fact that I have a record. I'm a convicted felon."

Mr. Murphy was silent.

"A nonviolent offense. I didn't commit murder... nothing like that. I didn't... I didn't beat someone bloody." *Not until after I was behind bars and had to survive.* "It doesn't matter what I didn't do. I broke the law, and I was arrested."

"They say confession is good for the soul, but this is hard for me to hear."

"I'm sorry to have to tell you that I was—"

"Is it possible you did something truly unforgivable at nineteen, like jump in the back seat of a car without first asking your friends politely whether or not they had perhaps stolen the car? Did you commit a felony as heinous as that?"

Connor's head snapped up. "You didn't forget. How long were you going to let me go on like that?"

Mr. Murphy laughed so hard as he slapped his knee that he almost spilled a drop of whiskey—but he didn't.

Connor tried to think of something Irish enough to please the old man, exasperating as that man was. "Best watch yourself. The devil won't take you if you get meaner than he is. He doesn't want to be outdone, and that's the truth of it."

This made Mr. Murphy absolutely howl with laughter.

It was good to see him breathing well enough to laugh so damned long. Connor finished his whiskey and stood. "As someone reminded me, it's Friday, so I've got to get going."

"Stay, stay a minute—I'll stop, I swear it, or my father never called me Seamus—" He couldn't finish as the laughter rolled through him.

Connor crossed his arms over his chest and shook his head.

Mr. Murphy got himself under control. "So, lad, I was waiting for you to hold up that old conviction. Now, let me knock it down. I've been keeping up with the news better than you have. The law that says you can't be on a ballot has fuzzy legal terms in it about 'remedies,' so people like yourself have been testing it. A felon in Austin filled out the application to be on the ballot, and the city decided since he'd served his time and could vote again, there were no legal 'remedies' left for him to do. They put him on the ballot. It made the news, and I thought of you, didn't I? I did."

"That doesn't mean the city of Masterson would do the same."

"They will, I'm certain of it."

What could Connor say in the face of such unfounded optimism? He carried his glass over to the kitchenette and set it in the sink.

Mr. Murphy was on a crusade. "You don't believe me, then fine. But there's another way, too. You can run if you get a judicial decision to put you on the ballot. Any judge with eyes to look at you would clear you as a candidate. But you have to start it, Connor. Turn in an application to be a candidate for the next election. The city will either accept it, or they'll get a judge to decide."

Connor was not going to voluntarily walk into a courtroom to see a judge about anything. A middle-aged man in a billowing black robe could have decided to give a nineteen-year-old, first-time, nonviolent offender a deferred adjudication probation—Connor knew the legal lingo now—and not the formal conviction that would haunt him forever. Connor had spent two weeks in the county lockup waiting for his five minutes before the judge. He'd pled guilty to joyriding. Those two weeks could have been punishment enough.

Instead, Connor had been given a felony conviction and sentenced to six months of hell. He'd walked in that courtroom wearing county jail handcuffs. He'd walked out five minutes later wearing state prison handcuffs. He'd survived, but he was not going to go back.

He put on his jacket so he could bury his fists in the pockets. "I appreciate your faith in me. I always have, even if I didn't show it when I was nineteen or twenty. But you taught me that I can't go through life like I'm the only one who matters. I've got fifty-three people on the payroll. If I try to get on the ballot, an ugly past will be resurrected, and people will take sides. Some will see me as you do, but some will call me a criminal. Business will drop, maybe by fifteen percent. Maybe by fifty. People will lose their jobs."

He walked to the window. He didn't see the same rosy future Mr. Murphy saw. He could only see what he had now, what he couldn't stand to lose. "The Tipsy Musketeer will become a place of controversy, a line in the sand. I can't do that to your legacy."

Mr. Murphy stroked his beard thoughtfully. He didn't actually have a beard, but he always stroked his chin as if he did. "After that stirring speech, I can see why city council might not work. Someday, you're going to be the mayor."

Connor could only shake his head at the familiar obstinacy. "I'm just trying to keep pedestrians from getting hurt outside our pub."

"Go get on your way, but be sure to come back Monday, and we'll have ourselves a talk about what's really bothering you."

"Everything else is going well. Cash flow is fine. Business is good."

"There's a problem with a woman."

"There's a problem with an intersection," Connor said. "There is no woman."

"That's a more difficult problem, then. You can't kiss and make up with no woman."

"What makes you so sure there must be a woman?" Connor asked. Mr. Murphy always knew too much about him.

"Your knuckles are scraped up. They're healing, but two or three days past, you weren't punching that bag of yours for some exercise, were you now? You didn't take the time to wrap your hands or put on your gloves."

Connor took one hand out of his pocket and flexed it. Mr. Murphy should have been Sherlock Holmes.

"When you come to drink whiskey with an old man at noon on a Friday, I know something's afoot. Friday is payday, don't you know? You should be getting the pub in order. Folks will be wanting to end their work week with a pint."

Connor buried his fist back into his pocket. "I do know that. I was taught by the best—and his father called him Seamus Murphy. I'll be back Monday."

Seamus Murphy waited until the door clicked shut before he reached for the whiskey. He added just a drop more, then raised his glass to admire the color.

One hundred shades of brown in a woman's hair? In the sunlight, no less. It was a wonder he hadn't dropped his glass when those words came out of his boy's mouth.

Seamus might be getting up in years, for that was what happened and no man could stop it, and his memory might not always be what it had been, but he could still read young Connor like a book. When that stubborn McClaine of unfortunately Scottish descent had raised his glass and spoken as poetic a toast as any Irishman on the Isle had ever spoken, Seamus had known there was a woman. Finally.

That boy could charm any woman into ironing his shirts, if he desired to. The fact that he was sitting here and not even trying could only mean one thing: he didn't think he was good enough for the woman in question.

Seamus sighed and raised his whiskey high. "To the fair colleen who has caught my boy's eye. He's as fine a man as anyone has met on this green earth, but I cannot make him see the truth of that. May the woman with one hundred shades of brown in her hair have better luck than Seamus Murphy at breaking through Connor McClaine's infernally thick skull."

Chapter Eight

"She's back!"

Rembrandt? Where?

Bridget roared into the pub through the employee entrance. She'd quickly recovered from her Tuesday hangover, so Hurricane Murphy had been back in force the past few days.

"Who's back?" Connor asked casually, coming out from behind the bar, determined to keep the foolish pounding of his heart his own secret.

"Me." Bridget dumped her backpack on a chair, then slammed her fist onto the table theatrically. "O God, that I were a man! I would eat his heart in the market-place." She pulled an imaginary heart out of an invisible man's chest and took a giant bite.

It was the next level of Delphinia's ominous intonation, *Finish him*. The women in his world relished bloodthirsty lines—not that Delphinia was part of his world.

Which was for the best.

"What are you back from, Hurricane?"

"I'm back to normal after the temporary insanity that made me pick Juliet's sappy balcony scene. I'm changing to Beatrice from *Much Ado About Nothing*. She's *sooo* much more like the real me."

"Eating hearts in the marketplace? You're into public executions by cannibalism?"

"Revenge tastes sweet, don't you know?"

"It's best served cold."

"Who has time to sit around and wait for things to get cold?" She tossed her red hair. "Not me."

Connor grinned at that. As she got older, Bridget was losing her girlishness, but none of her feistiness. The right kind of guy would appreciate having her keep him on his toes. Kristopher was an idiot if he didn't see it.

It wasn't really any of Connor's business. Still, every time he read a novel that had an overprotective older brother, the character's thoughts felt familiar. It was just as well that Connor had never had a sister, considering how much it took just to keep Bridget pointed in the right direction.

Bridget's smile was too smug. "My new piece is a solo. Kristopher's going to have to come up with something solo, too. Quickly."

Connor stopped grinning. "That's wrong of you, Britt. You know that. What is this really about?"

"Nothing."

"Something happened. You got your first hangover, and he tried to use his professor to make you jealous on the same day. Now, you're trying to get some kind of revenge."

The change in Britt's expression was instant. "That's why he was all over Dr. Dee? You think he wanted me to be jealous?"

Connor managed not to wince at the idea of another man being all over Dr. Dee. "Yeah, I do. Judging by your sudden change of heart about playing Juliet, I'm guessing he succeeded."

"We'll find out. I asked Dr. Dee to come hear my new role, and I told Kristopher to come if he wanted her to go over whatever his new piece is, too."

"She's coming," Connor repeated flatly. "Today. Here."

Rembrandt! Here!

"Yeah, I sent her an email, and she said she could meet me here." Bridget took her script out of her backpack with a defiant flourish. "It'll be just me, Kristopher and her, because I didn't tell anybody else. It might be good for him to see how old she is compared to someone his own age."

Connor was knocked speechless for a second. "That woman didn't do a thing to you, and you're trying to make her part of some petty revenge game. You're nineteen. She's a professor. You need to send her another email and tell her thanks, but no thanks, and apologize for taking up her time."

"Too late. She'll be here any minute. She said she was looking forward to it, so chill. I'm not pissed off at her. I don't even care what Kristopher thinks anymore, not after the way he treated me at the party."

All of Connor's pseudo-big-brother instincts kicked in. "What happened at the party?"

"*Nothing.* I thought he liked me, because he followed me the whole night, until I figured out he was babysitting me. Every single time I talked to a cute guy, he'd walk by and hand me a bottle of water and tell me to hydrate, like he was my dad or something. I hope he eats his heart out while Dr. Dee and I are working together on a speech about eating his heart out. Get it?"

It sounded like Kristopher had been jealous. The protective way he'd shown it at the party restored some of Connor's good opinion of him, but Bridget's attitude sucked.

Bridget held up her script. "I really do want her help. She's, like, my favorite professor I've ever had, so far."

Connor crossed his arms over his chest so he would neither explode nor wring her neck. "You like her, but you're making her waste her time and even her gas to drive here from BCC. It was rude of you to ask. I can't believe she said yes."

Why did she say yes?

Bridget shrugged, but she looked a little embarrassed, finally. An embarrassed Bridget was a defensive Bridget. "She's not coming from BCC. She was just our sub last semester. She teaches at Masterson. She can walk here from Hughes Hall, if she wants."

A professor at Masterson University. When he'd stood on the roof and wondered where Delphinia was, the answer had been that perfect green square and blue fountain. So near, and yet so very far.

"It's not like professors have that much to do," Bridget said. "They teach like one or two hours a day. It's not like she's going to get fired or something for leaving her office hours early. Her dad's the dean of my college."

Of course he is.

If Connor's coffin weren't already nailed shut, that would have done it. Dear old Dad would just love a high school dropout for his brilliant daughter.

"Her mom's something big, too. Like the person in charge of the whole English department."

Of course.

"They're all named Dr. Ray. That's why I know they're related. Everyone does. It's not like I've been creeping on her or anything."

Which meant Bridget had definitely been creeping on her. *What else did you learn?*

Bridget waved her script toward the stage. "I've got to memorize this. You want me to unlock the front door while I'm over there?"

Connor checked his watch. "Ten more minutes."

Unlocking the door ten minutes before opening time wouldn't normally faze him, but now he wanted those ten minutes to get his head on straight. The warning was good, at least. He'd be ready to do what he needed to do. Be polite. Offer her a drink. No leaning into one another. No eye-gazing. He'd be her biggest mistake. Ten minutes.

"Will do," Bridget called back on her way to the

stage. "I told Dr. Dee to use the employee entrance if the pub wasn't open yet, so she'll just go around the back if it stays locked."

"You did *what*? Damn it, Bridget, where's your head?"

"What'd I do now?"

"She's already doing you a huge favor, and you told her to go into the alley to use the back door?"

"Well, yeah, it's better than making her stand outside on the sidewalk, isn't it?" Bridget had reached the front door, and she strained to look this way and that through the gold lettering and etched swirls. "I don't see her out here. She could have just not gotten here yet."

"Or she could be standing in the goddamned alley." Connor quickly strode the length of the bar, around the corner, down the hall, past the storeroom. The storeroom might be a reminder of a stark place where he'd once lived, but the alley was the actual place where Connor had lived some hard, hungry days huddled by a dumpster. He didn't want her there. He couldn't stand the thought of her there.

The day he'd been released from prison, he'd had only the clothes he'd been wearing the day he was arrested. That was fine with him; most of the guys had been released early and wore ankle monitors. Not Connor. He'd served every day of his full sentence, so he got a check for one hundred dollars from the state and a voucher good for a bus ticket back to his county of residence.

He wasn't going back to that county.

No one had been waiting for him at the prison gate.

He'd never had a father. His mother had checked out of his life for good when he was fifteen. And his friends? They'd ditched the stolen car and run for it while Connor had been following the cops' orders. He'd gotten out with his hands up, only to be thrown to the ground to eat a mouthful of asphalt as two cops handcuffed him. His friends hadn't been caught.

Connor had walked out of the prison and kept walking.

The check-cashing place had charged him a fifteen-dollar fee. He'd bought burgers and fries at the first fast-food franchise he came to, so he didn't feel guilty about adding handfuls of their ketchup and sugar packets to the sad sack the state had provided to hold his few possessions: comb, toothbrush, the art history book—the librarian had given him permission to keep it—with the GED certificate tucked inside the cover, where it wouldn't get wrinkled.

He'd walked to a cheap motel, where he'd taken the longest, hottest shower of his life and then catnapped his way through the night, waking at every unfamiliar sound. It had been no more and no less restful than being in prison, but by the bed there'd been a ceramic table lamp, a breakable item, beautiful in its fragility. It could be smashed into sharp shards for weapons, and yet he was allowed to be in the hotel room with it, unsupervised. Prison was over.

The next morning, out of money, he'd started walking across Texas. He'd hit the interstate two days later, out of sugar and ketchup packets, and hitchhiked as far as a truck stop. He'd seen a car with Masterson Mus-

keteer window stickers, approached the driver, a guy
who was his age, and asked for a ride. Wedged into
a rich kid's car that was stuffed with an entire dorm
room's contents, Connor had arrived at a gas station
on Athos Avenue.

Connor hadn't eaten in days. He could have slipped
the twenty-dollar bill into his pocket, the one the rich
kid had casually stuck in his sun visor. It would have
been easy to palm a candy bar at the gas station, but
Connor had been scared to break any law. Another
cop, another set of handcuffs, and his whole nightmare
would begin over again. He'd rather starve.

He'd stayed on alert in the alleys, catnapping through
a few more nights. In the dumpster behind the Tipsy
Musketeer, he'd had some luck: a half-dozen sourdough
rolls that were stale but not moldy. He'd had one stuffed
in his mouth and was shoving the rest into his pants
when the employees-only door had opened. He and the
old man had stared at each other.

Mr. Murphy had extended a hand. Connor had
thought he wanted his rolls back. His instinct had been
to run, but he hadn't known if the police would come
after him for stealing trash. Before he could decide,
Mr. Murphy had reached for his arm to tug him up the
single step. *Come in, come in. No man eats like a rat
at my pub. Spit that roll out. We have Irish stew, hot.*

It had been the lowest, hungriest day of his life when
Connor had eaten out of a dumpster. Then Mr. Murphy had opened the door, and it had become the day
he was saved.

Connor reached the employee entrance and yanked

the door open. There she was, a step below him, looking small and lost with the dumpster looming behind her.

"Rembrandt."

"I was just about to knock." She sounded nervous. "I didn't want to just barge in, even though—"

"Come inside." He didn't wait—he couldn't wait—for her reply. He just took her by the arm and pulled her up the single step and through the door.

The hallway was crowded, the dolly behind him, cardboard boxes of napkins and coasters stacked three-high down one of the walls. To close the door, he had to pull Delphinia closer. They took another half step together as he shut the door, shuffling in sync. The awkward little dance elicited an awkward little chuckle from her.

His heart was pounding again. He *hated* that she'd been in that alley. She had a lovely life, a professor's life. He didn't want her living his. "Don't ever come here like that."

Her nervous smile faded. "I'm sorry. When Bridget asked where we could meet, I suggested it. You'd said I should come back again, but... I guess you don't want us using your stage all the time."

It took him a second to realize he'd been too intense. "I mean if the doors are locked, knock on a window. I'll let you in." She felt healthy and warm under her soft burgundy sweater, not shivering from hunger, from low blood sugar, from dehydration. The reality of her body, the normalcy of her presence, pushed his memories back into the past where they belonged. He gave her arm a gentle squeeze. "Because yes, you should come back. Anytime."

I'm losing my mind, anyway. Might as well get to look at you.

"So, it's okay to come, you just don't want me using the friends and family entrance?"

"I don't want you in an alley with a dumpster," he said, careful not to sound angry this time. "The main entrance *is* the friends and family entrance. This is the door we use to take out the trash."

The door opened inward with a swoosh. Kristopher walked in. "Hello."

Connor and Delphinia shuffled a few swift steps back, together.

"What are you guys doing back here?"

"Nothing," she said quickly, sounding as guilty as if they'd been caught doing something a hell of a lot more fun than they had.

That was interesting. What had she been thinking about while he'd been thinking about dumpsters?

She hastily backed away from Connor to put another inch of space between the two of them.

Well, well, well. Delphinia the Professor had been thinking about something better than he had. Not anything innocent, either. That blush looked like she'd been checking out his tattoo again.

Hell, yes. But that thrill of triumph died immediately. If she'd come to check out the bartender and pick up where her hungry eyes had left off Tuesday evening, then he was in trouble.

"Let me get you to the part of the pub you should be

in." He turned to lead the way. As he let go of her arm, he fought a bizarre impulse to slip his hand down her soft sleeve to interlock their fingers.

Only a minute in her presence, and he was losing his mind. Less than an hour ago, he'd had to rehash for Mr. Murphy the reasons he could not run for office like a regular citizen.

Connor paused by the utilitarian stairs that led up to the third floor and gestured for Kristopher and Delphinia to keep going. "Have a good rehearsal."

Connor headed up to his apartment, as desperate to lose himself in a good book as if he were a prisoner all over again. It was the only way he could block out everything surrounding him—or anyone two floors below him.

He'd told Mr. Murphy there was no woman. He was going to keep it that way.

Chapter Nine

Juliet Capulet was less foolish than Delphinia Ray.

For starters, Juliet had known her crush's name. Delphinia had been acting like a love-struck teenager since Tuesday, no matter how much she tried to employ logic and reason. She was obsessed with a man whose name she'd never asked.

The email from Bridget Murphy had given her the perfect excuse to return to the pub and fix this insanity. If she saw her alpha male in person again, well aware of the difference between science and magic this time, she would prove to herself that there was nothing there. It was a trick of hormones. An influence from a novel. She would see him, be no more impressed by him than she would be by any other reasonably attractive man, and she'd be able to return to her regularly scheduled life.

Then he'd reached out and pulled her through the door, up to his strong chest, and it had taken two seconds for her to feel the magic.

It had taken him two minutes to hand her off to his employee and leave.

She might as well be the nerdy ugly duckling and he the handsome high school quarterback who didn't know she existed—something which had never actually happened to her. She'd skipped the lovesick teenager phase while she was busy being the academic pride and joy of the Drs. Ray. It frankly sucked to finally go through the love-struck phase when she ought to be fretting about turning thirty.

She'd tried to pretend everything was normal while tutoring Bridget and Kristopher. She'd had them sit in the snug with her, *both* of them, and they'd flipped through their books on the little table and talked about the plays. Delphinia's radar was definitely not to be trusted. She'd thought Kristopher was flirting with her on Tuesday. Today, he was polite to the point of formality. He'd even called her Dr. Ray instead of Dr. Dee.

Unlike Tuesday, a few people had come into the pub. Since the sexy, sizzling bartender was gone, Kristopher had left to take care of the customers. Bridget had thanked Delphinia for coming—several times, with an almost comical emphasis on being *so* aware that she really had *no* right to ask her, but she was *such* a good professor, so she *really* appreciated her time. Then she'd left in whirlwind of college-sophomore energy, off to conquer something or someone else.

Delphinia's energy level was nonexistent in comparison. She had no desire to walk back to Hughes Hall, where her sturdy desk sat on sturdy, institutional carpeting. She'd rather sit in an Irish snug and admire the patina of the wood floor and feel sorry for herself.

Alone.

Not with a bartender who'd invited her to come back but hadn't actually cared if she did. Not with a law professor who invited her to places she couldn't refuse to go.

She didn't want to anger Vincent again, not after Tuesday. When she'd come downstairs in her most modest dress, they'd made their late entrance into the library. Joe Manzetti had already left. No matter how many *sweethearts* Vincent had thrown her way, she'd had the horrible feeling that if she'd been a door, he would have kicked her.

She didn't want to think about it. From her book bag, she took out the newest edition of the textbook for EN313, an advance copy which the publisher had given to the English department. She'd planned to review it this evening at home to determine what had changed from the current edition. She could do that here, instead. She stacked the new Victorian on top of her old Shakespeare, then took off its cellophane shipping wrapper.

As the book's spine flexed for the first time, the glue made a distinctive crackling sound. There was a joy in being the first to open a new book, to separate glossy pages and smell that fresh ink and paper. She smoothed her hand over the title page before turning it, hoping for something new.

A man in a black neck scarf that looked like it was choking him stared up at her from the book. It was the same photo of John Ruskin that had been in every prior version of the textbook, that had been in every version of every compilation of Ruskin's essays that she'd ever read. Ever.

How foolish of her to hope for anything new. The man was dead. It wasn't like somebody would discover a new photo of him any more than they'd discover a new essay or letter or sketch.

She closed the book. She was not going to require next year's students to purchase this edition. If they could buy a used one from this year, let them.

She was such a rebel. So wild.

With all the defiance her inner puppy could muster, she turned sideways on the bench and stretched her legs out. She crossed her ankles and made sure her gray skirt was tucked around her knees, then she pulled out her paperback. She wanted to get back to her lone wolf and his mystified heroine. Their kiss had changed something. The heroine was getting more rebellious by the page. Delphinia smoothed her hand over the hero's bare torso, a moment of anticipation, then she opened the book.

A Greek god walked right past her snug.

He stood at the front door and looked out for a minute, hands on hips, an impassive god surveying his world. He looked so supremely confident, or rather, so comfortable with himself and that perfect physique, so *capable*. And yet, she still imagined a sense of loneliness about him. He was both an ancient god and a modern wolf without a pack.

His expression wasn't so impassive after he watched the street for a minute. He was displeased by whatever he saw.

She was not displeased by what she saw. Instead of jeans and a tight T-shirt, he'd changed into semiformal attire, the most common dress for events at Dumas House. He wore black slacks, a crisp, ivory dress shirt, and a black suit vest. Without a tie or jacket, he gave those semiformal clothes a sexier appearance, like he was about to strip off the rest of them. Or perhaps he'd already stripped them off to do something less civilized, and just hadn't finished putting them back on again yet. Either way, if he walked into her parents' soiree, the ladies would all drop their wineglasses.

Science.

He watched the street outside. She watched him. He undid the button on his cuff and started folding the material back, casually exposing one strong forearm. He unbuttoned the other sleeve and started cuffing it back, too, as he turned away from the door.

He looked right at her.

She dropped her book.

He paused, then finished cuffing up the sleeve. "You're still here."

Delphinia really, really wished she knew if she could trust her radar, because she could swear he sounded surprised, but not disappointed. He didn't smile at her, but she imagined there was warmth in his calm expression. Even heat.

In your dreams, Delphinia Acanthia Beatrix. In your dreams.

The door opened behind him, and Bridget came back in, walking backward as she spoke rapidly to another young woman whom she had in tow. "It's not illegal to serve alcohol, so if he says that's a problem, it really isn't, no matter what he—jeez!" She turned around just as she was about to back into the bartender. Her nose nearly smashed into his shoulder. "What are you doing here?"

Delphinia did not imagine the way he looked up to the ceiling briefly, as if divine patience were available up there.

"I own the place," he said. "I'm here all the time."

"Duh. What are you doing by the front door?"

"I own the front door, too." His deadpan reply was said with a twist to his lips that meant he was trying not to smile. He and Bridget were obviously family. Bridget had said her great-uncle was the Murphy on the door's sign. If this bartender was the owner, then he must be a Murphy, too.

Bridget looked like she wanted to tell off the bartender—brother?—owner, but she forced a bright, fake smile. "I'm glad you're standing here. I wanted you to meet my friend, Allison."

"Hi," Allison said breathlessly, then her gaze skittered away as she blushed bright red.

Delphinia couldn't blame her. She was probably ten years older than Allison, yet she felt flushed every time she saw the bartender, too. The *owner*. Yes, being the owner suited him.

"Hey, there's Dr. Ray," Bridget exclaimed. "Hi!"

Delphinia was suddenly the focus of the three she'd been observing. Bridget couldn't be surprised she was here. They'd finished only fifteen minutes ago. Something was up—so Delphinia sat up and swung her feet to the floor.

Bridget turned to her friend. "Do you know Dr. Ray? She's amazing at Shakespeare. I took her class at BCC. You should take her classes if you can. She's really, really nice about being available for extra tutoring." Bridget turned back to Delphinia. "Like today. Thank you so much."

This was said as Bridget stole some anxious looks at the man who owned her great-uncle's place. Delphinia was being thanked for a reason that had nothing to do with gratitude, and she knew it. Her radar when it came to student-teacher dynamics wasn't broken.

"It's not necessary to keep thanking me. If I hadn't wanted to come to the pub, I wouldn't have."

That earned her a long look from a hot bartender.

"To tutor you," she clarified, because her inner wolf was a wimpy puppy.

Bridget smiled brightly at the bartender, who was not amused with her. "Hey, since you're standing right here, let's sit down for a second. Allison and I were just talking about something, and we wanted to talk to you."

Delphinia found herself in the middle of things as Bridget grabbed Allison by the arm and herded everyone into the snug. Delphinia had to slide over to make room for Bridget on the bench. Allison was pulled in after her to sit on one of the chairs. The bartender pulled out the other chair with a sigh. Her knee nearly brushed against his as they sat around the little table with her books in the center. Only two of her books— she'd dropped her paperback.

"My book." She sounded panicked as she dived for the floor.

Bridget reached down. "I can get it for you."

"No. Don't." She snatched it up and pressed it against her thigh, her hand covering as much of the cover as possible.

The bartender was watching her too closely. She fumbled with the opening of her book bag, then gave up and just laid it over the paperback as if she were laying a napkin across her lap. She smiled at Bridget with as bright and fake a smile as Bridget had used. "What are we all here to talk about?"

Bridget encouraged her friend. "Go ahead, Allison."

Allison braved eye contact with the bartender once more, since their chairs were opposite one another. Delphinia and Bridget sat on the bench and looked between them like they were watching a ping-pong match.

Allison served first. "Well, I just was thinking, this is such a nice place. I was thinking that I need somewhere to work weekends and nights, you know, when I don't have classes, but a lot of the bars aren't really the best place for a girl to work, but this is such a nice place. It's pretty. Bridget says the people don't get totally crazy here and nobody throws beers and things."

Almost there. You have to actually make the request to work here. It's not the boss's job to guess what you want. You can do it.

But Allison fell silent. She just looked at the owner as if he ought to take it from there.

Delphinia and Bridget looked at him. After a moment, he took pity on the girl and picked up her awkward attempt at a job request. "Are you twenty-one or older, Allison?"

"I'm nineteen. Same as Bridget."

"Then I appreciate your interest, but you have to be twenty-one to work here."

"That's not true," Bridget said, exasperated all out of proportion to his calm statement. "That's not the law. You have to be twenty-one to drink alcohol, not to serve it."

"At the Tipsy Musketeer, you have to be twenty-one to serve it."

"You let Kristopher work here before he turned twenty-one."

"As a busboy and dishwasher only." His expression was no longer entirely neutral. They must be related, because Delphinia would never have been so pushy with a person who looked at her as sternly as the owner looked at Bridget.

He redirected the conversation to Allison. "Would you be interested in washing dishes and busing tables? I can use an extra person weekend nights."

"She won't make any tips that way," Bridget said. "There's no money in busing tables."

"The waitstaff give ten percent of their tips to the busboy."

"But still—"

He pointedly turned back to Allison. "Kristopher

bused tables here for a long time. He's here now, at the bar. Why don't you go ask him what the job entails? It's not an easy one. If you're still interested, come back and talk to me."

"Kristopher?" Allison looked at Bridget. "Kristopher Newell works here?"

Delphinia wanted to laugh at the way Allison perked up at Kristopher's name a hundred times more than she'd perked up at the possibility of working here as a busboy. Delphinia exchanged a look with the bartender. He was as amused as she was, but neither one of them let themselves smile and embarrass the students. It was weepy Othello all over again.

Allison left for the bar with alacrity.

"Now, you can apologize," the man said to Bridget.

"For what? For bringing you somebody who would make a great waitress?"

"For dragging Dr. Ray into this. She's a guest. You made her sit through this excuse for a job interview for no reason."

"Yeah, but I got you to sit," Bridget bragged. "That lasted longer than the last friend I brought in here. She wasn't twenty-one, poof, goodbye."

"Now that you've *admitted* you manipulated a guest, you can *apologize*."

"I'm sorry, Dr. Dee. And *thank you* for helping Allison get more than a one-sentence interview."

From the direction of the bar, Allison's trilling laugh was joined by Kristopher's lower, amused chuckle. Bridget leaned over to see the bar beyond the wood partition. Way over. She frowned. "I'm just going to go see…"

And then, it was just Delphinia sitting in a cozy alcove with an alpha male who had the sleeves of his dress shirt cuffed up.

It was magic.

Chapter Ten

Connor couldn't just get up and run away like Allison and Bridget had. It would make Delphinia feel like nobody wanted to talk to her.

That couldn't be further from the truth. He did want to talk to Rembrandt. Only talk. But definitely, talk.

The two girls laughed simultaneously beyond the wood partition. Connor knew that type of laugh. Women were competing to show a fortunate man that each got his jokes better than the other. Connor only needed to glance at Delphinia's amused expression to know that she was aware of the situation, too.

"The course of true love seems to be running as smoothly as ever," he said.

"Running straight into a green-eyed monster," Delphinia answered.

He smiled at her joke, or she was smiling at his. Either way, Connor knew that the green-eyed monster was a Shakespearean phrase. "Play, act, scene?"

"You want me to do my bar trick?"

"We are in a bar."

"*Othello*, act three, scene three."

"Much better than a cherry stem."

He could leave now. They'd made polite small talk. He'd thank her again for her tolerance and tutoring of Bridget, then he'd get himself back behind the bar, where he'd have two feet of mahogany as a buffer between him and a woman who looked as touchable in her burgundy sweater as she had in her navy one.

He lingered too long; she started a new conversation. "Is Bridget your sister?"

"No."

"Your cousin?"

It was odd for her to think they were related. They didn't look alike. Bridget was a redhead. Connor was a basic brown-haired, brown-eyed guy. "No, she's a Murphy."

"But you're Mr. Murphy. Aren't you?"

"Not even close. Most people would say he either looks like a very large leprechaun or a small Santa. He put the Irish in this Irish pub. I'm a McClaine, which is Scottish. Mr. Murphy would be the first one to make that distinction. He sold me the pub two years ago, but I didn't change its name."

She tilted her head and smiled a little. "What's in a name? A pub by any other name would still be as sweet."

"What's in a name here is marketing. 'McClaine's Scottish Pub' doesn't really have a ring to it. But 'Murphy's Irish Pub?'" He winked at her. "That's catchy."

Maybe he was giving himself away by remembering every word of their Tuesday conversation, but that smile of hers made him reckless—that smile, and the fact that she wouldn't have gotten his joke if she didn't also remember Tuesday as clearly as he did.

Keep your wits about you, lad. He'd planned to treat her like any other customer. That meant he'd now stand, offer her a drink and leave her to her pleasure. But first, she had that book hidden in her lap. He'd told himself that he would find out the title, if she ever returned to his pub. That much, he'd allow himself.

"What are you reading?"

Her fingers tightened on the bag in her lap. With her other hand, she turned the hardcover books on the table toward him.

"Shakespeare for Bridget and Kristopher. *Selections of Victorian Prose and Essays* for everyone else I teach."

The *Selections* book on top had an eye-catching watercolor on its cover. It reminded him of his art history book, the one he'd found in the prison library, thick with dust on the outside, brilliant with color photos of paintings on the inside.

Connor touched the shiny, new textbook that had never seen a speck of dust. "May I?"

"Sure. It's the new edition for next year."

He leafed through it, bold titles catching his eye: *Venice, Heroes, Impassioned Truth*. The pages of close-written text were almost tissue-thin. They were punctuated every so often by thick, glossy pages printed with full-color reproductions of landscape paintings. His hands looked too rough, his knuckles too bruised, to hold such a pristine book.

He kept flipping through the book, anyway. He recognized a few of the paintings from his own books, but he paused at the painting of a woman who was standing in a circle of tiny people who held glowing plants and globes. The forest behind her was dark. The light on her face and throat was otherworldly, lit only by the fairy lights.

"Ah, Hughes," Delphinia said. "The nephew, not the uncle."

Connor had no idea what she was talking about, but she'd angled her body to see the book. Her head was tilted to see the photo from his angle, to see it at the same moment he was seeing it.

It was disconcerting. He read alone. During high school and the GED classes, he'd never liked it when a teacher would stop by his desk to see what page he was on. He'd even hated being expected to share a program or a hymnal during the prison's religious services. They'd been another good way to get out of the violence of the common areas for an hour a week, but if he was supposed to hold half of a hymnal while another inmate held the other half, he'd rather sit there with his arms crossed over his chest and read nothing at all.

"A Midsummer Night's Eve," she said. "Hughes didn't explicitly say the painting was inspired by Shake-

speare's play, but that's its common title. I'm glad they left it in this edition."

Connor was too aware of her closeness. It wasn't like the physical closeness in the back hallway. Reading the same page at the same time was not sexual in the least, yet it felt utterly intimate.

"She looks too sweet to get teased by all those fairies," Delphinia said, her eyes touching the page his fingertips were touching. "But I guess there wouldn't be much of a play if the course of true love ran smoothly. Bridget doesn't need any meddling fairies. I think Allison's throwing her for enough of a loop."

Connor kept his eyes on the page. "This woman has Bridget's hair color." But the lighting reminded him of Delphinia, of the way the sunlight had reflected from her book's pages up to her throat and face.

"She does," Delphinia agreed. "Maybe she's just as mischievous as those fairies, like Bridget would be, and they don't know it yet. I'll never look at that painting quite the same way now."

Connor turned the page, then another, quickly, until Delphinia sat up and no longer tried to see the pages he was seeing.

His relief was very real. Closeness, connection—these were not feelings he needed to have with Bridget's professor. They were not feelings he needed, period.

Another illustration stopped him for a second, a watercolor by Turner. He knew this one, knew its storm clouds over the sea, a thing of beauty created out of turmoil.

"It's yours, if you want it," she said.

He didn't look up from the page.

"The book, I mean. If you think it looks interesting, you're welcome to keep it."

She meant well. She couldn't know—but an old fury roiled through him. Rich people so easily gave away their possessions. They had so many, it didn't matter. The college student who'd picked him up as a hitchhiker—*You want a can of Coke? There's a six-pack in that cooler at your feet.* So many customers: *Send a round of drinks to those pretty girls over there.* When he'd been nineteen, with the taste of a stale sourdough roll still in his mouth, a man wearing a sports jersey and a Rolex had smacked his team's ball cap onto the bar. *Another loss. I hate this hat. Keep it or trash it, I don't care.*

None of them had ever saved ten pudding cups from a month's worth of state-provided meals in order to barter for a worn paperback copy of a twenty-year-old Tom Clancy thriller. Their generosity cost them nothing.

Connor couldn't look at Delphinia.

She sounded happy. "You gave me a free drink. This would pay it back."

Again—again, again—he was reminded of the disparity between them. The professor with her lovely life, the ex-con with the dark past. They had no connection.

He closed the book. He was one of the rich people now, and he knew it. He also knew he would never truly feel like he was. "You're being too generous. Textbooks like this cost more than a hundred dollars."

"I'm not being generous at all. That bourbon and Coke cost you more than this book cost me. We receive free sample books all the time. If a professor likes one, then hundreds of students will need to buy it as part of the course, so you can see why the publishers try to tempt us."

"This doesn't tempt you?" He ran his fingertips down the colorful cover, because if he looked at her, he'd be tempted by something that had nothing to do with books. He loved her hair, her face. He could look but not touch—but he remembered the feel of her sweater under his hand, the warmth of her body in the close hallway. "Then what's your pleasure?"

"Shakespeare is my first love." She smoothed one fingertip along the spine of the book lying underneath the *Selections*. "This is my own textbook from my undergrad years."

She'd nearly touched his hand. The scrapes on his knuckles reminded him of the fistfight he'd had with himself on the roof, so he folded his arms on the table and leaned forward to hide his hands. It was a dangerous trade-off, though. The last time he'd leaned into this woman, he'd been ready to give up everything to have her.

It was impossible not to think highly of her. She was his Rembrandt. But if he could frame her differently in his mind, so that she was just an intelligent woman, very pretty, sitting here in his snug, then he should be able to enjoy a conversation with her, before everyone came in to enjoy their Friday paychecks.

He smiled at her. "The harder you try to hide that book in your lap, the more curious I get."

"Oh, that. It's nothing. Just something for pleasure."

"But that's exactly what I'm asking the one and only Delphinia. Shakespeare is always good, but that's not what you're hiding. What's your pleasure?"

"What's yours?"

Seeing you.

He said nothing.

"You must have a favorite book that you read over and over." She looked at him with eyes that held as many shades of brown as her hair. It would be too easy to fall into that spell between them again.

He joked, instead. "Is this an 'I'll show you mine if you show me yours' kind of thing?"

"Yes. What's your favorite book?" She hadn't picked up on the innuendo, or she was deliberately ignoring it. She really wanted to know what his favorite book was.

He looked into her eyes, fell under her spell, and told her the truth. "A textbook like this one. It's an art book I found lying at the back of some library shelving when I was…younger. It was covered in years' worth of dust, but when I opened it, the color pages… I felt like I'd walked into some kind of oasis. The librarian let me keep it, because it had been missing for so long, it was no longer in the catalog system. I couldn't believe no one had noticed that a book like that had gone missing. I looked at the paintings for a week before I got around to reading the text. Then I had to look at all the paintings again, once I'd read about the subjects and the techniques."

"That sounds magical. Don't you love books?"

He wouldn't say he felt magic right now. He felt pain, actually, an unfamiliar pain, the vulnerability of revealing something so personal. He needed a little vulnerability of hers to balance his. "Your turn. What are you reading today?"

Her smile disappeared as she pressed her lips together.

It's not easy, is it?

"Go ahead," he said. "You can tell me."

"It's a novel."

"Is it, now?" He sounded like wise, old Mr. Murphy. Not the most seductive way to speak to a woman, but this wasn't anything like flirting. She felt vulnerable revealing her book. He understood.

"It's a romance. A paranormal. She's human, but he's a shape-shifter. They come from different worlds, but… well, it's a romance. They'll be together in the end."

"How do you know? Are you one of those people who reads the last page first?"

"Oh, never. I know it will end that way because that's the only right way for two people in love to end up. Together."

"Romeo and Juliet couldn't live without each other, so they ended up together. I suppose that's romantic."

"They ended up *dead* together. That is not a romance. It needs to end happily-ever-after together, every time. I wish real life could be that way."

"I see."

It was a childlike wish, that happily-ever-after. Parents wouldn't disappear when kids needed them. Mr. Murphy wouldn't get pneumonia. No one would ever be hit by a car. Everyone who broke the law would be caught, instead of one guy taking the fall.

Connor couldn't dwell on the injustices of the world. These were his precious minutes with the most intriguing woman who'd ever walked into his bar.

"Actually, I don't see," he said. "You're still hiding the book. We had a deal."

"I said I'd show you mine if you showed me yours. You didn't show me anything. You merely described to me how magnificent it was."

She spoke with a perfectly straight face, but she had to be making that sexual innuendo intentionally. Didn't she?

Her exaggeratedly innocent blink gave her away. "Men always claim theirs is magnificent, so…"

He burst into laughter. "I believe *you* said it was magical. That's a new one for me."

She laughed with him. "What's your art book called? If you don't remember, then I'll know you haven't really read it over and over."

He shouldn't tell her, but she'd come back to see him. She'd made him laugh. It would reveal far too much, but he told her the truth. "My favorite book is called *Rembrandt: Passion in Full Color.*"

Her eyes widened. "Rembrandt? But—oh." She spoke in that breathy voice a woman used when a man touched her just right.

"Your turn, Rembrandt."

Neither of them was laughing now. This still wasn't a flirtation. He didn't know what it was. Unintentional seduction, maybe.

She was silent for an eternity before she took a deep breath. "My book is called *A Mate with Destiny.*"

The silence was profound, sexually charged, emotional. Everything felt profound, that he should call her Rembrandt, that she should be reading about two lovers' date with destiny—

Wait a minute.

"A…mate? *A* Mate *with Destiny?*" Connor sat back, but he rubbed his jaw so he wouldn't laugh. "With a title like that, you know I've got to see it."

"You can't judge a book by its cover. Or its title."

He held out his hand, palm up. "It sounds magical."

She slapped the book into his hand with a huff.

Finally, he got a good look at the blue cover. He kept looking in a kind of numb surprise, while his brain rearranged a few preconceived notions about genius professors.

"It's really very good," she said defensively. "Very atmospheric, lots of mysterious lakes and fog under the moon."

He tapped the cover. "This guy is ripped."

She tried to grab it out of his hand, but he was too quick.

"I've got to read this." He turned his shoulder to her and opened the book, smiling unguardedly now at this unexpected side of Delphinia.

She came out of her seat a bit as she made a more determined grab for it, but her fingers only grazed his wrist.

"Is he supposed to be a wolf?" He flipped to another random page. "He's a *wolf.*"

"Give it back." There was a desperation to her voice. No laughter, no friendliness—only panic.

It chilled him. He handed her the book immediately.

She practically hugged it to herself. "I just… It's just that I haven't finished it yet. And it's not that recent, so it might be out of print, so if I lost this copy, I wouldn't ever know how it ends. I usually finish a book once I get more than halfway into it, and—"

"Delphinia—"

"It's not really mine. I borrowed it, really, and I should put it back on the swap shelf when I'm done."

"You don't have to justify yourself. It's your book. You wanted it back."

She stilled, looking surprised he'd said that.

She wouldn't be surprised if she knew the real him. If he'd learned anything in prison, it was how important possessions could be—and how harrowing it was to have someone take yours, someone bigger and stronger than you were. Someone more vicious.

"I'm sorry, very sorry." He barely recognized his own voice. He never spoke this gently, but he didn't want her to think he was some kind of brute. "I didn't realize how much you didn't want me to see it."

"I'm overreacting." She pressed her thumb into the groove of a carved rosette and scowled at her own hand. "I don't know why. It's been a long week, I guess."

He wanted to cover her hand with his own, so she couldn't scowl at herself.

He had no more right to touch her than he had to touch her book. "Don't apologize for fighting for something you love. That book means something to you."

"It doesn't mean anything to me."

He knew that wasn't true. The first time he'd laid eyes on her, she'd been absorbed by it.

She pressed the pad of her thumb harder into the edge of the carving. "It doesn't even make me happy."

That could be true. She'd looked so very unhappy Tuesday. She was so unhappy now.

It was time for him to go, because she was unhappy, and he didn't know what to do or what to say to make it better for her. He wished he did—and because he was wishing such an unfamiliar kind of wish, he needed to get back to work, back to real life, back to bartending and customers and the kind of temporary happiness his pub provided. Everything with Delphinia was too unfamiliar.

He scooted his chair back, a scrape of new wood over old, but he didn't leave.

"It makes me want things I shouldn't want." Her voice had taken on a harder edge.

He tried a bartender's smile, a little friendly charm, hoping to interrupt this sudden, fierce misery she was directing at herself. "It makes you want what? A wolf?"

"*Yes*. Exactly that." She cut her gaze from the carving to him. "It makes me want a lone wolf in my life. A man who's so strong and capable that he doesn't need anyone else. But he *wants* someone else. Their eyes meet across a crowded room, and the attraction is instant. It's destiny."

The intensity of her words made the hair on the back of his neck stand up. It was almost a challenge. He couldn't run away now. He'd been conditioned years ago to never be the one who backed down—but to never be the one to antagonize, either. Pouring fuel on a fire got one burned, so he returned her fierce gaze with a carefully blank one of his own. And waited.

"I know the book cover is sexy. Their relationship is sexy, but there's so much more to it than sex. The reason it's sexy is because they belong together. It's an intense kind of love, the kind you scale mountains for, the kind you'd give up everything for. They're soul mates." She frowned at the cover as she riffled the book's pages at a corner with her thumb, a few quiet zips, before she set it on the table. "But it's only a book. That's not really how love goes."

It wasn't? That had to be one hell of a book, then, because she'd sounded pretty convincing.

She slid the Shakespeare out from under *Selections* and reloaded her book bag. She pulled the strap onto her shoulder and sat on the edge of the bench, ready to leave, but she didn't get up, just as he had not. They were sitting at a right angle to one another, so as she looked straight ahead, out of the snug, out to the world she would return to at any moment, he looked at her profile.

She stared, unblinking, at the empty stage. "I'm seeing someone."

Too many emotions made his heart pound too hard, as if he needed to fight, as if there were something to fight for. But he was a bartender; he'd learned not to interrupt folks at his bar. He kept listening.

"Love isn't a struggle," she said resolutely, addressing the stage. "It's simple, really. Most people meet someone who suits them, someone they work with, or someone who knows the same people they know. Someone who lives where they live."

His hands were in fists.

Of course she's seeing someone. Of course.

Fists were useless.

She looked down at her own smooth hands, her own unscarred knuckles. "Your lives are already running along the same course. You fall into step without any effort or angst or drama, and the next thing you know, you've been dating for half a year, and those colleagues and families are looking forward to the next step. It's simple, and it's nice, and it's real life. I need to stop reading books that make me want something more."

But you want more. She deserved more. He also knew *more* was not a man with a criminal record who had no idea what her career involved, who her friends were, where she lived—or what she needed to be happy.

She stood, so he did, too. They both stepped toward the open side at the same time, but there was no awkward, shuffling dance. They simply stopped and faced one another, nothing between them but air and emptiness.

"I don't know your name, Mr. McClaine."

"Connor." *My father never called me Connor McClaine, not that I can remember...*

"Connor McClaine," she said.

For a moment, the sound of his name spoken in her voice filled the empty space.

But only for a moment. "I need to get back to campus and let you get back to business, too. You've been very generous about the stage, but I won't impose on you again. I think Bridget and Kristopher are through with me."

"You're welcome back at any time."

"But use the main door?" She made a sad attempt at a smile.

"All my friends do."

He didn't have any friends, not really. He had Mr. Murphy, his mentor and lifesaver, a man old enough to be his grandfather. Otherwise, he had acquaintances. Customers. Business associates, from the city council members to the students he employed to the delivery drivers who stacked boxes three-deep in the back hallway, which forced people to stand close together.

But no friends.

Now that Delphinia was leaving, it occurred to him that he would have liked to have become friends with her. He might have adjusted to that unfamiliar closeness as they'd shared a book.

I'm seeing someone. He'd absorbed the one-two punch of those three words without flinching. Disappointment couldn't hurt him. If it could, he wouldn't have lived to see twenty.

"Have a good weekend," she said.

"You, too."

She walked out the door and out of his life.

It was automatic for Connor to turn back to the snug and push in the chairs, putting things in order for the Friday night crowd. Delphinia had left the new textbook on the table for him, so easily giving away something that had come so easily to her. He picked it up, and there it was, the book with the blue cover. She'd left that, too.

That book had cost her something. A piece of her heart.

But she'd said she hadn't finished reading it yet. As much as he wanted to believe she was the kind of person who gave away things she valued, she'd only left it behind in the hope that she'd leave a little of her pain behind when she left his pub. Everyone tried to leave their pain behind them when they left the pub.

The sound of screeching tires blew his thoughts apart. *Not again—*

The sickening crash of impact, this time. *She just walked out there—*

He was already yanking open the front door when a woman screamed.

Chapter Eleven

His heart stopped at the sight.

A car was crumpled around the lamppost in front of his pub. Its front tires were on the sidewalk, its engine still running, steaming. Beside it, Delphinia was on her hands and knees.

His heart must not have stopped, because he could run.

"Delphinia." Other bystanders scattered as he dropped into a crouch beside her, putting his hand on her back, ducking to see her face. "Are you all right?"

"It wasn't me," she said, but he'd just glimpsed a twisted bicycle and knew that. "It wasn't me."

A few feet away, a young man managed to sit up with help from bystanders. His bicycle helmet was still on, but his clothes were torn, and the exposed skin was raw and bloody. He held his arm and rocked in pain.

Connor felt Delphinia take a deep, deliberate breath under his hand. She was okay. It wasn't her. He could go check on everyone else now.

He stayed at her side.

He looked up at the gathering crowd. "Who called 911?"

"I did," a young woman answered. Another man, too.

"Good. See if you can turn off the car."

The driver had run to the cyclist, loudly telling everyone that there'd been no way he could have stopped in time, and the cyclist hadn't been using the crosswalk. Two women put themselves between the driver and the cyclist.

The cyclist's backpack had gone flying. Papers blew along the crosswalk. A book had landed open. Its pages fluttered as traffic started moving again, driving around the crumpled car and twisted bike.

Connor pointed at a young man who was just gawking. "Get his books together for him. The ambulance will be here in a second." The sirens were already close.

"It wasn't me," Delphinia said under her breath, still on her hands and knees, looking at the sidewalk.

Connor rubbed her back as police and ambulance arrived at the same time. "Let's get out of the way."

She nodded. He could stand from his crouch easily, but she had to get up from a more awkward, crawling position. She picked up one hand and shook it.

He wasn't going to watch her crawl; he slipped his hands under her arms and lifted her to her feet.

She held up her hands between them and looked at her palms. They weren't just dusty from the sidewalk. They were bright red from a hard slap on the concrete.

He moved closer, until the backs of her hands rested on his chest. He kept his hands under her arms, as if he might lift her in the air over his head, like every couple in TV reality shows. In reality, he didn't want her to drop to the ground if her knees gave out.

Or the devil could take him for a liar. The reality was that he needed to hold her unbroken ribs between his palms and feel her breathe, so his own breath would return to normal.

"Are you sure you weren't hit?" He'd never been more grateful to look into a woman's eyes. She took another intentionally deep breath, her ribs expanding between his hands.

"I jumped back and lost my balance and tripped, that's all." She sounded more confident, more like herself. "My reflexes are not exactly catlike."

"Your reflexes must be fantastic. You're standing here, talking to me." He had to fight his own reflex, which was to squash her against his chest, scraped hands and all.

He let go of her. Wanting to feel a woman breathe wasn't an acceptable excuse to hold her on a public sidewalk.

The paramedics wheeled a stretcher to the cyclist. The sheriff's deputy was a familiar face from the bar, Deputy Kent Grayson. When he spotted Connor, he came to him first. Why the hell did cops always want to talk to him?

"Did you see it happen?" Deputy Grayson sounded hopeful, but Connor shook his head.

"I did," Delphinia said, but she frowned at the lamppost. "Or not really. I heard something, and I turned, but the car was already coming at me. I don't know how I got out of the way."

"Wait here," the deputy ordered her. "Don't go anywhere until I can get your statement."

"No," Connor said, a reflex. He was not leaving her out here on the sidewalk for the next hour. "She'll be inside my place."

"Sure. Thanks, Connor." The deputy turned to the rest of the crowd and started canvassing for witnesses and sending bystanders away.

Connor stopped worrying about everyone else in town and focused on Delphinia. "Come in and sit down for a minute. You could use a glass of ice water, or anything else you want."

"My hands are shaky."

"Yeah." *Mine don't feel so steady, either.*

"Just leftover adrenaline from having a scare, right?"

"Right." *The scariest five seconds of my life.*

Good God, what if she'd been on the other side of that lamppost? What if?

"My knees hurt. I might have landed on my knees first, do you think? Because otherwise my hands would hurt worse." She started to bend down to get her book bag, but Connor picked it up for her. She froze with her head down, looking at nothing.

"Delphinia?"

"My skirt." She picked up a bit of the gray chiffon delicately between her thumb and finger, lifting it away from her on one side. On the skirt was a fat, black smudge. "It's from the car tire. That's—that's how close it—that was a close one, wasn't it?" She looked up to him, too pale. Her expression started to crumple. "Connor?"

He swept her up into his arms and started walking toward his door. Damn the sidewalk crowd and to hell with whatever he did or did not have the right to touch. He needed the weight of her in his arms. He needed to hold her close to his chest.

One of his waiters had come outside, so he ran ahead and held the door open as Connor carried Delphinia over the threshold. It was all he could do not to take her straight to the staircase, up three flights of stairs and into his apartment, so he could slam the door on the rest of the world. It was visceral, this need to hide her away from danger, to drag her into his own dark cave and keep her there, safe and his, all his, like he was some kind of caveman.

Or some kind of wolf.

He wasn't a damned animal. He was a man with self-control, a man who took no risks, because he already had everything he needed in life. Delphinia was a nice, normal woman, and he didn't need to clutch her to his chest just because she was alive. All of this was too much, too emotional, and it did no one any good for him to keep losing his mind.

He set her on her feet by the snug.

She blew on her scraped-up hands. "I feel like such a wimp. I'm not going to freak out, I promise."

He set her bag on the table and took her hands in his, to evaluate them for first aid, nothing more. "You can wash them in the restroom. We'll get some ice for them while you're waiting for the deputy. What would you like to drink?"

"Ice water? Or is that too wimpy? A bourbon and Coke might be better."

"You don't have to choose. I'll have my crew bring you both."

"We're a matched set. Look at us." She turned their hands over. "You're scraped up on the knuckles, I'm scraped on the palms. Between the two of us, we still have one good set of hands."

He smiled politely at her observation, squeezed her fingers very gently, then let go. "Go wash up. I'm glad you weren't hurt worse."

He let himself watch as she crossed the pub, passing through the sunlight from the window into the darker back of the building, one more time.

Then he returned to his job. A guest had been hurt. He gestured for the nearest waitress to come over. "Go check on her, just in case she needs any help."

"Sure thing. Nobody was killed out there or anything, right?"

"Maybe a broken arm. Not as bad as last year."

She left and Connor gave more orders. "Gina, go in

the back and fill a plastic bag with ice for her, please. Kristopher, bring her an ice water and a bourbon and Coke." He barely hesitated. "Sit with her, *if* she wants company while she's waiting on the deputy. DeAndre can handle the bar by himself. If she doesn't want to talk, then leave her alone."

Kristopher made a gesture of surrender. "I got that message loud and clear the first time."

Connor turned on his heel to head outside. He needed to see what he could do to expedite things. It was Friday, payday, and as Mr. Murphy had told him—twice— folks would be looking for a place to buy a pint. Having a police cruiser and a wrecked vehicle in front of his pub was bad for business, and that's what Connor was, a businessman.

That was all he was. He wasn't a caveman or a wolf or a godforsaken Romeo. He wasn't looking for the kind of love that made people so miserable they had to scale mountains to be together, not the kind of love that led to something so much more than sex, whatever that might be. No wanting, no needing, no soul mates. He wasn't looking for any of it.

He was checking on the cyclist because he was a businessman. He was watching out for Dr. Delphinia Ray because she should be safe when she was in the Tipsy Musketeer. All of his customers should feel safe in the Tipsy Musketeer.

It wasn't magical. It was business.

But an hour later, when the deputy had come and gone, and Delphinia had iced her knees while drinking two bourbon and Cokes, he left his place of business during its busiest hour to walk her to her home.

He didn't want to, but he needed to, because if she walked out that door and he heard tires screech again, then carrying her up to his apartment and locking the door on the rest of the world would feel like a sane thing to do.

Chapter Twelve

"This is where you live?"

"I'm afraid so." Delphinia felt a little helpless as she gestured at the imposing white columns.

Beside her, Connor was quiet for a long moment. He took a breath to say something—nope. He stayed silent.

"It's called Dumas House," she offered, as they stood on the sidewalk by the historical marker which declared that same fact.

"It's…nice."

She kind of snorted at that. "You don't have to try so hard. It's not mine. The university owns this."

He looked from the white pillars to her. "That's one heck of an employment perk."

She'd never felt more like a teenager. "I live with my parents. My father is Dean of the College of Liberal Arts. I just…" She pointed at the portico side of the house. "I have a bedroom over there. And a salon. To watch TV in."

Brilliant. Because having a salon in one's parents' house made one sound so mature, compared to having only a bedroom.

Connor was slowly shaking his head. "This is where you grew up."

She wasn't sure that had been a question, but she answered him. "No, I grew up in a small house near Princeton when my parents were more junior professors. We moved to Masterson when I started high school. Father was only the department chair of archeology then. This is the dean's house. He didn't become dean until I was working on my bachelor's."

Connor squinted just slightly at that, never taking his eyes off the white columns.

She didn't want him to think she was incapable of independence. "I lived on my own while I got my bachelor's degree. I went all the way to Taunton University in New England. I'd only just turned seventeen, but my parents had no choice except to let me go. My great-grandfather founded Taunton. I thought it was very clever of me to back them into a corner that way. They couldn't insist that Taunton wasn't as good as an Ivy League, could they? Especially not when the president of Taunton came to see us to recruit the founder's descendent."

Connor finally looked away from the white columns as she spoke, but his expression was as perfectly neutral as a statue. He could have been hurling a thunderbolt or composing on a harp. It was impossible to tell.

But she knew what he was thinking, because she'd made this same mistake with kids in high school. "Never mind. I know how that sounds. Being the fourth generation of college professors and presidents and deans and whatnot is…not cool. It makes me sound like a stuck-up brain, doesn't it?"

"Not at all. Why shouldn't you have grown up in a respected family? Why shouldn't you enjoy a settled life? I'm glad you live with your parents."

"You are?"

"You had a close call this afternoon. If it starts to bother you later, I'm glad to know you'll have someone around."

"They're somewhere on the other side of the building from me, but I know what you mean. Thank you." Weren't her manners just so sweet? All her *pleases* and *thank-yous* had made adults in collegiate settings approve of the elementary-aged girl in their adult world.

She didn't want her time with Connor McClaine to end here, to end now, to end like this. He was going to go back to his world. Like this house, his building was big and historic, yet it had felt safe and snug when he'd carried her there—when he'd literally swept her off her feet and carried her there.

What was it like to be cradled against the chest of an alpha male when you were feeling shaky and scared?

It was the best feeling in the world, that's what it was.

She was ruined. She wanted Connor, wanted to talk with him about books and bourbon, to watch him carry kegs and recite Shakespeare. She wanted him to carry *her* instead of a keg, using his strength—not even needing all of it, just some of it—to make everything so easy for her when even crawling felt too difficult. She wanted him to murmur words that were more intimate than *wash your hands*, although when he'd murmured that, she'd gone weak in her scraped-up knees.

But he was leaving, because she was only the brainy girl with a hopeless crush on the handsome all-star. He'd walked her home, because he was a nice person. He'd carried her books for her, too. If she were fifteen years younger, this would be the pinnacle of romance.

She was nearly thirty, and she wanted more.

"Won't you come inside?" She heard herself issuing a gracious invitation like a grown woman who'd been raised in the most civilized settings. "You've done so much for me. I must owe you at least one drink."

He was shaking his head before she could finish her sophisticated sentence. "I have to get back to work. It's Friday night. I just wanted to be sure you were steady on your feet."

He sounded like her father, restricting the ladies of the family to petite glasses of sherry. "An adult can drink a bourbon and Coke without being in a drunken stupor and unable to find her house, even if she's a *lady*."

"I meant because you hurt your knees." He said it so kindly, she was embarrassed at her petulant remark. He handed her book bag to her. She felt the square edge of the paperback through the thin cloth.

He'd given it back. He didn't want to read her book.

He didn't want to know more about her. What more was there to know, after all? She was only a professor, as she'd been born to be. She wasn't a heroine, inspiring and intrepid—or sexy.

She tapped the lump of the paperback. "You weren't tempted to read *A Mate with Destiny*."

"You said you like to finish books you've started, and you said this one was guaranteed to end happily. I thought you might need that this evening."

He humbled her. His thoughtfulness touched her. But he was leaving her, because he had an entire life that didn't include her.

"You're a very kind man, Connor McClaine."

She rose on her toes and kissed him on the cheek. It wasn't a peck, nor was it passionate. Just a soft kiss on his cheek. Her heels were already back on the ground before she realized that he'd shaved recently, before beginning his Friday night workday.

"Take care of yourself, Rembrandt."

He walked away.

O that I might touch that cheek.

She had. She'd kissed it.

She watched him go and told herself it was a poignant, sweet moment, but the truth was, her lips burned from the heat of his skin. Everything burned for everything about him that was virile and masculine and dangerous and protective and kind. And adult.

Then she turned to go inside and tell her mommy and daddy how her day had gone.

* * *

Mother and Father were not all that interested in her grand entrance to their salon.

Mother was reading a book with a pen and notepad balanced on the arm of her chair. The notepad was always at the ready, should she find some discrepancy that required her further investigation. Next to her, in his own armchair, Father was reading his newspaper, the real kind, nothing digital on a tablet or phone.

When she'd been a child, Delphinia had loved playing on the floor by his chair, loved the green and blue and yellow diamonds on his argyle socks, loved the polished leather of his loafers, and most of all, she'd loved the anticipation of that moment when he'd lower just one corner of the paper and address her mother. "This is interesting, Rhea," he'd say, and then they'd discuss something wonderfully adult about traffic or politics or scientific discoveries.

Delphinia stood before them and took in the familiar scene. This was their life, their marriage. As Connor McClaine had said, why shouldn't they enjoy a settled life?

But should she? She was ready to move on, to move out, to move into her own life, to throw away other people's routines and find her own.

She was second from the top of the waiting list for the apartment now. Someday soon, these evenings would be a thing of the past. She should try to appreciate them while she was still here. She took a seat on the settee across from them.

"One would think," her father said, as he turned the

page and his newspaper made that distinctive rustle, "that we would have taught our child to knock when entering our salon."

"I wanted to tell you about my day," Delphinia said.

"If only etiquette allowed for a polite greeting before launching into one's own concerns," Mother said.

They didn't look at her. They didn't *see* her, didn't notice her ruined skirt.

Delphinia had spent hours with drama majors this week. They were exciting students. They demanded attention. She decided to channel Bridget Murphy.

"Apparently," she announced, "today was not my day to die."

Her mother looked up from her book. Her father lowered one corner of his newspaper to observe her. He looked at his wife. "Well, that sounds rather dramatic, Rhea."

"It *was* dramatic. There was an accident." Delphinia held out her hands. "A car drove onto the sidewalk, because it was trying to dodge a bicycle. It didn't hit me, because I jumped out of the way, but I fell hard on the concrete. The cyclist was hit, and he was taken away in an ambulance. I was so lucky that only my hands and knees got scraped up. So lucky. The wheel missed my legs by a millimeter. Look at my skirt."

Without quite knowing how, she found herself with her mother sitting next to her, her hand patting her back as she looked at her raw knees, saying, "Oh, Delphinia." Her father was beside her, handing her a glass of sherry. His newspaper was on the floor.

All Delphinia could think was that Connor McClaine

had been so right. It was a good thing to have family around after a bad scare.

She took the delicate sherry glass with her undamaged fingertips—and then Vincent was there. He hadn't been there a minute before, but he was dropping to his knee in front of her, which blocked her father from coming closer.

"I can't believe this." Vincent took her free hand and kissed her knuckles, which reminded her too much of the way he'd done that by the stairs. He squeezed her hand. "How terrifying."

She hissed and pulled her hand away. He looked so crestfallen, she apologized. "I'm sorry, but my palms are scraped up."

Her mother stayed next to her, but she'd taken her hand off her back. Delphinia wished with all her heart that she could be fussed over a little longer by her parents, but Vincent was here now.

"Where did it happen?" Vincent asked.

"Athos Avenue."

"Be a little more exact, sweetheart."

Such a commanding man, her mother always said. She meant it as a compliment.

"At the Stadium Drive intersection, by the Irish pub."

"That pub!" Vincent exploded to his feet. "It's that damned pub owner's fault. You know the pub, the Irish something-or-other." He was speaking to her father now, not to her.

"Are you referring to the Tipsy Musketeer?" Father asked.

"Yes, that's it. I knew you'd know it. You know everything about Masterson. There's a real problem with the owner."

Delphinia forgot about her hands. The owner?

"Oh, that building is lovely." Mother turned to Father. "What is the owner's name? Murphy? We went to that wedding reception there. He was so affable, we returned a few times."

Delphinia couldn't remember her parents partying anywhere except the library or the music room or the president's house, not since Father had been made dean. This wedding must have been while she'd lived in New England.

"Yes, it's Murphy," her father said. "Fine old Irishman."

Vincent set her parents straight. "It's been sold. The new guy is some upstart, younger than I am."

I'm younger than you are. Do you think I couldn't run a business? But Delphinia didn't interrupt. The conversation was clearly between Vincent and her parents now. No one was looking at her or her knees.

"What a shame," her mother said. "A young owner probably installed a bunch of televisions for the sports fans. I'm afraid to see what the students have done to the place. They damaged the student union after that football game in November."

"No, it's still beautiful inside," Delphinia said. She was suddenly the focus of all three of them. It shouldn't have been more unnerving than being the focus of Connor and Bridget and Allison, yet it was. "The chandelier, the stained glass—it's very authentically Victorian."

Vincent was just a fraction cooler as he spoke to her.

"I wasn't aware you patronized the place. We've never gone there together."

Her mother chuckled—elegantly. "With all those Tuesday and Thursday evenings, I assumed you two had tried every restaurant in town by now."

Delphinia braced herself. Vincent was going to demand to know what her mother was talking about, and everything was about to explode into a big shower of confessions.

The beat of silence was terrible.

"They've had quite a few accidents involving MU students at that intersection," Vincent said.

"There was quite a bad one last year," Father said. "It nearly left a young lady paralyzed."

"Yes, that's the one I'm thinking of."

That was it? Vincent was letting her mother's comment about Tuesdays and Thursdays go? It didn't seem possible.

Delphinia took a sip of sherry to sneak a look at Vincent. He was looking back. His expression left no doubt that she was going to be required to explain things later.

Vincent turned his attention back to her father. "That new pub owner isn't helping matters, I can tell you that. The city council voted to fund fresh paint for the crosswalk, but what does this yahoo do? He tells them it's not enough. He wants some kind of grand, million-dollar bridge to go from the campus to his side of the street, so the council went back to the drawing board, and no one repainted the crosswalk. Now, look what a tragedy we almost had."

"Paint couldn't have stopped it," Delphinia said—

or interrupted, really—but Vincent hadn't even been there. "Paint won't prevent a sedan from swerving into people."

The beat of silence that followed was even more fraught with tension. Vincent did not like to have counterarguments made, yet he was supposed to love her. Then again, her father did not like her to interrupt, either, and her father definitely loved her.

"Did you attend the last city council meeting, and I just didn't see you there?" Vincent chuckled at his rhetorical question before he turned back to her father. "Imagine the game-day crowd leaving the stadium and being funneled over a bridge to the door of his bar."

"Quite a transparent motivation. I'm surprised the city council hasn't picked up on it."

"Perhaps…" Vincent walked away to pour himself a glass of port. He topped off her father's glass. "Perhaps I should make a point of bringing it up the next time the mayor attends a university event. Joe Manzetti, too, should I run into him. I understand he's been approached to consult on the construction."

"You just missed him on Tuesday," her mother said. "He was here."

"Did I? What a shame." Vincent looked at Delphinia over the rim of his glass as he drank her father's port.

Now that she was home, sitting still, Delphinia ached all over. Wrists, shoulders, back—everything hurt, not just her hands and knees, and she wanted nothing more than to take a hot bath in silence.

She set down her sherry. "If you'll excuse me, I think I need to go rest for the evening."

"I'll walk you back to your room," Vincent said.

"There's no need. You must have come to speak to my father about something besides my accident."

"I came to see you." Vincent stood where he was, too close, watching her as she bent down to pick up her book bag while trying not to brush her face against his slacks. "Your side of the house was empty, so I came here. I overheard your story just as I was coming in. Quite a shock for me."

"I'm sorry about that, Vincent, but I need to retire for the evening. Good night."

She left. She hadn't made it to the central staircase when she heard Vincent's decisive footsteps behind her.

"Delphinia Ray. We have things to discuss." His words were as clipped as his footsteps. He passed her by a pace and then turned to face her, forcing her to stop. If he'd been a sheepdog, he would have just positioned himself to force her to change direction.

Which made her the sheep.

All she wanted to do was go into her bedroom, shut the door and hide from the rest of the world.

"*What* Tuesdays and Thursdays?" he asked.

She wasn't his sheep to herd around. She called upon what little inner wolf she'd discovered she had this week. "It was nothing. I was asked to cover a few classes for a professor at BCC, that's all."

"At BCC? You were teaching at the community college?"

"Don't say it like that. It's a good school."

"Don't say it like—?" He snapped his mouth shut

and cupped her chin. "Aren't you just full of surprises, my lady professor?"

Delphinia didn't answer. His hand was holding her face like a lover's, but it seemed as if he had grabbed her chin to force her to look at him. When she tried to pull away, he tightened his hold on her chin, holding her in place for a beat, and then, he kissed her.

It was a real kiss, mouth on mouth, a sudden display of more raw passion than she'd known he was capable of. His mouth demanded her mouth to open, to allow him to explore her intimately. He'd kissed her many times before, and he kissed well, but this was…more. More sexual. More dominant.

It ought to be thrilling.

She felt so very little.

He finished kissing her and spoke quietly in her ear. "I love you."

He'd never said that before. She shut her eyes and braced herself for who-knew-what, but Vincent only kissed her forehead. "You're the perfect woman for me. I've always thought so, since I first heard the Rays had a daughter."

"This is kind of—I'm kind of overwhelmed. I had such a scare today."

"I did, too. Your accident made me realize I've been moving too slowly, so let me say it again. I love you."

She couldn't look away, not when he still held her chin, forcing her to look at him.

"I'll keep your little community college secret. You won't give me any reason to tell your parents, anyway. I know you."

She'd barely heard her mother's kitten heels on the wood floor behind them, when Vincent tilted her chin up and kissed her again, closemouthed this time.

Her mother must have gone back into the salon, because Delphinia heard her say, in a disturbingly singsong voice, "I think I just interrupted something in our hallway, Archibald."

Delphinia jerked her chin out of Vincent's hand.

Her parents both came into the hallway, and Vincent shoved his hands in the front pockets of his slacks as he gave her parents that sad-puppy look. "I'm sorry, Dr. Ray. Truly. Delphinia is so special, and the realization that I could have lost her today… Well, it's making me rethink things, rethink my priorities, and…" He laughed at himself. "Listen to me. I wasn't doing much thinking at all a moment ago, was I?"

"Please." Her mother dismissed his apology. "You're nearly forty. Delphinia is almost thirty, for goodness' sake. Don't mind us. We're just going out."

After they passed Delphinia, her father said to her mother, "You remember what it's like to not be able to keep your hands off one another when love is in its first bloom."

Her mother pecked him on the cheek as they headed down the stairs.

Delphinia would be home alone with Vincent in a moment, and the thought made her stomach clench. "Mother! Father."

Her parents stopped.

"Could you see Vincent out as you go? I need to retire, and I don't want to be rude and not see him out myself, but…" She lifted the black-smudged side of her skirt, truly miserable.

Her parents and Vincent all seemed surprised for a moment, but then Vincent, being the gentleman he was, did the only gentlemanly thing he could do. "Of course, sweetheart. You relax for the rest of the evening."

He gave her a peck on the cheek like her mother had just given her father, then he walked down the stairs with her parents.

Delphinia made a beeline for her bedroom and shut her door. She locked it, just in case.

In case of what?

She was going to have her hot bath and lose herself in a book that was guaranteed to end happily ever after, because she didn't want to think about Vincent or her parents or relationships that happened unintentionally, without disturbing the routine of one's life, and with the approval of everyone who knew the couple. She didn't want to think about how Professor Delphinia Ray's life was destined to turn out.

She needed to escape for a few hours. Thank goodness, Connor had thought to give her back her book.

And that, she thought later, while lying in her bed and staring at the dark, might just be the sexiest thing about him yet. The man had known what she needed before she had.

Everything about him was sexy. The way he'd swept her up into his arms—so much strength—and held her close to his chest—so much tenderness—and carried her to the shelter of his pub—so protective. He was just like the hero of the romance she'd finished in the tub. The hero's *I love you* had meant that everything in the world was going to be all right, now that he and the heroine had found one another.

She rolled onto her side and began drifting off to sleep with a smile on her face, until she remembered that the man who had said *I love you* and kissed her passionately today was Vincent Talbot.

Chapter Thirteen

Delphinia sat in her classroom, brooding.

It was Friday afternoon. Her students had turned in their midterm papers and bolted for the door to begin their spring break. The building was empty, and the city of Masterson itself would feel like a ghost town while twelve thousand students and half the faculty were away. The businesses that thrived around the college would be operating with only a few employees this coming week. That was life in a college town.

Her parents had resumed their teasing manner with her—or a little worse than normal, now that they'd seen Vincent kissing her in the hallway. Delphinia had disrupted their sherry-and-port tête-à-tête last night to inquire if they had any bourbon in the house, declaring that she'd developed a taste for Irish whiskey.

Their resulting amusement—bourbon was apparently not made in Ireland—had made her feel like that awkward teenager all over again, younger than everyone else at school, more naive than everyone else she knew.

Vincent had been as busy as she with midterms, but he'd met her for coffee one morning and lunch another day. Both dates had been on campus because of the midterm schedules, so there'd been no passionate kisses or declarations of love. Professors lived at the pace the university set. She and Vincent were from the same world. They understood this.

But…

In her imagination, there was a lone wolf who was alone no longer, now that he was living happily ever after with his heroine in a castle by a lake. If the two of them were separated by something as trivial as an acre of smooth grass the way she and Vincent were, not one day would pass without them seeing each other. Not one day would pass without them being in one another's arms, not one day without a kiss.

Fiction.

Delphinia stacked and restacked her pile of midterm exams. The Victorian essayists had done their agriculture-versus-industry thing. Her students had written their essays about those essays, and now Delphinia needed to read and grade every single one.

Make me.

She needed a serious attitude adjustment.

It was five o'clock. Quitting time. Happy hour. Would the Tipsy Musketeer be busy enough during spring break to need Kristopher there? It would be nice to stop by and find out how his Shakespeare performance had gone. Bridget's, too.

Vincent hadn't requested Delphinia to be his plus-one this evening, so she would not need to plead her case to him if she spent time at the pub. She could justify it, though. A Friday evening cocktail was a socially acceptable norm. She was far over twenty-one. She wasn't driving. She wasn't going to drink to excess. She didn't have to go to work tomorrow. She didn't have to go to work for a *week*.

Connor's calm voice interrupted her litany. *You don't have to justify yourself. It's your book. You wanted it back.*

A man could make her melt into a puddle by saying things like that.

It was five o'clock on a Friday, and she was going to take a detour to the Tipsy Musketeer on her walk home.

Because she wanted to.

Delphinia walked into his bar.

Connor knew he was in trouble, because her hair was smoothed into a tight bun at the nape of her neck, and the refrain from "Hot for Teacher" ran, unwelcome, through his brain. She looked very professional in a black pantsuit, very sharp.

She took the seat at the far end of the bar and gave him a little wave.

"Oh, my *God*, Connor. You are *so* funny."

Connor returned his attention to the two women in front of him. One was an assistant diving coach at MU. The other, her friend. Both of them? In the mood to flirt, and Connor was the current target for their affection. He didn't take it personally. It was just part of being a bartender.

The coach leaned onto the bar and crooked her finger in a *come here* motion.

Connor remained standing as he was. The woman wouldn't care.

She didn't. She was all sly smiles. "We need a round of lemon drops."

Connor smiled slyly, too. "That's Kristopher's specialty. Hey, Kris. Come here. These ladies deserve the best lemon drops in town." He wiped off his hands and tossed his bar towel into the laundry bin, then he headed toward Delphinia.

He stopped on the way to refill a soda for a guest. Delphinia had taken the seat at the end of the long bar, where it ended at the wall—or where it began. That barstool was seat one. The wood paneling at her left shoulder had propped up many a person in seat one. Given the way Delphinia liked the snugs by the stage, he guessed she preferred to sit out of the way.

Connor couldn't ignore all the customers between them. He could feel her stare as he made a quick vodka on the rocks for the woman at seat four, the executive assistant to Dr. Marsden, the university's president.

"You're the perfect man," Ruby said. "You always know what I want."

He winked at her. "A splash of cranberry in the next one."

Ruby turned to her friend. "See? The perfect man." Delphinia had her chin in the air now, displeased about something. He didn't know what. The bar was full, but thanks to spring break, it wasn't the usual crazy Friday night. She hadn't been waiting long for a drink.

He turned to the mirrored shelving behind himself and picked up the sweet bourbon he'd served her the past two visits. It wasn't hard to catch her eye, since she was blatantly watching his every move.

He raised the bottle with the label toward her. *Bourbon and Coke?*

"Were you aware that was made in Kentucky?" she called from three seats away. She sounded indignant.

Connor walked over to her, finally, and set the bottle on the bar. "Yes, I was."

At seats eight and nine, the two lemon-drop women were shrieking in delight. "Oh, my *God*, Connor. Connor! Look at this."

He turned to look. Kristopher had twisted a lemon slice tightly, so that it untwisted in the glass and stirred their drinks. The pub was loud and about to get louder. Connor's best musician this year, a senior at MU, was a singing cowboy named Buck. He'd set his microphone up on the stage and was giving his acoustic guitar a quick final tune.

Delphinia gave the bar a little slap. "Bourbon is from Kentucky. All of it."

"Almost all of it. Everyone knows that." He tried to suppress his smile, but he could swear she'd slapped his wrist instead of the bar, like a schoolmarm getting a bad boy's attention. *Yes, ma'am.*

"No, everyone does not know that. When someone asks an Irish bartender in an Irish pub to recommend an Irish whiskey, they do not expect to be served something from Kentucky."

She was lecturing him. Damn, she was cute. And sharp. But cute.

"I'm Scottish, if anything, but I get your point." He was having a hard time playing it cool. He hadn't been sure if he'd ever see her again. One week ago, he'd walked her to that brick mansion and left her where she belonged—but she'd come back.

There was an expanse of mahogany between them, and the crowd was a decent size for the first Friday of spring break in a college town, so he felt safe enough to risk another one of those intense *Are you thinking what I'm thinking?* moments. He braced his hands on the bar and leaned in. "What's your pleasure, then, Rembrandt?"

The crowd and the noise didn't matter. He felt it, and he knew she did, too, because that offended-professor posture began to ease from her shoulders. Then the lemon-drop women down the bar got a little loud, and she looked toward them and sat back, still miffed.

"I want an *Irish* whiskey and Coke, please."

He had other customers waiting, plus the waitstaff's orders to fill at the opposite end of the bar, but he set a coaster in front of her. "Bourbon goes better with Coke. Maybe Southern Comfort or Jack Daniels tonight?"

"Even I know those are not Irish. You're patronizing me."

"I'm suggesting something that you'll enjoy."

"I'd enjoy it if I wasn't made a fool of again."

The implication wasn't cute, even if she'd said it like an offended schoolmarm. "Who treated you like you were a fool?"

She pressed her lips together. Women were laughing up a storm all along the bar, from the executive assistant to the diving coach, such a contrast to the woman before him.

He studied her for a minute, then answered his own question. "That someone you're seeing. He laughed at you about bourbon?"

"No. Can I just have my drink, please? Your strongest, most Irish of Irish whiskeys and Coke."

Connor gave her what she wanted. He knew it would taste awful with the soda, but he was willing to bet that Delphinia would not admit it—not as long as the lemon-drop ladies were irritating her.

As Connor moved down the bar, checking on other customers, he kept one eye on her. She choked on the drink as much as on her pride. It would have been pretty funny, if he could get the idea of that *someone* out of his mind. *Someone* might know the people she knew, and he might fit into her life seamlessly, but if the man had humiliated her over something as trivial as bourbon being from Kentucky, Connor didn't like him.

But he'd already known that.

"A Guinness for my friend. Best way to end the week." The city councilman, Ernie, had returned with another member of the council.

Connor obliged. A glass of Guinness had to be partially filled, then allowed to sit for a minute or two to let the nitrogen gas in it settle before being topped off.

"Heard about the accident," Ernie said, as they waited.

"It could have been worse. The city won't always get lucky, if you can call a cyclist getting broken bones 'lucky.'"

The cyclist could have been killed. Or Delphinia could have been. If there'd been blood on her skirt instead of tire dirt—Connor couldn't go there.

"You know Kurt already," Ernie said, referring to the man beside him. "That cyclist was the last straw. We came here to let you know that we're not going to let your proposal get tabled again."

"Glad to hear it." Connor set the glasses in front of the councilmen. He'd believe their promises after they came true, but the bridge might happen sooner rather than later, after all.

The evening picked up. Buck performed, the crowd sang along, and all would be right with the world, if only he could steal more time with Delphinia.

The opening to go in and out from behind the bar was at the opposite end from Delphinia, twenty long seats away. He headed that way. As the owner, he always made a few rounds of the tables throughout the evening. He'd do so now, then end by talking to Delphinia while he was on her side of the bar, so he could see all of her as they spoke. She looked sharp in the suit, but he wondered why the switch from skirts.

Her knees. Of course. She didn't want to wear a skirt and have everyone ask why her knees were scraped up.

Connor didn't make it out from behind the bar.

"A toast!" The call was picked up along the bar. "A toast!"

As Buck finished his song and the guests at the tables turned toward the bar, Connor poured himself a splash of beer in a highball glass. This was one part of the job he'd never master like Mr. Murphy, but he was the publican now. He couldn't refuse.

He stepped back to stand in front of the antique mirrors. Every eye in the place was on him, every glass raised in anticipation. Connor appreciated the sight of regulars and visitors all united for the evening, here to shed some cares and spend a little time in camaraderie with their fellow man. That was what a good pub could do, and Connor wanted to run a good pub. He'd learned from the best.

He raised his glass and spoke in a voice meant to carry. "May there always be work for our hands to do."

"Here, here!" came a voice from the crowd.

Connor smiled as he delivered the punch line. "And may there always be coin for a beer when we're through."

This was met with laughter and a few cheers, but the glasses stayed in the air. The regulars knew that was far too short for an Irish toast. Connor hadn't said anything properly poignant yet.

"May the roof of the Musketeer never fall in, and may the friends gathered below never fall out. *Slainte.*"

He threw back the ounce of beer and thunked the glass down, an action repeated by eighty or so guests on the floor and in the loft. He could forget his plan to walk the floor; now the orders for fresh drinks would pour in.

But he'd been looking forward to another minute with Delphinia, and he was going to take it, even if he had to stay behind the bar to talk to her. He walked back to her seat quickly, stopping only for a handshake for a well-done toast.

Delphinia gestured toward the center mirror. "That was a wonderful toast."

I'm glad you liked it was his usual reply, but this was Rembrandt, with whom he'd laughed over *Othello* and talked about books. "It wasn't Shakespeare."

"But the crowd loved it like it was. Shakespeare was a crowd-pleaser. You are, too." Her smile was real, reaching all the way to those intelligent brown eyes.

"You liked the toast, but you didn't like your drink. I saw your face."

"I should have trusted you. The bourbon was better."

"With Coke, yes. Don't go anywhere, and I'll teach how you to enjoy Irish whiskey properly once the rush is over. It's about to get real busy here for about twenty minutes."

She turned to look over her shoulder. He wondered if she could see what he could see, every server filling trays with empty glasses throughout the main floor, all the guests who gestured at the half-full glasses on their tables, *Another round, please,* all the guests who were nodding as they recognized the song Buck began to play, settling themselves in, not even thinking about leaving.

"You know it's going to get busy?" Delphinia sounded doubtful.

"Yes. Can you stay?" He felt like a little boy asking if a friend could come outside to play, or a teenager asking a girl if she could go to the movies. Both absurd analogies, and far more wholesome than his actual childhood had been, but he owned enough books with Norman Rockwell paintings in them to get the general idea for how an innocent first love would have felt.

His heart sped up as he waited for her answer, at any rate. *Can you spend a little time with me?*

"Where would I go? It's Friday, and I'm in a pub, so I'm already where I should be."

She was with him. He couldn't throw her over his shoulder and hide her in his cave, but he liked seeing her tucked in safely at seat one, and she wasn't going to leave, not yet. It felt good.

"Before I take care of the rest of the floor, what would you really like to drink?"

She wrinkled her nose. "Maybe just a plain Coke to get the taste of that awful stuff out of my mouth." Then her eyes widened at her own words. She reached out with her hand again, setting her palm on the bar. "I didn't mean that drink was awful. I'm sure it was good whiskey, very good whiskey, truly."

He covered that hand with his own, then turned it over. Her hand was completely healed. He ran his thumb lightly over her perfect palm. "Do your knees look this good?"

"Oh."

Oh, that *oh*, from his lightest touch. He hadn't meant

it that way. He'd been thinking only of undamaged, healthy skin, but at that *oh*, he lowered his voice. "I don't mean that they were awful before. I know for a fact they weren't. They're good knees, very good knees, truly."

Her eyes narrowed just a bit. "You're being very charming, Connor McClaine, with me and with every other woman at this bar." She pulled her hand back and sat up just a bit, a touch of that lecturing tone back in her voice.

Her earlier, prickly demeanor suddenly made sense to him. It wasn't that she'd been kept waiting too long; it was that she'd seen him talking to other women while she'd waited, and she hadn't liked it. She was jealous.

Jubilant, victorious—the idea that she wanted him all to herself made him feel all of it, all at once.

"'Charming' doesn't mean I'm lying, Rembrandt. I'm glad to see your hands are healed, and I hope your knees are, too."

"They're fine."

"I won't really know until I see them again, will I? To quote a certain English professor, you haven't shown me anything. You've only described them to me as fine, and women always say they're fine, so…"

Her laugh was light and bright. "You are too charming. You ought to be a bartender or something. People would love to come and spend time at your place."

He was in real danger here. He'd told Mr. Murphy there was no woman, but there was absolutely, definitely a woman. He was looking right at her, but he couldn't have her, not without making her life more difficult for her.

The back of his neck prickled with a different sense of danger. He looked beyond Delphinia's shoulder, to a table he should have noticed sooner. Two men, early twenties—one he recognized as a recent graduate, a football star who'd become an assistant coach when he failed to make it in the NFL. Their voices didn't have the right tone of male one-upmanship. This was straight-up anger.

His waitress was trying to interrupt and diffuse the tension, holding the check in her hand, probably asking if they wanted her to split the tab. The former star reached up and put his hand on her hip and gave her a squeeze. His fingertips grazed over her backside as he let go.

"Excuse me." Connor had to walk the length of the antique bar to get out from behind it and head for that table. Twenty seats. Thirty feet. Too long—but he couldn't vault over the bar without causing absolute chaos. That wasn't what the Musketeer was all about. But it wasn't about a couple of men shouting at one another in a public pissing match, either, and it sure as hell wasn't about his employee getting manhandled.

As he passed Kristopher, he gave him a nod. The waitress had already been coming to get Connor, as she should, so she met him in the middle of the floor. "I don't want to serve table eighty-seven."

"I saw it." When Connor reached the table, he stood between the arguing men and Delphinia—a reflex. "Gentlemen, let's take this outside."

The former star sneered at his friend. "Get your ass out of here. I'm staying."

Connor smiled congenially and set his hand on the man's shoulder. "Nah. We're all going outside."

The man tried to jerk his shoulder to shake Connor's hand off, but his shoulder didn't move an inch, because Connor didn't allow it to.

Kristopher strolled up, all smiles to keep things looking friendly for the rest of the pub. "Gina gave me their check. Fifty-two fifty."

Connor took the check and tossed it on the table. "This could be your lucky night. I might make the drinks on the house for a new coach of the mighty Masterson Musketeers. You and your friend can make it out the door before I change my mind and decide you should stay and pay."

The coach glared at his friend, but the combination of carrot and stick—free drinks and a bartender who was strong enough to keep him in his seat—had him saying, "Let's go."

Exactly as Connor had intended.

Connor walked them outside and waited until the door closed behind him. "You are banned from the Tipsy Musketeer for life. Don't come back."

They got loud again on the sidewalk. Indignant. Connor silently crossed his arms over his chest and stood in front of his door. He was well aware that his white shirt and black vest gave him something of a gentleman-boxer look, which was classier than an ex-con and just as effective. He'd also spotted a patrol car parked at the corner. Connor was a magnet for cops. He only had to stand here.

Sure enough, the deputy walked right up to them. It was the same officer from the bicycle crash, Kent Grayson. Again, he talked to Connor first. "Anything exciting going on?"

"Just informing these two that if they set foot in my place again, I'll be calling you to report trespassers."

The coach appealed to the deputy. "This is bull. He has no reason to throw us out. We didn't do a damned thing in there."

The deputy crossed his arms, too, over his bullet-proof vest. "He doesn't need one. It's private property. He owns it."

Connor was faintly surprised at the support from a man in uniform. It wasn't the first time it had happened, but it caught him off guard to have the law on his side.

Kristopher came out to update him. "Gina doesn't want to press charges for them touching her."

"Isn't that fortunate for you?" Connor asked the coach. "Before you go, you owe me fifty-two fifty for your drinks."

"You said it was on the house."

"I said it might be, if I didn't change my mind. I changed it. Pay your bill. Cash only."

Facing Connor and Kristopher and a uniformed deputy, the two had no choice. They pulled out their wallets. One had a fifty-dollar bill.

Connor accepted it. "We'll call it even. If you don't mind seeing them off my sidewalk, Deputy Grayson?"

Once inside, he took Gina aside, stopping at the

employees-only hallway just past seat one, where Delphinia still sat, watching him like a hawk.

"They'll never be back," he told Gina. "They're taking a walk with a deputy right now."

"Thank you."

Connor held up the folded fifty-dollar bill. "Might be kind of a shame, actually. Turns out they were very generous tippers. This is yours."

Gina squealed like one of the lemon-drop ladies as she hugged him and told him he was the best boss, ever, but when Connor glanced Delphinia's way, she was beaming at him with an expression on her face that was nothing like her earlier schoolmarm disapproval.

What a night. The cops were on his side, and now he was the teacher's pet.

The night was still young. He had a promise to keep. He was going to teach the teacher how to enjoy Irish whiskey.

Chapter Fourteen

The crowd got smaller. Those who remained were paying attention to the music more and hollering jokes at one another less. It was all part of the ebb and flow, the pulse of a Friday evening at the Tipsy Musketeer.

Connor picked up two whiskey glasses in one hand, poured two fingers of his favorite in each one, then headed toward the open end of the bar. He clapped Kristopher on the shoulder as he passed him. "Bring an ice ball to seat one, would you?"

Delphinia spotted him as he walked toward her, winding his way through the tables. She stood, shook her suit jacket off her shoulders and hung it over the back of her barstool.

Connor's thoughts took a hard turn from whiskey to the bedroom. She was wearing a silky sort of tank top, a rich burgundy that looked almost as smooth as her skin. He didn't even glance at the rest of his guests. She stayed standing as he walked straight toward her.

Keep a cool head, lad.

Burgundy was one of the Masterson University colors. This was probably an outfit she wore to official university functions. She wasn't trying to seduce him—but she was still succeeding.

"Are you ready?" He handed her one of the glasses.

She gave him a little *I don't know* shrug with those newly uncovered shoulders. "How does one get ready for something like this?"

For a woman like you to walk into my bar and turn my world upside down?

Rather than answer, he stood so they were shoulder to shoulder, and raised his glass toward the chandelier. "First, you admire its color."

She moved closer to hold her glass at the same angle he held his. Her bare shoulder brushed his shirtsleeve.

"Like a wine tasting? I know the drill. What colors am I supposed to be seeing?"

He was the one who shrugged this time, another brush of shoulders. "What do you see?"

She squinted thoughtfully at her raised glass. "Amber? A touch of black, like walnut. Some ochre. Sienna, definitely, and russet. Rich sepia tones."

He turned his head just enough to look at her instead of the whiskey. It didn't take much, as close as they were.

"And umber." She nodded decisively, never taking her eyes off the glass. "Umber and amber, both."

"Are you pulling my leg?"

"About what?" She frowned as she tilted the glass this way and that, but her lips twitched. "Smoky topaz."

"That's some vocabulary, Professor."

She looked at him and batted her eyelashes.

He burst into laughter—not for the first time around her. The moment left them looking at one another, inches apart, smiling, breathing.

"Smoky topaz would better describe your eyes than the whiskey," she said, bold and apologetic at once, like she was sorry she had to tell him the truth, but the truth was, she thought his eyes were special.

The rest of the world disappeared. Rembrandt was everything.

"I see one hundred shades of brown." He was looking into her eyes, because he was talking about her eyes, and devil take the whiskey. His voice was husky, but that didn't matter, because her gaze had dropped to his mouth. She was going to kiss him. There wasn't a single reason why he shouldn't let her. There were only two of them in their world.

The entire bar erupted as Buck hit the chorus of "Sweet Caroline," everyone shouting the famous three notes: "Bah, bah, bah!"

The spell was broken. He was in his bar, out on the floor.

He didn't kiss women in public. The flirty ones and the regulars might kiss him on the cheek as they hugged him in greeting, but he'd never kissed a girlfriend on the job, and Rembrandt wasn't his girlfriend in any way, shape or form. She was *seeing someone*, some idiot who was a snob about bourbon and didn't take her out on a Friday night.

The crowd chanted: "So good. So good. So good!"

Rembrandt sat on her barstool and looked up at him. "Now what?"

He felt off-kilter. He glanced around the floor, at the amount of empty and full glasses, at the waitstaff and guests. This was the real world, and there were rules to the game. Connor didn't go after other men's girl-friends, even if he knew he could win. Even if the other bastard deserved to lose. Connor wouldn't be a great replacement prize for Delphinia, anyway.

He shielded himself with some bartender charm. "The nose would be next, but don't bury your nose in the glass like they do with wine. It's too strong."

She sniffed it tentatively. "Wow. That will wake you up."

Connor felt like they were talking in code. Yes, they'd both just woken up. They'd both snapped out of that spell. She must know it as well as he did.

Kristopher had placed a glass with a single ball of ice, larger than a golf ball, on the bar. Connor took Del-phinia's glass from her, poured her whiskey over the ice and handed the new glass to her. "It will melt very slowly, but a little melt is good. A touch of water makes the whiskey burn less, so you can taste it more."

"Now what?" She looked at the glass apprehensively, bracing herself, thinking too hard. She'd never enjoy anything like that.

"That's it. You're now officially enjoying Irish whis-key."

That earned him a look of disbelief. "Shouldn't I taste it at some point?"

"It's not necessary. Relax and enjoy the music, watch the crowd. You entertain yourself a bit by rolling that ice ball around. You watch the shades of brown change with the melt, hold it up to the light again if you like. Enjoy the colors."

"But…" She rolled the ball in the glass.

"There's no trick to it. Stay as long as you like, but if you're here for Buck's last song, be ready. He leaves everyone teary-eyed with 'Red River Valley.' It's even worse than when my Irish singer does 'Danny Boy.'" Connor winked at her and walked away.

From a distance, he kept an eye on her for the next song, and the next. She toyed with the ice. She didn't hold the glass up to the chandelier, but she sat with her elbow on the bar, held the glass up to her eye and looked at the mirror through it.

She listened to "Red River Valley," lost in thought. So lost, she raised her glass and took a sip. Connor saw the faint surprise in her face as she realized she'd done it. She looked into the glass, and she smiled. She took another sip. She liked it.

Of course.

He liked her—but he'd already known that.

They'd had nothing in common, except a love for books. Now, there was more. They both enjoyed whiskey when it was savored. They shared a physical attraction; that was a certainty. Most dangerous of all, she made him laugh. They got each other's jokes. He could glance at her and tell when she was amused by the same thing he was.

It was not enough. She knew nothing about him. His childhood. His incarceration. His education, or lack of it. There was no need for her to ever know, because this would not become a love affair. They were not soul mates. They were not going to scale mountains.

This story was much simpler.

Once upon a time, a girl walked into a bar. The bartender enjoyed their conversation, and then she walked back to her lovely life. The bartender mopped the floor, turned off the lights, climbed the stairs and went to bed.

The end.

"Don't you look nice, dear? Are those sandals new?"

Delphinia turned from the sink, surprised to see her mother in the kitchen on a Sunday. It was surprising to see her in the kitchen at all, really. Dr. Rhea Acanthus-Ray wasn't the kind to slave over meat loaf and mashed potatoes, but when Delphinia had been a child, her mother had perfected the basic grilled cheese sandwich for her. She'd served it dozens of times on a porcelain plate, alongside a pickle and a handful of potato chips. It was still one of Delphinia's favorite meals.

She gave her mother a peck on the cheek. "Thank you. I went to Austin and bought myself some things."

Everything was new. Her shirt was bright blue. Tiny, embroidered dogs were scattered on the material of her shorts. The sandals revealed her freshly pedicured toes. Even her haircut was new.

The changes must not be obvious. Her toes were

polished with a subtle pale pink, after all, and her hair was still all one length. It was probably hard to see that it was six inches shorter. Still, her mother had noticed her sandals. That was something.

"Buying yourself new things? You and Vincent must have plans this afternoon." Her mother sounded delighted.

"We don't, actually." Delphinia didn't want to kill this happy kitchen camaraderie, but it irked her that her mother assumed any positive change was due to Vincent. "You know, Vincent and I don't see each other very often." *He won't cross a few acres of grass.*

Her mother only laughed. "You've been exclusively dating him for seven months, practically every Tuesday and Thursday evening."

Delphinia winced. "That was only for the last half of the fall semester."

Her mother's delight died. "Oh, Delphinia. Did you have a lovers' quarrel?"

"No, of course not." *We're not lovers, for one thing.*

And for another, she hadn't been dating Vincent on Tuesdays and Thursdays. But it was true that she'd been dating Vincent exclusively for seven months, so confessing her substitute-professor role at BCC would serve no purpose, now that it was over and done. Habits were hard to break. She still wanted to please her parents.

"Your accident had him quite shaken. I'm sure Vincent wants to spend time with you now that midterms are over."

Delphinia cleared her throat. "Yes, he's taking me out to dinner Thursday with some friends of his who just got married." *He sent me a text. We have an appointment.*

But her mom was delighted once more. "Dinner with newlyweds. Let's hope they are deliriously happy. That could get a young man thinking that he'd do well to be a newlywed himself."

"That's not the point of the evening."

"It's never the point, dear, but it happens more often than you'd think." Her mother spoke in a bizarre, conspiratorial tone, as if the two of them were trying to lure Vincent to the altar.

Delphinia hated to be a disappointment, and her inner wolf was still more of a puppy in her mother's presence, but she couldn't let this go on. "Please, don't get your hopes up. Vincent and I do go out socially, but that doesn't mean we're at an…uh…intimate point in our relationship."

"I stumbled upon that kiss in the hallway." To Delphinia's shock, her mother pretended to fan herself with one hand. "You have nothing to worry about on that score. I'm glad to see you so happy, dear. You've been looking so vibrant lately."

Happy? She wasn't happy at all. Was she?

Her mother pecked her on the cheek as she left.

Delphinia turned away from the kitchen sink. Perhaps she did feel happier lately, but it was the happiness of anticipating being happy. She was going to propose some changes to her Victorian Essay course. *Not yet.*

She was going to move into her own apartment. *Someday.*

Her inner wolf howled louder now. *Do something.*

She was going to go to the Tipsy Musketeer again to enjoy some music and whiskey, and to soak up a joyful atmosphere—this very evening.

Wear something sexy!

Sunday evening at the Musketeer had an entirely different feel to it than Friday. The spring break ghost town effect had kicked in. There were only a quarter as many people in the pub as there'd been on Friday, and no live music.

Delphinia loved it. She had Connor all to herself, or nearly.

He stayed on his side of the bar. That meant he couldn't see her sexy new jeans or pink-painted toes, but she hadn't come here to seduce him. She'd just wanted to be near him.

Since he always scanned the pub, she'd turned around her barstool so she could see what he saw. She'd taken the seat on the end again. From here, she could see partway into the snugs, enough to see a couple in the middle one, kissing as much as they were talking. That carved rosette was witnessing one more love story.

So was she. So was Connor. So was anyone who walked by the snug.

"I don't see how the snugs gave women privacy to drink. They're not hiding that couple very well."

From behind her, Connor answered. "There were curtains. Up close, you can see the nail holes where the curtain rods were."

"But people must have seen the women when they walked in the door, before they had a chance to hide."

"I imagine everyone knew what everyone was doing. It was important to appear like a proper lady or gentleman, or else we wouldn't have the snugs. But it was only on the surface, or this bar wouldn't have been the first building in town to be built out of brick instead of timber."

Delphinia rolled her ball of ice around her glass as she listened to Connor. She felt so content. She was in the right place. She was *happy*. Not looking forward to happy things in the future, but actually happy now, right here.

The couple in the snug were even happier. They started seriously snogging. Delphinia turned around to face Connor. "Voyeurism isn't really my thing."

He smiled at her. He'd smiled at her a lot this evening. "If they don't come up for air, I'll have to walk over there and hand them a glass of ice water."

"Have you had to do that before?"

"This is a college town."

She raised her glass in a little toast to that fact.

"I'm not the first owner to cool off guests. There are some legendary tales. Men drank in those snugs, too. Things could get dicey if you had groups of women in one and men in the other. There was a lot of curtain-hopping."

"What did the men and women sneak into each other's snugs for?"

He rested his forearms on the bar, perfectly serious. "I'll give you one guess."

She sat up straighter. Surely that rosette hadn't witnessed couples actually having sex on that bench. "In the Victorian era? With all the corsets and bustles?"

"They made babies back then, didn't they? Mr. Murphy will tell you there was too much of that still going on in the sixties. The *nineteen* sixties, not the eighteen. Don't get him started on what the devil should do with 'those kids who think this is Woodstock.' He took the curtains down. The only private snug left is this one." Connor pointed at the wall next to her.

"This isn't a wall?" She rapped her knuckles on the paneled wall. It sounded hollow. When she looked up, she saw that it stopped about eight feet up and didn't reach the ceiling.

"It's a snug for the VIPs. There used to be a side door, before Mr. Murphy added the back hallway and the storage rooms. People came in the side door, snuck right into this booth, rang a bell and got their drinks served privately, see?" He pushed himself off the bar and slid open a small piece of paneling on his side. "Only the bartender would know who was in here."

"This is just the coolest building." Delphinia braced her hands on the bar to lift herself up so she could lean over farther. If she craned her neck, she could peek through the small window. "It's pretty big in there."

"It'll hold four men easily. The mayor, the doctor, the minister…" His voice trailed off.

She looked at him. His eyes snapped from the deeply scooped neckline of her new blouse back to her face.

"…and the college professor."

Her position must have given him a clear view down her blouse. Her mistake, an accident, but that new bra made of smooth, blue satin seemed like such a smart purchase now.

She tossed her hair back as she sat down. "We professors are moral pillars of the community."

"So I see."

I see. That might have been a reference to her unintentional peepshow. Matching wits with him was too fun. "Would you like to check out the snug with me? You'll be perfectly safe. I have a sterling reputation to uphold."

"Yes, you do." The change in his mood was subtle, but she felt it. "You go ahead. The door's around the corner."

She stepped down from her barstool and found the door to the snug, which had a stained-glass inset. The benches had cushions.

Connor slid the paneled door open. "Can I get you anything, madam?"

"I love the stained glass."

"It lets in light, but it's not see-through. They were pretty clever about it all. Mr. Murphy said the university president and the sheriff were regulars in there well into the 1980s. They were ticked off when he added the addition, because it forced them to walk through the pub to get to the booth. He told them if they weren't man enough to walk through the pub, then they weren't man enough to drink at the Musketeer at all."

"I can't imagine saying that to the president of any university. Then again, the president wasn't his boss."

"No, not his boss." He turned away from her. "Not his father, either."

"My father's only the dean."

Connor said nothing.

She placed her hands on the little sill. "You know so much about this building. It makes the Victorian era come alive. I would love to have you teach as a guest lecturer."

He tilted his head as if he hadn't heard her correctly.

"I could have my classes meet here once a semester, and you could lecture on the architectural features and how they prove that it was common practice to circumvent all those infamous Victorian social restrictions."

"That would be a short lecture. People like to drink. People like to have sex. Always have. The end."

He was being funny, surely, but his expression was perfectly neutral, the unconcerned Greek god once more. But he had a scar on his eyebrow; he was only human. She could persuade him with a sound academic argument. She'd been persuading adults that way since childhood.

"Just look at this place, all this brass and glass. Ruskin praised the innocence of farmers in his essays, like they were children in the Garden of Eden who needed to remain unspoiled. But when those virtuous farmers came to town, they spent their money in a showy bar that made them feel like they were part of all the materialism that came with the Industrial Age. It would make such a good class."

"I'm not interested, but thanks." He slid the door shut.

Had she—had she *offended* him? By the time she came around the corner, he was already walking down the bar to check on one of the few other customers. She hustled after him. They were each on their side of the bar, like racers at a track meet staying in their assigned lanes. "Connor, wait."

He seemed startled—irritated?—but he stopped.

She gripped the back of an empty barstool. "I'm not asking as a favor. I should have made it clear that the university would pay you. Nobody expects faculty to work for free."

"Faculty?" Connor said it like it was ludicrous, not humorous. "I'm not going to be on the faculty at Masterson."

"I meant there's money in the faculty budget for us to bring in guest speakers. You submit a quick outline of the learning objectives. You're the subject matter expert, so it doesn't matter what your degree is in. Business, art history, whatever. The department chair will approve it. The money comes out of the dean's budget."

He looked up to the ceiling, as if he needed to find patience to deal with her. "Your mother and father sound very generous."

Delphinia could be offended, too. "I don't get special treatment from the chair and the dean. Any professor can request funds."

They exchanged a heated look. "I'm not going to have a dozen PhDs in here, asking me questions about *Ruskin*."

"It's only a 300-level course. Why not?"

"Because." His hand had been in a fist. She only noticed because he flexed his fingers and studied them for a moment. "Because I don't know enough about

Ruskin to answer all their questions, all right? Listen, your whiskey is on the house. It was a pleasure to talk to you this evening. You're welcome back at the Tipsy Musketeer any time."

With each sentence, he put more invisible space between them. He was once more the owner of the bar. She was only his customer. From across the impenetrable mahogany, he nodded at her as he would at any customer. "If you'll excuse me, I need to go serve some ice water to a certain couple."

She wasn't special to him at all.

He hesitated. "By the way, the shorter hair looks good on you. Good night, Rembrandt."

Or maybe she was.

Chapter Fifteen

Delphinia had a stack of midterms that needed graded.

The day yawned before her. She'd bought her new clothes and she'd had her mini-makeover, but she had no one to appreciate it.

By the way, the shorter hair looks good on you, Rembrandt.

Connor had appreciated it—but that conversation about the guest lecture had gotten testy. Leave it to John Ruskin to ruin things. There'd been no way to smooth things over yesterday, because the pub was closed on Mondays, but tonight, she could stop in.

Go now. Go see him. Go.

She had the perfect excuse: she could grade her papers at the pub. Her new Bermuda shorts were modest enough, should a professor run into a student in town. Connor had wanted to see her knees all healed up, hadn't he? She could use that as a casual way to strike up a conversation and pick up their joke about fine and magnificent body parts and books. She'd just take a quick shower first, maybe wash her hair…

An hour later, she waited at the crosswalk for the light to change. She was just seconds from seeing Connor, just a few feet from standing next to Connor, giddy with anticipation.

The light turned green, and she headed for him, armed with her red pen and her stack of midterms, so he wouldn't guess why she'd really come. Professors who graded papers always wore makeup and had freshly blown-out hair at two in the afternoon, right?

Wrong. She was being as subtle as that boy-chasing, love-struck teenager she'd never gotten to be.

She'd nearly kissed him on Friday night, under the chandelier. He'd left her alone with her whiskey. On Sunday, he'd kept the width of the bar between them for hours. Yes, he'd walked her home after the accident two weeks ago, but when she'd kissed him on the cheek, he'd left her on the brick walkway.

As she crossed the sunbaked asphalt of Athos Avenue, the facts were chilling. Every single time she'd thought their connection was romantic, he'd backed away and given her space. She couldn't walk in there again, like a puppy begging for his attention. It was going to be so obvious: *look at my knees!*

Good grief, she'd even shaved her legs.

Feeling foolish, she waited by the lamppost for the signal to cross Athos Avenue again, back the other way.

"Dr. Dee? Hey, hi. Wait up." Bridget Murphy's voice carried outdoors as well as it did from a stage. She held a bag from the Mexican cantina. "Are you coming to Murphy's?"

Delphinia couldn't think of any other reason she'd be standing in front of the pub. "I was considering grading some papers here, instead of going into the office."

"We don't open until four during spring break."

Thank goodness. It had been insanity to think Connor would want to see her new clothes and her stupid, unromantic knees. "In that case, I'll just—"

"So when I saw you, I thought I'd better come get you. I'll take you in around back."

"But if it's not open—"

"Connor won't care if you sit at a table and do paperwork." She started walking, talking over her shoulder as if it were a given that Delphinia would follow. "This is like my second home, you know. It's all cool."

Like most MU students, Bridget wore a lanyard full of keys and her student ID. One of the keys unlocked the employee door. They walked up the single step and into the hallway that was crowded with boxes.

No one was there.

Delphinia let out the breath she'd been holding. The main part of the pub was empty, too. All the chairs were turned upside down on the tables.

"You want to be by the window again?" Bridget walked over to the table and pulled the chairs off it like she owned the place. "There you go. What do you want to drink?"

She headed to the bar, got out two glasses and filled

them with ice. She did it with the kind of nonchalant grace that came with repetition, just like Connor did it.

"Do you work here?" Delphinia asked.

"My parents told me to study instead of work, but I end up here all the time, anyway. They ought to know by now that the only person who ever gets me to study is Connor. When Uncle Murphy owned it, Connor used to read everything out loud to me, even stuff like biology. If I have to sit down and read by myself, I won't make five minutes, I get so bored." Bridget closed the ice bin with a flourish. "Want a Coke?"

Delphinia decided to stay, if only because leaving would have been more difficult in the face of Bridget's enthusiastic hospitality. She could sit here and grade papers for a couple of hours, then leave before four, before Connor arrived. That sounded safe.

She was halfway into her third essay, eyes glazing over at the same old thesis, when she glanced up to see Connor McClaine, every gorgeous, Greek-god inch of him, heading straight for the bar. He was mostly naked.

Her red pen slipped out of her hand.

His skin glistened with sweat. His hair was soaked, black rather than brown, and he was breathing hard, like he'd just come in from a run—a run in the sun, for his muscular legs were tan, bared by his athletic shorts. His chest and back were visible, too, all kinds of interesting—no, *sexy* was the correct word—all kinds of sexy lines on display, thanks to the extra-roomy armholes in his loose-fitting tank top.

Bridget was bending down to scrounge through a refrigerator behind the bar, oblivious to his presence, but

Delphinia was riveted. Connor moved with an animal grace—never had a line from *A Mate with Destiny* been more accurate—yet he didn't have that lone-wolf aura today. He was relaxed, his guard completely down, as he twisted open a water bottle and took a swig, while simultaneously walking up behind Bridget and kicking her in the butt.

"Ow! Dweeb."

"What are you stealing now?" He chugged half the bottle.

"Where'd the olives go? The ones with the blue cheese stuffed in them?"

"They'll reappear when you get out the blue cheese and the olives and stuff some more of them. Funny how that works."

"As if."

"I'm serious, Briddy. No olive-stuffing fairy came to replace the ones you ate yesterday. You need to make more."

Delphinia listened with only half an ear. She was too consumed with using her eyes. His tattoo was fully revealed. The black swirl was the bottom flourish of a Celtic design. Geometric curves, twined into intricate knots, formed a capital letter *M*. It covered most of his upper arm, moving in a fascinating way with the bunching of his muscles as he lifted the water bottle for a drink.

"Be nice," Bridget said. "Dr. Dee is here."

That beautiful male body went still for a fraction of a second, and then Connor spun around to stare at her.

"She just wanted to hang out and grade some papers." Bridget returned to her fridge-scrounging.

Even his smoky topaz eyes could not keep Delphinia's attention on his face. Her gaze slid over his shoulder to the stylistic letter *M*, but she managed to murmur a mundane response. "I didn't know you were closed."

"Yes, we're closed."

That startled her into looking away from his body. "I'm sorry. I'll go."

"No—no, stay. You're welcome to stay. I'm just going to go shower and get some clothes on. Not that I'm not dressed right now. I'm just going to go get dressed." He looked down at himself. "In something different."

As he frowned at his running shoes, it hit her: he sounded almost flummoxed.

Fascinating. The idea that a man like Connor could be knocked off balance for even a second by a woman like her—well, that was intoxicating. Impossible, but intoxicating.

He looked up. Their eyes met.

It's not impossible.

She got so quickly drunk on the taste of feminine power that, for once, she was the one to wink. "By the way, nice knees."

He burst into laughter. "I'll be back." He gave Bridget another nudge as he walked away. "A little heads-up next time, Hurricane."

Delphinia watched him until he disappeared around that corner.

"I'm going to run back to the cantina," Bridget said. "They forgot my guacamole."

A minute later, Delphinia heard the employee door open and close. She picked up her red pen and tapped it on her papers. There was no reason not to resume her work. Connor was gone.

Again.

She stopped tapping. She'd admired his bared body, winked at him, flirted with him, and he'd left, giving her space. He always left. It was a fact, a pattern, a scientific observation.

She didn't want that space.

He did.

He wasn't intoxicated by her presence, irresistibly drawn to her, dying of loneliness without her. The idea of destined lovers was only fiction. The reality was, the man was a bar owner, polite and charming to every woman who walked in the door, polite and charming to her. Nothing more.

Nobody had hurt her, but tears stung her eyes, anyway. She'd hurt herself by wanting something she couldn't have, by falling in love with a man who—oh, dear God. She was falling in love with him.

She couldn't fall apart here. She turned over her paper napkin and used her red pen to write a note. *Thank you for everything. I had to run—Dr. D.*

Delphinia reloaded her messenger bag, fastening the flap shut as she headed down the hallway toward the back door that would lock behind her and lock her out for good. She'd hurry back to the lamppost, back to the crosswalk, back to the campus and her house and her bathtub. She'd fill it up, slide down until she was under water, and then, *then*, she could cry where her tears couldn't even fall.

Hurry, hurry, before the tears fall.

A man appeared out of nowhere, and she crashed into him—into Connor, shirtless, his skin warm everywhere her body touched his, her palm, her cheek, her chin, the tip of her nose. It all registered as one big, warm impact. *Wham.*

"Whoa." He steadied her with a hand on her arm.

She couldn't back away in the crowded hallway. Her hand fluttered around for a moment, but she couldn't stand there with her hand in the air, so she set it on his arm. His skin was smooth, but the muscle it covered was as hard as marble.

"You scared me. I thought you left to take a shower." If she sounded angry, it was better than bursting into tears—or nuzzling her face into the rounded muscle of his shoulder, just to feel that curving black ink against her cheek.

"I take quick showers."

She registered the smell of soap and clean, dry skin. He was wearing jeans now. He had a brown T-shirt in his hand, sort of—his arm was halfway through one sleeve, like he'd been putting it on when she'd crashed into him.

"So…you're already back?" she asked inanely. There was an open door behind him, a washer and dryer visible through it. "Or, you never left? Is there a shower in there?"

"The shower is in my apartment. I live on the top floor. The laundry room is down here, for the bar towels and aprons, and you weren't leaving, were you?" His hand tightened on her arm.

"Bridget's gone. I was alone."

There was a beat of silence. She was holding his right arm, but she was looking at his left, at his tattoo, because if she looked into his eyes, he would be able to look into hers, and she was still on the verge of crying, because she'd fallen for a man who didn't want to be this close to her.

"I can keep you company now," he said. "No other guests to check on, for a change."

Damn her broken radar. It sounded like he wanted her to stay, but she didn't trust the instincts of her stupid little untrained inner wimpy puppy.

She needed to remember the facts. He always put space between them. She ought to let go of him now. She ought to *go*. She shifted her weight restlessly, and her hip bumped against his, because...

Because he wasn't putting any space between them, not this time.

His voice was as warm as his skin. "I'm just guessing here, but if grading papers is anything like writing papers, then I know some people don't like too much silence. Bridget can't stand to be all alone at a table."

Delphinia held on to his hard arm and kept her gaze on his bare chest. He'd lifted her from the sidewalk with this arm. He'd held her close against that chest. She could lean in so easily and take a taste of his golden skin, a sip where it dipped above his collarbone. Golden, amber, tawny... They'd laughed together under the chandelier.

She watched her own fingers reach for his tattoo and caress it lightly. The tattoo didn't feel different from his un-inked skin. It was just a part of him.

"*M* for McClaine," she said. "I like it."

His spoke more quietly. "It won't be as busy as a coffee shop, but if you want to keep grading your papers—"

"Connor."

He fell silent.

She finally looked at his face, and the heat in his eyes matched everything she was feeling, too—didn't it? She wanted to believe that her fantasy was real. The longing blurred her vision. Hope was painful.

If he didn't want to kiss her, then she was about to make a huge mistake.

"Connor... I don't want to grade papers."

Chapter Sixteen

Connor didn't move a muscle.

Rembrandt had been holding his right arm, but now she clutched his left, too, standing squarely in front of him. *I don't want to grade papers* echoed in the air as she looked at him with brown eyes that held one hundred layers of complexity. Sexual awareness was clear within that tangle of emotions.

Hunger. Desire. More—it was the *more* that made him hesitate. She wasn't looking at him as if she simply liked him, as if she admired his body and wanted to play. This look was different. He'd offered her a table and chair for grading papers, but she was looking at him as if he could offer to touch the moon and stars for her just as easily.

He wouldn't try. He already knew he could not. She shouldn't look at him like he could.

Her eyes filled with tears.

"Are you okay?" he asked.

"No," she whispered, and she kissed him.

It was a soft kiss, like the one she'd pressed on his cheek by her house in the night, that impossibly sweet kiss that he hadn't known how to receive. Just hold still? Just feel the softness? He'd walked the mile back to his place in the dark, unsure how to think about it or where to store it in his memory: thank you, goodbye, first kiss, something new?

Now, that soft kiss was on his lips, and he knew how to receive this kiss and how to return it. Hers was a mouth to appreciate like whiskey. He savored the shape, the curve, the feel—until she slid her hands over his shoulders and looped her arms around his neck, as if she needed him to hold her up.

She was pulling him under. He was half-undressed, drowning in arousal. Conflicting sensations assaulted his senses. As she pressed herself into his body, the crisp material of her shirt abraded the skin of his stomach and chest, but that abrasion was an innocent, cotton caress. She hugged his neck hard, but the skin on the inner sides of her arms was impossibly soft. The slightest touch of her fingertips on his back, unintentional taps between his shoulder blades, clamored for his complete and undivided attention—which was impossible to give, because, with a nudge of her mouth against his, she opened their mouths and the sexual, intimate slide of her tongue blotted out every other sensation.

They could drown together if he brought her upstairs to his bed. She would look like a work of art, beauty and mystery, with her rich hair on his pillow. They would make love for hours.

Then, she would think she knew him so well. She'd say she was in love. She'd want to make it exclusive, to see him every day. *Him*: the business owner, the bartender, the body tattooed with an *M* for McClaine.

The *M* didn't stand for McClaine. It stood for Murphy and it stood for Musketeer, for the only things that made his life worthwhile. Why would he honor McClaine?

McClaine was a dropout. An inmate who fought dirty to survive. A convicted felon until the day he died.

She thought McClaine could teach Victorian literature with her, because she didn't know him at all.

He'd be her biggest mistake, an embarrassment she'd have to defend against everyone's judgment, the weight she'd have to drag through a life that should be lovely, until the day she gave up and let him go, feeling guilty for failing to love him like she'd promised she would while they'd been in bed.

He'd never do that to her, but he'd memorize the feel and taste of her before he let her go. He wrapped his arms around her, holding her up the way she wanted him to. He let one hand enjoy the silk of her hair, let the other slide down the dip of her lower back, over the curve of her firm backside, a reverent touch, because she felt like a miracle in his arms.

Then he lifted his head, separating their mouths by those few, critical inches. "No."

She pressed her forehead against his cheek, her arms still clinging to his neck, her breaths swift, soft, shallow.

He moved his hands to rest lightly on her waist, an innocent touch, friendly.

"No," she repeated, as if it were an unfamiliar word she needed to repeat to get the pronunciation right.

"Delphinia…" But he breathed her in when he said her name. The smell of her hair and skin and crisp cotton shirt were more important than whatever he'd been about to say.

This time, she whispered. "I thought you liked me."

He squeezed her waist, a reflex. *"I do."*

She frowned at his emphatic tone, a little scrunching of her eyebrows against his cheek.

"I do," he repeated, more controlled. "But this would be a mistake for you."

He dropped his hands and backed up, then started fumbling for the other sleeve in the T-shirt on his wrist.

She said nothing. He stopped with both wrists captured in his T-shirt and looked at her. Really looked.

Passion looked so good on her. Her color was high, her lips were full from the kisses he'd given her. No, damn it, she'd given *him* kisses. She'd started the kiss.

It made him angry, but not at her. He was angry with the universe for giving him fantastic chemistry with a woman who was fantastically wrong for him. He pulled his shirt on over his head, and he caught sight of that constant reminder, that badly drawn purple tattoo near his inner elbow. He bent his arm, hiding it instinctively.

"Why?" she asked.

He could give her an easier reason why. "For starters,

you're seeing someone. He moves in your circles. He's probably a professor like you—he is, isn't he? Of course he is. Your friends and family approve, even though he made you feel like a fool over bourbon."

He was angry at the universe, but he was angry at her, too, for that one thing. "Why do you put up with that?"

"It wasn't him. It was my parents."

Her parents.

Connor scrambled to reframe the Norman Rockwell picture he'd drawn around Delphinia and her parents. A parent who made you feel like a fool? The universe wanted him to have even more in common with her, just to make it more painful to resist her.

"They love me," she said. "They're very proud of me."

That much was different from his life, at least.

"They enjoy being very clever, but it can be a cutting sort of clever. Maybe they think I'm still their ten-year-old little bookworm, and their jokes will go over my head. I'm twenty-nine. They don't."

Connor nodded, for he couldn't speak. He braced his hand against the wall, for he couldn't touch her.

She tugged her shirt into place. "I'm moving out, very soon. I'm next on the list for a faculty apartment on campus. My parents keep listing the convenience of living on campus as one reason for me to live in Dumas House. That takes care of that much of the argument. I'm babbling, aren't I?"

She was preparing to fly out of the proverbial nest. She was about to embark on a new phase in her life, just like every other woman who took her diploma and left Masterson behind. Just like every other woman who wanted a boost in her self-confidence after a divorce, every woman who wanted to reassure herself that she was still sexy as she faced a milestone birthday. Just like all of the women he'd liked, let leave, and didn't miss.

Delphinia, he would miss. And yet, she'd be the one who wouldn't leave Masterson when she moved on. Their paths might still cross. She'd smile, even kiss him on the cheek, but he'd know when he looked into her eyes that she'd moved on, and it would hurt.

"A new apartment," he said. "Good luck with that."

She frowned at him, and—and *petted* him, smoothing her palm down his chest, because, of course, now she thought she had the right. He'd kissed her intimately, openmouthed. He knew her taste now, and she knew his.

"I'll tell you when I get the apartment," she said. "You can come over."

And be the charming bartender in her bed? Discuss the business degree she so blithely assumed he had? Plan field trips for her 300-level classes?

He didn't know what *300-level* meant, and she didn't know him. Those brown eyes weren't looking at the real Connor. She hadn't kissed the man who'd eaten out of a dumpster. She was touching the wrong tattoo.

"That's not going to happen," he said. "I won't let you make that mistake."

Her hand stopped. "How can seeing you be a mistake? Are you seeing someone?"

He looked up at the ceiling and laughed. "No, but you are."

That thrum of arousal was still strong between them, so she leaned close to kiss him again, as if that would make everything okay between her and the man she thought he was.

He stopped her with his hands on her pure, ink-free arms. "The honest truth, Rembrandt, is that I am very sorry I kissed you."

Her lips parted in silent shock. She searched his face, and he let her, because then she'd see he was sincere. He would never be able to get her out of his mind now. He'd never be able to stand in his own hallway without remembering this moment, her taste, her touch, how it felt to pull her body into his. It was too late to change it, and he regretted making that memory already.

She recoiled slightly, hurt all over her face, but her eyes didn't fill with tears of want and hope again. She didn't beg him to change his mind.

Instead, she stiffened her posture and put a little schoolmarm into her voice. "You didn't kiss me, Connor McClaine. I kissed you."

She turned on her heel and walked to the employee exit, three angry paces, before she whirled around, eyes fierce and chin defiant. "And I'm not sorry."

"Don't go out that door," he ordered—or begged, an angry kind of begging.

She hesitated, hand on the door, a touch of hope in that defiant expression. Hope, because she wanted him, and he'd said something that sounded like *stay.*

The universe was cruel. Connor hadn't meant to be.

"I'll unlock the front door for you."

She slammed the employee door open and stomped

down the single step. Connor was at the door in a second, stopping it with his palm before it swung shut, but he only watched as she marched past the dumpster and out into the sunshine on the sidewalk. With a swish of shining brown hair, she was gone.

He waited an eternity, but no tires screeched. She was gone, but she was safe. That mattered.

It would always matter.

But he'd already known that.

On Thursday, Delphinia wore her little black dress.

It fit her perfectly, hugging her waist and her hips, stopping just above the knee to show some leg without sacrificing an inch of elegance. The portrait collar exposed a generous amount of décolletage in a classic, silver screen way. She'd spent her empty hours pinning up her hair to complete the look. She did not look like her parents' little bookworm. She did not look like the fourth generation of college professors.

She wished Connor could see her in this dress, because she wanted him to think she was beautiful.

She wished Connor could see her in this dress, because she wanted him to eat his heart out.

Vincent was the man who would see her tonight. He'd said this dress was too distracting when he wanted people to notice him, but tonight was a dinner date, and the other couple were already his friends. He'd appreciate that she'd dressed to impress this evening. Maybe.

Maybe not. Her instincts sucked. Her gut feeling was that Connor wanted her and Vincent cared very little for her, but the facts pointed the opposite way, and facts did not lie.

She'd asked a man to share her kisses, her passion, her future, and he'd said no. Connor hadn't left her any room to hope. *That's not going to happen* was blunt. *I am very sorry I kissed you* had been said with brutal honesty.

Fact: Connor did not want her.

Vincent wanted her to meet his friends. At the end of tonight's date, he would kiss her, and he would not say he regretted it.

Fact: Vincent wanted her.

Delphinia stood inside the portico doors, consciously keeping herself as together on the inside as she looked on the outside. It shouldn't be so difficult to do, but a piece of her had broken loose after kissing Connor, and she couldn't force it back into place.

It rattled with impatience, threatening to explode out of her. She was fed up with her job, she was tired of Vincent's cool control, she wanted her own damned kitchen, she wanted to tear her hair down and scream at the world.

She could quit working, stand Vincent up tonight, pack a suitcase and move to a random spot on the map. She could run barefoot across the green and howl at the moon, but it wouldn't change the way her heart ached for Connor. It would only derail her life.

She touched her hair. Her pearl-tipped pins were holding nicely.

"Don't you look lovely, dear?"

She turned, surprised to see her parents leaving the

house dressed as they were. Her father's blazer was his most casual tweed. "Where are you going?"

"We thought we'd take a cue from you young lovers and go out to dinner before tonight's get-together," her father said. "Several councilmen want to know the university's position on the pedestrian bridge your Vincent told us about. The new sheriff will be there. We haven't met him yet, have we, Rhea? There should be a lively discussion."

The bridge—the accident—Connor picking her up from the sidewalk.

She ignored the rattle of that broken piece inside her and smiled politely at her parents. She could do this. Her life was still heading in the right direction, slowly but surely, toward classes she was more interested in teaching and toward a place where she would be more comfortable living. "I didn't realize there was an event this evening. I didn't see any caterers in the kitchen."

"The meeting is not being held at Dumas House." Her mother slipped into that bizarre, new conspiratorial tone. "So, if anything exciting happens this evening, you'll need to reach me on my cell."

"What kind of exciting thing?" The jagged edges of the broken piece tore at her throat, but she swallowed it down. "Not a proposal. Mother, we discussed this. He didn't ask you already, did he?"

Her mother admonished her father. "Don't you dare say one word, Archibald."

Her father rocked on the balls of his feet. "I'll only say that I cannot imagine our daughter marrying a more suitable man. She'll soon understand why I removed her name from the waitlist for faculty housing."

"*Father.* You did not. Tell me you did not. You had no *right.*"

"I have every right to review your benefits. I am the dean. One of the faculty apartments came open today. Imagine my surprise when your name appeared on the list. It would have been a complete waste of resources to have you move into an apartment and then right back out again."

"Move out again? To live with whom?" A sharp sliver escaped, not in rage, but in despair. "You assumed I would say yes to a question that I don't even want to be asked."

But this marriage proposal was her destiny. She was going to be asked, sooner or later, to marry a man against whom she had no more rational objection than *I don't want to.* Everyone would be disappointed in her, angry at her, disgusted with her—and there would be no escape, because she would still be living under the same roof with the two people who would be the most upset.

She wished a hero would appear, lift her out of this mess and carry her close to his chest, because she was his heart, and his chest was where his heart should be.

What a useless, adolescent wish that was.

Vincent pulled into the portico. Dully, she said good-bye to her parents. Dutifully, she got into the car.

Then Vincent drove her where he wanted her to go, because her fantasy that she had taken control of her life was over.

Chapter Seventeen

Vincent's fellow attorneys were not deliriously happy newlyweds.

They were a pair of sharks, and Vincent enjoyed swimming with them. With an expensive bottle of red wine on the table and rare meat on their plates, Vincent and his rivals wrested respect from one another by telling stories that proved their prowess at manipulating people. They talked about it like it was a sport, wins and losses tallied in courtrooms, high scores awarded for getting valid evidence dismissed or for convincing a jury to ignore a reliable witness.

Delphinia cut her potato into even, precise pieces. Nothing jagged. Nothing torn. "Perhaps you would be happier if you went back to your law firm."

"And go back to billing eighty-hour weeks?" Vincent laid one arm on the back of her chair, but he rolled his eyes with his friends at her suggestion. "Being a professor gives me control of my time. There are other opportunities to enjoy the thrill of the kill. Political opportunities."

"You're considering running for office?" She ought to be told these things before a man asked her to share his life. Then again, that might be the point of this dinner. Mother knew best.

"Not running for office. Controlling those in office."

Vincent casually fondled the back of Delphinia's exposed neck. She couldn't stop the shiver he triggered. It was a reflex, undignified, unbecoming.

The shark husband challenged him. "You're delusional if you think you can pull the puppet strings in Masterson. You haven't lived here a year."

"It only took me a semester to make the right connections. It's time to strengthen a select few. A bridge project has split the city council. I'm going to help kill it, and those who wanted it dead will become my grateful allies."

Mr. and Mrs. Shark nodded in grudging approval. "Who's opposing it?"

"The sheriff, for one. He was appointed after the elected sheriff resigned—cancer, whatever it was." He dismissed a man's life with a wave of his hand. "The new sheriff's appointment was a political favor, naturally, but he has to win the next election in a matter of months. The system has given him an incentive to do favors now for those who can help him get elected later. Having a sheriff in my pocket will be...entertaining."

With a subtle hiss of his name under her breath, Delphinia pleaded for him to stop saying such outrageous things. *"Vincent."*

Vincent's fingers circled the back of her neck and stayed there, a steady pressure. "The sheriff tells me Joe Manzetti isn't in favor of the bridge, either. Since I still haven't been introduced to Manzetti, I'll have to take his word for it. Won't I, sweetheart?" Had his hand been on the front of her neck, it would have choked her.

She wasn't imagining this.

"Just think. Manzetti is the wealthiest man in town. If he opposes the bridge and I oppose the bridge, you'll be on my arm at his Christmas party next year, my pretty Miss Ray."

That's not going to happen. Connor had said those words to her with calm sincerity. She wanted to stand and scream them at Vincent. *I am very sorry I kissed you.*

But his hand was heavy on her neck.

"You have my father convinced that the bridge is a get-rich-quick scheme for the Irish pub. He's meeting with Dr. Marsden this evening to discuss it."

"Is he? What a coincidence." Vincent took his hand off her neck. His slow, satisfied smile was for his friends, not her. "The bridge is dead."

"Even though the woman you love was nearly hit at that intersection," she said under her breath.

Vincent's hand settled on her knee under the table. "Speaking of your father, is the dean pleased with your classes this semester? Any difficulties with your Tuesday and Thursday schedule?"

"None at all."

I'm going to teach Shakespeare at BCC again, starting this Saturday. Othello, to be exact.

She wished she could say that, but Vincent had a way of swaying her father's opinions. He would ensure her father pressured her to quit teaching *Othello* if she argued with Vincent in front of those he wanted to impress.

"That's good to hear." Vincent's smile was charming. Under the table, he gave her knee a quick squeeze. It was not approval; his thumb and finger dug into pressure points for a harsh second. He let go to dash his signature on the check. "Shall we call it an evening?"

There was no question this would be the last date she'd ever have with Vincent Talbot. He manipulated people as a game. He was as ruthless as the villain in *Othello*, who'd ingratiated himself with all the right people, who'd whispered in all the right ears at all the right times in order to convince Othello that his devoted bride was cheating on him and laughing at him behind his back.

Delphinia had been critical of the play as a doctoral candidate, because Shakespeare had failed to give the villain a motive. The villain had destroyed an honorable man just because he could.

She would not criticize the play again. Shakespeare had been right. For some men, that was motive enough, and she was looking at one of those men now.

Vincent drove her home in silence. Her role was now hideously plain to see. Her parents were respected and influential at Masterson University, which meant they were influential in Masterson, the town. As long as Vincent pretended to adore their daughter, they would think he could do no wrong—which meant Delphinia had value to him.

He was not going to let her go easily.

Without any explanation, he drove past the turn that would have taken them back to campus. She looked at the dark road ahead of them, so aware of her vulnerability. If Victor didn't stop the car, there was no way for her to get out.

Don't panic. Stick to the facts.

This was real life, not a Shakespeare play. Vincent Talbot was not a murderer. He was a normal man, a colleague of hers and her parents. He relished manipulating them all for his political ambitions, but he was not going to physically harm her. She was not a door.

She rubbed her knee. "Where are we going?"

"I thought we'd get an after-dinner drink."

It was shocking that he could resume courting her, as if she hadn't heard his chilling plans. He picked up her hand and kissed her knuckles, as if she hadn't felt his fingers wrapped around her neck.

"You mentioned that your parents are meeting Dr. Marsden this evening to talk about bridges. It sounds stimulating, doesn't it?"

"We weren't invited."

"Your parents aren't going to refuse when you ask to sit with them."

"They aren't at the house. I don't know where they're meeting Dr. Marsden."

"I know where." Vincent turned onto Athos Avenue.

"Haven't you guessed? I thought you were a fan of the Tipsy Musketeer."

Connor. Relief left her light-headed. Connor might be sorry he ever kissed her, but he was still the man who'd carried her in his arms when she'd been vulnerable, the man who'd protected his waitress from an aggressive customer. He would not let Vincent hurt her.

But, as they circled the block, looking for a parking spot, Vincent was as focused as a shark who'd caught the scent of blood in the water. He was coming here to win. To do so, he was going to paint the owner of the Tipsy Musketeer as a greedy monster, sinking his reputation with everyone influential, from Dr. Marsden to the sheriff to her parents.

Delphinia wasn't Vincent's target. Connor was.

Connor knew he was in trouble.

When a woman walked into a bar wearing a killer black dress and a determined expression, it never meant she planned a happy and carefree evening.

When the woman was Delphinia, it meant—

Hell, it meant she looked amazing in a little black dress. He couldn't think beyond that as she walked toward him.

But he had to. He was standing right in front of her mother and father.

"Mr. Murphy gave the most charming toasts," Dr. Ray—the mother—said to him. They stood with the city council members who'd congregated around a large corner table.

"Long toasts, but nobody minded listening to that

Irish brogue." Dr. Ray—the father—clapped Connor manfully on the upper arm. Connor expected him to say *Isn't that so, old chap?*

They were friendly people, in their amusingly formal way. That Delphinia's parents were the third generation of college presidents was easy to believe. That they'd produced a daughter who was so passionate about life, about her books, her students, his architecture and *him*, was harder to grasp. Delphinia did not kiss like she was the fourth generation of college presidents.

She stood before him now, glamorous but silent, as her father made introductions. His hand was still on Connor's arm as he gestured to her. "This is my daughter, Dr. Delphinia Ray. She's the youngest professor Masterson has ever placed on a tenured track."

Delphinia was white-knuckling a small purse, but her voice was perfectly polite as she said, "Yes, we've met. It's nice to see you again."

Her father pulled the man next to her forward with a hand on his upper arm, too, bringing Connor face-to-face with the man who'd escorted Delphinia through the door.

"Vincent, I don't believe you've met the current owner. Connor McClaine, this is Dr. Vincent Talbot, Masterson's newest professor of law and my daughter's devoted swain."

Connor had to shake the man's hand, damn it.

"I think boyfriend will suffice," Vincent said, before pausing to look over Delphinia with exaggerated appreciation. "Proud boyfriend, obviously."

The proud boyfriend shook hands in a predictably

competitive way. Connor wanted to catch Delphinia's
eye to see if she noticed, but he didn't look at her. They
weren't on the same wavelength like that, not any longer, so he simply returned the show of strength with
ease and kept his expression neutral. *And may the devil
take you to hell tonight, Vincent—sideways.*

Connor didn't miss the way Vincent spotted someone beyond Dr. Ray's shoulder, the way he took Delphinia's elbow, the way he whispered urgently, "There
he is. Introduce us."

"If you gentlemen will excuse me, I need to…ex-
cuse myself."

Vincent tugged her elbow back an inch. "Five minutes, sweetheart. Introduce me first, then you can go
while we chat."

Connor saw the way she forced a smile before turning to her boyfriend. "Excuse me, please."

She walked past Connor, close enough that she would
have brushed against him if he hadn't shifted out of her
way. The sound of her high heels faded away.

"I hope she's feeling all right," her mother said.

"I'm sure she is," Vincent said. "She's been fine all
evening. I see that Joe Manzetti is here. Would you do
me the favor of an introduction, Dr. Ray?"

Her boyfriend was an idiot. Delphinia hadn't looked
fine. She'd looked pale and acutely uncomfortable, but
Connor knew what was ailing her. She was petrified
that he was going to ruin her relationship with her
swain.

Connor would never tell, he'd never even hint, that
he'd kissed her—or she'd kissed him—in the hallway,

so temptingly close to the staircase that led to his bed. Connor had learned to keep secrets in prison. Snitches got shanked. People who witnessed too much were silenced. Connor wouldn't say a word.

But Delphinia didn't know that, because she had no idea who the real Connor was.

Nobody in this town did, and he was going to keep it that way.

Chapter Eighteen

"What's Dr. Dee doing in the VIP booth?"

Connor continued shaking a batch of cosmos, but the question caught him off guard. "I'll take care of it."

Connor poured the cocktails and served them to some appreciative ladies while he kept an eye on that corner table of Masterson heavyweights. The new sheriff had been the last to arrive, swaggering into the bar in his uniform, gun in his holster, handcuffs on his belt, about fifteen minutes ago.

Connor had left the group to go check on the rest of the house. He had a business to run. If the sheriff wanted to meet him, he'd find him; law enforcement always did.

The proud boyfriend was still over there, talking to

everyone. What he wasn't doing was checking on his girlfriend.

Connor walked down to the VIP booth, bracing himself to be hit again by the sight of Delphinia looking like a star for another man's approval. This was the way things had to be, but Connor hadn't expected her to move on quite so easily, not in his own damned pub. He hadn't expected to have to *watch* her with another man.

Connor slid open the panel. There she was, a punch to his solar plexus, a vision in black, her dark hair studded with pearls.

She had the bench cushions in each hand, and she threw one down when she saw him in the window. "It's about time."

"What are you doing with my cushions?"

"I'm looking for the damned bell so I can get the damned bartender's attention. That's you. Where is the bell?" She threw the other cushion down.

"I got rid of that bit of authenticity."

She nearly stamped her foot. "Why?"

"Would you want drunk people ringing bells at you?"

She sat down on one of the benches with a thud. "I need to talk to you. Not through the window."

"It would take me five minutes just to get to the other end of the bar and walk back around to that door." He was not going to enclose himself in a small, private space with a woman he wanted as much as he wanted Delphinia Ray.

"This is important. I came to warn you. This evening—"

"That's not necessary. I'm not going to say a word." He slid the panel shut.

She banged on the wood from the other side. Seats two and three were keenly interested now. He slid the panel open and turned his back to his guests.

She was standing again, so she put her hand on the edge of the window. "You're not going to say a word about what?"

"The boyfriend. The kiss. You want to act like we've met just once before? Fine."

She blinked at him, a sad reminder of when she'd intentionally batted her eyelashes playfully.

It made him impatient. "Drama isn't necessary. I'm not going to screw up your life."

"Vincent is going to screw up yours."

He backed his face away from the window an inch. "What?"

"He's playing a game, trying to rack up political favors. He's going to kill the bridge project. The sheriff and Joe Manzetti want it dead, so he wants them to be grateful. More than that. *Indebted* to him."

"To your boyfriend?"

"He's been working on my father since the day of the crash, telling him you had nefarious intentions to funnel the student body of Masterson into your trap."

"*Funnel.* That was his exact word?" Connor didn't mean to laugh, but what an arrogant piece of garbage that Vincent Talbot was.

"It's not a joke. He's going to make you the villain, so the town will oppose you."

She was truly distressed. She thought Connor was in

danger, and she had snuck away from her friends and family rather than silently going along with their plans.

The implications sobered him. "And you came to warn me. Despite…everything?"

She made a helpless kind of gesture. "Did you think I cared about you *less* after kissing you?"

Yes. Connor's last words to her had been an emphatic *no.*

They looked at one another through the small window, and he felt it again, that spark between them, that anticipation of more. It was anticipation for something that would not happen, because he cared for her, too.

"I appreciate the warning, but it's not going to happen the way your boyfriend thinks he can make it happen. You don't need to worry about me, Rembrandt. Don't defy anyone for my sake." With one last look, he stepped back and started to slide the door shut.

"Wait. Please, wait. I have something else I need to ask you."

He wanted to retreat behind his bartender persona. The pub was buzzing all around him, and he'd had his back to the rest of his guests long enough to be rude. But this was Delphinia, dressed so beautifully for another man, yet looking at Connor so earnestly.

He waited, hand on the panel.

"I'm going to break up with him. Tonight."

She looked like she'd just announced that she was going to the guillotine. Her life was supposed to be full of light, not full of conflict.

Connor wanted that for her, even if he wasn't the man who could offer any woman a light and happy life.

"Don't break up with him if it makes you unhappy. It won't change anything between you and me."

She studied the floor.

This little window was a terrible way to speak to someone. It was as frustrating as trying to communicate with an inmate in another cell by speaking through the slots for the meal trays. He'd never want Delphinia to know how isolating that felt, yet he was talking to her that way right now, a former prisoner treating her like a fellow prisoner. "It will always be a mistake for you to imagine that I'm good enough for you. I'm not sure anyone is, but I know I'm not."

She dragged her gaze up to his. "I wanted to ask you if you would walk me home after I break up with Vincent. I—I promise not to proposition you or tell you I love you or anything like that."

He'd never had a woman promise not to tell him she loved him. He probably would have liked hearing that from prior lovers. Hearing it from Delphinia hurt, no matter how much he'd practically demanded she say it.

Hurt tasted bitter. "You're going to walk a mile in those heels?"

"I don't want to get in his car again."

Something about the way she said it sent that prickling sensation along the back of his neck.

Danger. Pay attention.

"Your parents can drive you home."

"They might be…on his side. They'd want me to ride with him. I considered waiting to tell Vincent after he drove me home, but if my parents were on the other side of the house, they'd never hear me if I...well. I think this is the safest place for me to tell him goodbye."

The safest?

"Has he hurt you?"

She took too long to answer.

Connor fought a hot anger. He needed to stay calm, to get more information in order to help her, but he wanted to break through this stingy opening, to tear out the whole wall, so he could pull her hard against his chest and keep her safe from the rest of the world.

She touched her throat, trailed her fingers over the back of her neck, then finally shook her head. "Not really, but he's playing a game with that, too, I think."

Rage had to be controlled, doled out in appropriate measures at the Musketeer, so this would remain a civilized world, a respectable place of business. No need to throw a fist. No need for the police to get involved.

"I'll let Kristopher drive you home any time you want. He'll still be on the clock, so don't worry that you'll be taking him away from his job."

Delphinia's shoulders sagged slightly at his tepid offer, but it was a good solution. It would get her where she wanted to be, whenever she wanted to be there. There was no need for Connor to walk with her alone on a moonlit night.

"It could look bad if I were seen in a student's car late at night. It's not always what you're doing, it's what it looks like you're doing. Thank you, anyway." She picked up her little purse and left through the stained-glass door.

Connor felt like he'd kicked a puppy. It wasn't what

he'd done, but it was what it looked like he'd done, because as she'd turned away, her eyes had filled with tears.

She didn't know what kind of man he was, but he did. He never had been the kind who stood by and watched when an aggressor tormented a vulnerable person, not even when he'd been in prison. He had the purple tattoo to prove it.

He couldn't handle this situation the way he had back then. Instead of being awarded a tattoo, he'd get a set of handcuffs slapped on him, and he'd land right back in jail. No windows, no light, no liquor license, no Irish pub.

The devil would take it all.

It was closing time.

Delphinia perched on the bench in the snug, facing Vincent. Waitresses cleared empty mugs off the tables, carrying five or six in each hand by their handles as they walked past the snug, like a processional of bridesmaids with bouquets of beer mugs, but the carved rosette was not going to witness a love story tonight.

Delphinia began formally. "I need to speak with you, now that the evening is wrapping up."

"It's wrapped up, all right. Everyone congratulated each other on green-lighting that asinine bridge."

She didn't want Vincent getting more agitated before she could deliver her little speech. "'Everyone' included you. You came around to the idea, once you saw the plans. You were smiling and shaking hands with the rest."

Vincent looked disgusted with her. "I had no choice. How could you possibly miss that?"

Why was she still trying to placate him?

"I didn't miss anything. I sat by your side the entire time. I stayed neutral."

She'd had a front-row seat as Vincent had self-destructed. When Connor had unrolled a blueprint-sized drawing on the table, Vincent had taken one glance, then laughed. *Can you believe this guy? He wants to funnel our student body right into his bar.*

Her father, as practical as his daughter could be, had pointed out that the bridge had access ramps on each of the four corners of the intersection. Pedestrians could use it not only to cross the street, but to go diagonally from one corner to another. Did Vincent not see that?

I see delusions of grandeur. How about expecting people to obey the law, instead? One would hope that MU students are smart enough to use a crosswalk, but if they keep walking into traffic... Well, they might not be the kind of students we want at MU, anyway.

The sheriff had laughed, but Dr. Marsden had not been amused.

Connor had kept things positive. *I hired an architecture student to draw this concept. There's a lot of talent at MU.*

Dr. Marsden had been gratified, even more so when Joe Manzetti had joined in the praise. *A student? You have to put me in touch with her. She's exceptional.*

Vincent still hadn't realized how badly he was losing his own game, until he managed to insult all the players at once. *No one has bothered to conduct a study to prove it's necessary before wasting millions on it.*

The city council members had been offended by the accusation that they wasted taxpayer money.

Manzetti had said that he'd cover some of the expense himself, just to have his company's name attached to such a beautifully designed project.

Dr. Marsden had said, *The university can afford to invest in a bridge that will be a gateway to the campus. What we can't afford is a study that will tell us what we already know. We've had three students hit in three years.*

Connor had casually lined up the shot. *And one faculty member grazed.*

Manzetti had driven it home. *Your own girlfriend, Talbot. How much proof do you require?*

Vincent was still fuming. "I was made a fool of tonight, and it's your fault."

Delphinia swallowed the jagged piece that wanted to escape in stinging sarcasm. *I'm sorry for not agreeing that I got hit because I was so stupid that I don't belong at MU.*

"If you hadn't gone tutoring that night, I would have met Manzetti before—"

"I don't want to talk about the bridge."

"—and I would have been able to feel out his attitude—"

"*Vincent.* I don't think we should continue seeing one another."

He went still, but it was the silence of a rattlesnake who was done warning everyone to watch out. Now he was calculating whether it was time to bite or time to slither away.

Please, slither away.

He leaned into her so abruptly, she jumped. "You really know how to bust a man's balls when he's down, don't you? Nothing is ending, my pretty Miss Ray. You owe me—"

"I'm not your pretty Miss anything. I'm a professor. It is not my job to bring you to every university function and introduce you to everyone I know, and tonight was the very last time I will sit beside you silently."

"Is that what this is about? You didn't get to talk at dinner?"

"I haven't talked for seven months. I wish you well." She grabbed her purse and stood.

"Sit—" Vincent grabbed her wrist "—down."

She yanked her hand free. Her purse hit the floor.

Another man's voice filled the space, a single word of command. "Vincent."

Vincent jerked toward the man in surprise. Delphinia turned, too. There, framed in the open side of the snug, stood the man with the chiseled body, the Greek Ideal with the nicked eyebrow.

"I hate to interrupt," he said, in a voice that said he didn't give a damn if he was interrupting, "but I told Delphinia's mother I'd let her know she was looking for her."

He pushed aside one of the chairs and bent over to pick up Delphinia's purse. As he stood, he slowly, deliberately, took Vincent's measure, until he finished standing, looking down on him. Connor's expression was not neutral. He was an annoyed god, Poseidon irritated at a lowly human for being so aggravating that the god had to bestir himself to pick up his trident.

Connor turned to Delphinia, dismissing Vincent's entire existence. "You should go. You'll find her in the ladies' room."

She took her purse from him. "Thank you. Really. Thank you."

Vincent stood. "I'm going with you."

"To the ladies' room? Nah." Connor turned, a matter of a few inches, but it was enough to put his shoulder between them.

"Good night," Delphinia said, more to Connor than Vincent.

Vincent moved to follow her, but Connor casually set the back of his hand against Vincent's chest. "Let her go."

Delphinia brushed against Connor as she left, craving even the most humble touch of the man she loved.

Chapter Nineteen

"Don't tell me what to do."

Connor didn't bother replying to Vincent. He stood outside the snug, arms crossed over his chest, waiting for the ass to leave. He positioned himself so the path to the ladies' room would require Vincent to walk through him. The path to the main door was a short, clear shot. Any reasonable animal would take the easier path.

This made Connor a sheepdog, not the wolf of Delphinia's book. But game wardens captured rogue wolves. Sheepdogs remained free. That mattered.

Vincent tried to go through him. Not the sharpest animal in the barnyard.

"Not tonight," Connor said. "She's going home with her parents."

"Who the hell do you think you are?"

"Just the bartender. It's almost closing time. Let me see you out." He gestured toward the door and herded Vincent out. He watched through the etched glass until Vincent passed the lamppost, then Connor turned around to get back to his business, back to the one thing he had left that still mattered.

He stopped short. The sheriff was blocking his way. Badge, holster, handcuffs—Connor's reaction was visceral, but he didn't back away. This was his bar, his private property, damn it, but the flash of anger had to be controlled. Fists were useless.

"You managed to avoid being introduced to me," the sheriff said.

"Likewise. Busy evening." Connor extended his hand now. "Connor McClaine. I own the Tipsy Musketeer."

The sheriff shook hands with a bone-crushing grip and didn't bother to give his name in return.

Connor returned the grip, resisting the temptation to overpower it. "But you already knew that."

The sheriff did not let go. He put his other hand over theirs, one of those two-handed sandwich handshakes that usually meant a very warm, very enthusiastic greeting. It was odd, wrong for this situation. *Danger. Pay attention.*

The sheriff abruptly pushed up Connor's cuffed sleeve, exposing the purple tattoo.

Connor jerked his arm free, but the sheriff had seen what he'd wanted to see. "Ward, cell block number, state of Texas. Big fighter. Proud of yourself there, were you?"

"Ten years past."

"I know all about it. I run the names of everyone I might meet through the database before get-togethers like tonight. You're a felon with a liquor license. Judging from the love affair everyone had with you and your bridge tonight, nobody around here knows who you really are. Let's make sure we don't do anything to endanger that."

A common bully, which was all this sheriff was, wouldn't stop until he was told to stop. "If you want to threaten me, Sheriff, be specific. Otherwise, I need to get back to running my business."

"Fair warning. Bar fights will now result in arrests, every person, every time. Bouncers, owners, doesn't matter to me. I'm no pansy like the old sheriff. Voters want a sheriff who treats criminals the way they deserve to be treated. It'll be easy to win the election, once I make an example of a few troublemakers."

"You'll be busy at other places, then. You've got bigger problems than an Irish pub. The only reason your deputies come here is for some caffeine during a long shift. It's on the house for law enforcement, of course." The more puffed-up the sheriff got, the more relaxed Connor stayed, if only to enrage the man by not playing his game. "Did you need anything else? Coke in a to-go cup?"

After a long moment, the sheriff put on his cowboy-style hat. "I'm watching you."

Connor held his ground. If he gave this type of man an inch, he'd take a mile. The sheriff had to walk around him to go out the door.

Connor hated the victory. It would only add to the

sheriff's grudge, but caving in would only have emboldened the sheriff. There was no safe move, no way for Connor to win.

There'd been a moment earlier, as everyone had shaken Connor's hand and thanked him, when Mr. Murphy's prediction had seemed possible. Why wouldn't the city let Connor be on the ballot? As a council member, he'd be respectable enough to be seen with—to be the *proud boyfriend* of—a professor like Delphinia, despite the criminal record he had and the education he didn't. He could build a life with a woman whose very laugh would guarantee there would always be light in his life.

The sheriff had come out of nowhere tonight like a sucker punch in a prison chow hall. Nothing would ever change. It didn't matter who was elected, who came, who went, who was just passing through. Any sheriff who came to Masterson in the next fifty years could be worse. Any mayor could try to revoke a liquor license to force him out. Anyone who wanted to take what Connor had would always have a felony record to bludgeon him with. If he had a wife, a family, they'd get bludgeoned, too.

There's a lot in this world we cannot change, lad. Best to focus on what you can control. Get back to work with you now. Connor crossed the floor with the intention of heading to the storeroom. He had a bar to replenish.

But when he walked around the corner, he veered into the VIP booth and shut the door. He needed a minute, one minute to hide from the world. He closed his eyes and rested his forehead against the wood.

The devil hadn't taken Vincent Talbot to hell sideways this evening. He'd taken Connor.

Something was wrong.

Delphinia knew it the moment their eyes met. She'd come back to the VIP booth to wait until she was sure Vincent was gone, but Connor had already been in it, waiting just for her.

Maybe. When she shut the door behind herself, he crossed his arms, or rather, his wrists, putting the bulk of his arms between them, keeping space between them. It reminded her of the way he'd stood with his wrists trapped in his T-shirt, after their kiss—their one kiss.

It was a crime that she'd kissed this man only once in her life.

Her radar was spinning madly in every direction. He'd freed her from a volatile situation, but he didn't want her? He did want her, he must. He'd known she'd still be in the pub right now, alone. He'd arranged it that way. Maybe.

"My mother wasn't in the ladies' room. Did you know they'd already left for the night?"

"Yes."

Euphoria was like a drug in her veins. He had known he was stranding her here, with him.

"Vincent didn't know," he said. "It was the easiest way to get him to let you walk away."

"That, and you standing between us, ready to stop him if he tried to stop me again." She was resolved to stay firmly grounded in facts and reality, but the cold way Connor had said *Let her go* had been a hair's breadth from bared teeth and raised fur.

She didn't need to scale a mountain. She only needed to cross a foot of flooring to smooth her hands up the sleeves of that ivory dress shirt, over the Celtic *M* that she knew lay underneath. The backs of his crossed hands pressed into her soft stomach, because she pushed close to him. With her high heels on, she only needed to slide her hands over his powerful shoulders and up his neck to cup his face and tilt his head down an inch. As she closed her eyes to kiss that beautiful mouth, she felt the muscles in his jaw clench under her thumbs.

Fact: the last time she'd kissed him, he'd said no.

"May I kiss you?" she whispered against his lips.

He kissed her. Softly, gently, lips against lips. Her heart beat harder, waiting for more, wanting his tenderness to be a prelude to passion, when, with a little push of his mouth against hers, he lifted his head.

She opened her eyes.

Courteously, he reached around her to put his hand on the doorknob. "I'll drive you home. I'm not any better for your reputation than Kristopher, but you can't walk a mile dressed like that."

"Connor."

He opened the door.

"Connor, I don't want you to drive me back to my house."

He hesitated, but she knew, she just knew, he was going to come up with some pedantic transportation solution, as if he didn't know what she really meant.

She had no patience for polite pretenses, not tonight.

Not ever again. "I don't want to go home tonight any more than I wanted to grade papers the other day."

His expression was so aloof. Should he answer the mortal?

She'd give him the real question to answer. "Why won't you kiss me?"

He frowned, a brief movement of that perfectly, beautifully nicked eyebrow, her reminder that he was only a man—

"I just did," he said.

—and she was going to kill him for pretending he didn't know what she meant.

"You know, when you said you regretted kissing me, I thought my instincts were all wrong," she said. "For two days, I tried to convince myself that what I knew was true wasn't true. But my instincts are good. You like me as much as I like you."

He shut the door and pointed toward the top of the partition walls around them. "This snug isn't as private as you might think it is."

She stepped closer, right into his personal space. "*Like* isn't the right word for this. You *want* me as much as I want you. So why won't you kiss me? Really kiss me?"

"That kiss was real." His breathing wasn't any more steady than hers. "But yeah, I'm stopping this from going farther. You're on the rebound. The bartender is fun and available, but I'm only available for so much."

"Nothing about kissing you has anything to do with a rebound."

"You walked in here tonight on another man's arm. You're dressed to impress another man."

"I was thinking of you while I got dressed, but it wasn't a nice feeling. I wanted you to think I looked beautiful, because if you were going to regret kissing me, I wanted you to really regret it. I wanted you to eat your heart out."

He almost smiled, a lift of one corner of his mouth.

"It was an adolescent wish. I didn't think I'd actually see you tonight. The restaurant was out of town. But when I walked into your bar—"

"I ate my heart out. Believe me."

"No, that's not it." She couldn't force that loose piece to stay inside any longer. It was no longer jagged. Now that she was with Connor, it was a molten liquid that came pouring from her heart. "I'd been so afraid. I didn't know what Vincent was going to do, but when I walked into your bar, I thought 'thank God, I'm with Connor now.' But it wasn't because you wouldn't let a woman, any woman, be hurt in your bar."

He raised a skeptical eyebrow at that. "You stood in this booth and specifically asked me to protect you. The bouncer is no more available for a rebound fling than the bartender."

"It's not about bouncers and bartenders. It's about you. You're the reason I could breathe again, once I saw you. It was because you saw me. You *see* me. You notice me, you talk to me. You have from the start, so when I walked in tonight, I stopped feeling afraid, because when I'm near you, I'm not alone."

The truth filled the space between them.

She kissed the corner of his mouth that had smiled so briefly. "Being with you is not a mistake. It's magic."

He didn't let go of the doorknob, but with his other hand, he cupped the side of her face, running his thumb over her cheek with infinite gentleness. "This, whatever this is between us, is still a mistake. You want love stories to end happily, together forever, but that's not possible here. I'm not the man for you."

"I don't believe that."

"It's not a matter of belief. I know it for certain. I could prove it to you." His thumb stopped. A grim resolve touched the corners of his mouth. "You'll never believe me unless I do. Will you come with me? There's something I need to show you."

Chapter Twenty

Delphinia had no idea what Connor wanted to show her, but he climbed the stairs in grim silence. On the third-floor landing, he opened the door and stepped aside for her.

She walked right into a fantasy world.

White bookshelves ran from floor to ceiling on every wall, custom-made to frame the windows. The books upon them were an explosion of color. The spines of compact paperbacks stood between fat textbooks. Hardcovers, soft covers, every type of book, every single color—a joyful chaos contained in neat white rectangles.

She turned in a slow circle. "Did you build these?"

"Mr. Murphy didn't mind. I was only renting his spare bedroom, but he let me keep my books in his living room. I built one or two bookshelves a year, as I needed them."

"You lived with Mr. Murphy?"

"Until the stairs got to be too much for him."

A piece of the puzzle clicked into place. Bridget had said Connor had helped her with her schoolwork. He hadn't just worked at the pub. He'd lived with her uncle. No wonder they seemed like they were family.

"These are all yours? Have you read them all?"

His gaze glanced off her.

"You have." She trailed her fingers over the spines, stunned. Fiction, nonfiction, popular paperbacks propping up classic works, all kinds of books shelved in no particular order. "You read everything."

"Not enough. I've never read Ruskin."

"But you're going to now, aren't you? Because I gave you a textbook you haven't read yet. When I gave it to you, I had no idea—"

"This isn't what I wanted to show you." He looked down at his arm or his hand or his sleeve, at something, frowning, tense—motionless.

His hand was empty. She placed hers in his.

He closed his eyes, but his fingers closed around hers.

"I'm going to bring back *A Mate with Destiny* for you," she said. "You should read more happy endings."

That broke his stillness. He led her into a modern-industrial kitchen, not an interior designer's creation, but the real thing. The exposed ceiling revealed Victorian ironwork, including a ladder that was bolted to a weathered brick wall that must have been the original exterior of the building. "Can you climb a ladder in heels?"

Delphinia stepped out of her shoes, and they climbed up to the roof.

The city looked lovely in lights. She walked out to the middle of the roof to try to take it all in. The roof felt hard and smooth under her bare soles. She felt grounded, connected to everything, even as she tilted her head back and lost herself in the vast night sky above them. She was happy she was in her best dress, happy that pearls were in her hair when the stars were out, happy that Connor would share something so wonderful with her.

But when she turned to say so, she saw that he hadn't moved far from the ladder. Gym equipment was set up there, under an awning. He stood with one hand on a heavy punching bag that was hanging from chains, shaded from the moonlight.

Fact: he wanted to show her why they were a mistake.

"Do you see your house?" he asked.

She looked to the north. The fountain was lit up, too perfectly blue. She followed her daily path from Hughes Hall down a gentle slope to the stadium, dark tonight, then over several blocks. The trees and streetlights blurred together in the distance, but the four dean's houses were among them.

"That's your life," Connor said.

"For now. I found out tonight that my father won't authorize a faculty apartment for me, so I'll have to move off campus." The solution was obvious now. "I'm going to. I should have done that sooner." But she was watching Connor out of the corner of her eye.

He was looking at his arm. Then he clenched his fist and threw one punch at the body bag, a ferocious release of force. When the gods used all their strength, it was fearsome.

The look on his face was anguish, not anger. "You can put your furniture anywhere you want, but you belong to the university. You earned your place there. You have stability. Respect." Connor shook out his right hand, then held out his arm and cuffed his sleeve one turn more. "That's your life. This is mine."

Delphinia was baffled. "What's wrong with your life? This is an amazing place to live."

"All of this, everything I have, I only have because of Mr. Murphy. I was lucky, and he was kind. Nothing more." He held his arm out to her. "This is what Connor McClaine earned on his own."

She was glad for the excuse to walk back to his side, to touch him as she took the arm he held out. In the light that came through the ladder's hatch door, she barely made out some faded purple letters, a number, a squiggle of an upside-down triangle.

"I was given this tattoo on night one hundred and seventy-nine. I was released from prison on day one hundred and eighty."

The world stopped. It was only the two of them for a suspended moment, then she came crashing back to this new reality.

"Prison. Oh, Connor." Delphinia wanted to ask why, when, for what, but she didn't. After every sympathetic

Oh, Delphinia, her mother would ask a question that implied she'd done something to cause her misfortune. *Did you quarrel with Vincent?*

So she ran her palm over Connor's forearm in silence. The ugly little letters felt no different than the beautiful *M.* It was all skin, all part of Connor.

"I was stupid at nineteen. I got in a car with a couple of guys I shouldn't have been friends with. The car was stolen. I didn't know riding in a stolen car was a felony, but it wouldn't have mattered to me then. I thought I was tough. I went to prison and found out I wasn't."

The shaky triangle was supposed to be the shape of Texas, then. "I had no idea prisoners were tattooed by the state. That's obscene. I'm so—I'm so *angry* they did that to you."

"Texas doesn't tattoo inmates. The inmates tattoo the inmates. Sometimes. It was considered an honor on the inside."

"They respected you."

"For what, Delphinia? For what? The first month that I was in the state prison, I got jumped. A lot. You never knew when it was coming, or why. One beating landed me in the infirmary for two nights."

Her knees felt weak. Connor, beaten so badly he had to be hospitalized—she held his other arm, too.

"When I returned, someone newer was the target. He was skinny, scared. I sat in the chow hall and watched them surround him. They started eating his food off his tray, and I…"

She could only wait, hanging on his every word, hanging on to him.

"I snapped. I started wailing on them. Fists. Feet. Beating them off with a meal tray like they were a pack of rabid dogs. I fought, really fought, for the first time in my life."

"You still defend other people."

"I wasn't defending anyone. I was furious at—I don't know. Inmates get a skimpy lunch, and I wanted everyone to sit and eat what little they had, just shut up and eat and get through the day. I wanted some sense of order. To get it, I learned to be *vicious*. For the rest of my time, the guards looked the other way, as long as I was keeping their troublemakers in line."

"That's how you got that scar on your eyebrow? Defending someone?"

"Don't look at me like I'm a hero. I wasn't some kind of Robin Hood, protecting the innocent and weak." He jabbed his finger toward his eye. "This? I was siding with a man who'd held up a gas station at gunpoint. That skinny, scared guy in the chow hall? He'd set his mother's house on fire. I was sick of the violence, so I became the source of the violence. That's all."

He looked away from her, glaring at the night, at the city lights—but not at her.

Delphinia knew she'd never been wrong, not for a minute, not about anything to do with Connor Mc-Claine. That first day, she'd known he was a lone wolf, looking through a window at the world without being a part of it. Now, she knew why.

"It's hard to imagine you living like that, once upon a time. You're so warm to everyone now. You're generous. Everyone loves you. Your employees, your customers…" She ran her thumb along his cheekbone with as much gentleness as he'd shown her. "Me."

He covered her hand with his own, but only to stop her from touching him. He lowered her hand and let go.

"You might think you're falling in love with me. You're not. You're in love with the owner of the Tipsy Musketeer. He's a nice guy. Generous? You watched him get a bridge to protect students—but that's not why *I'm* doing it. I want that bridge because I hate the sound of those tires screeching. I don't want to scrape a human being off the pavement, because I don't want that image stuck in my brain. I'm not a hero. I'm selfish."

"That's not selfish. Any decent human being doesn't want to see someone hurt."

"But I used to hurt people. Don't you see that?"

"You hurt others and others hurt you. For one hundred and eighty days, you survived. It's incredible, the way you turned your life around after that."

He'd already started shaking his head before she could finish her thought.

"You need proof, or you'll never believe me," she said, using his own words. "That bridge is proof. Most people just hope nothing bad happens, or that they'll at least not be there when it does. Not you. You're doing something about it. You put your time into it. Your own money. You have the charisma to get others excited about your vision, and you're using that to prevent more disasters. That makes you a very rare kind of person."

"You sound like Mr. Murphy. You both overlook the fact that I have a criminal record." Connor's hands tightened on her arms, holding on to her as she was holding on to him. "It's not common knowledge. I don't think Bridget even knows what I did before I came to the Musketeer, but it's a matter of public record. The sheriff reminded me tonight just how easy it is, how easy it always will be, to call me up in a database."

"How did he—"

"It's a punishment I will never escape. I could get pulled over for something as simple as a broken taillight anywhere, in any city or state, and the cop would know as soon as he ran my driver's license that I am a felon. I guarantee they'd ask me to get out of my car. They'd pat me down, just to make sure I wasn't armed. They could handcuff me, detain me, while they waited for the dispatcher to check if any warrants were out for my arrest, because most criminals remain criminals. That's what would happen at a routine traffic stop. Can you imagine what would happen if I were involved in a fight?"

Connor in handcuffs. It would be an unjust humiliation.

"Don't worry about me," Connor said, as if she could erase from her mind the picture he had painted. "I don't break the law, ever."

"I don't, either. Am I allowed to kiss you yet?"

"No, you're not." At last, he let go of her arms and drew her against his chest, wrapping his arms around her to hold her close to his heart. But as he pressed his face into her pearl-dropped hair, he laughed a little. It was not a good laugh. It sounded resigned, hopeless. "Ah, Rembrandt. Can't you imagine your parents' reaction if you brought a felon home to meet them?"

"They've already met you. They like you."

His chuckle died. "*Don't*. You're only being stubborn now. I'm not the man who fits into your life. I didn't even graduate from high school. I passed the GED test years later. Guess where I passed it. One guess."

"In prison?" Incredible. This intelligent, well-read man had not graduated from high school. "I have so much respect for you. I'm speaking as a teacher. It's superhuman to be able to concentrate on a major test in a dangerous, unpredictable place."

Against her hair, she could feel him shaking his head no. "The library was safe enough. That was the only reason I studied. I learned to love the library really quickly."

"So, we come full circle. Books are magical."

He was silent. She closed her eyes and wished the moment would never end: his arms wrapped hard around her, his cheek resting heavily against her hair.

"We agree on that much," he said. "Come on, I'll take you back where you belong."

Connor shepherded Delphinia out of his home—or he tried.

She was looking at the bookshelves again, and she didn't care if he nudged her in the direction of the door. It didn't work when the person *hoped* he'd pick them up.

"Where's Rembrandt?" she asked.

Right here. He thought of her, a reflex.

But she was scanning the shelves. "I want to see it. I hear it's magnificent."

She was magnificent. She was still teasing him, unbowed, uncowed, unintimidated by him. Her enthusiasm for his pub and his life, for his books, for *him* was genuine, no matter what he told her about his past or his future. She was a magnificent temptation.

He needed to get her out of his house.

He stood by the door, ready to grab his pickup truck's keys from their hook beside it, but Delphinia walked down the longest wall, fingers trailing over his books, looking for the one that meant the most to him, the book whose title had revealed too much of his feelings toward her.

"I thought this was random," she said. "But they're shelved in the order that you read them, aren't they? The paperbacks get more yellow with age toward that corner. My gosh, Connor. You built a bookcase *or two* every year, to hold the one hundred books you read that year. How could you think you're uneducated?"

She didn't seem to need an answer, and since he'd already told her he was a dropout, he watched her in silence, cataloging her appearance as she cataloged his books. Her makeup had faded, but her cheeks were touched with rose from the cool night air. A few pieces of her hair had come loose from the rooftop breeze, or from the dangerous way he'd buried his face in her hair as he'd held her. She was still barefoot. As she touched his books with one hand, her fancy black shoes dangled from her other.

Some man was going to have the privilege of seeing her like this, late in the evening after a full day at work, *for as long as they both shall live*.

Maybe Connor wanted to watch her a little longer. Maybe he wanted to fantasize that she belonged to him, and this was how they'd live together. Maybe he just didn't want to say goodbye for one more minute. Whatever it was, it made him say, "*Rembrandt* is on the far left, bottom shelf."

She set down her shoes as she crouched low and found the book, the very first one all the way to the left. She looked at the cover for a moment, at the crumbling plastic with which the library had protected it, at the letters stamped across the sun-faded cover art, *TDCJ*. She must know they stood for Texas Department of Criminal Justice. She sat down on the floor, right on her backside in that elegant dress, and opened the book.

"*Oh.*" The colors inside were still vivid, even from where he stood. "Oh, it's beautiful."

It was something, watching this woman touch the pages he'd learned by heart more than ten years ago. He couldn't have pictured a woman like her back then, but here she was, a teacher who cared about her students, a scholar who was passionate about Shakespeare, a woman who appreciated whiskey and who made him smile every time they were together.

So, this is love.

"This is where it starts?" she asked. "*Rembrandt* is the very first book you put on the first shelf?"

She was as clairvoyant as Mr. Murphy. Connor needed to get her out of here. He held out his hand. She took it, and he pulled her to her feet. Her shoes and his book lay on the floor. He picked up her shoes and left the book, then took her hand and walked her to the door.

"Now, I'm your Rembrandt," she said. "I want to be the start of something good, too."

Loving her made it easy to choose to do the best thing for her. "This is the end. Put your shoes on. It's time to go."

She knew he meant it; he could tell it in a glance as she stepped back into her shoes.

"Well, then." She pressed her back against his door. "Aren't you going to kiss me goodbye?"

Chapter Twenty-One

"You'll regret this," Connor whispered, mesmerized by the color of Delphinia's lips.

"No, I won't."

She thought he was talking to her.

He was going to regret this kiss more than any other, but he had to kiss her again, one final taste. If he maintained control, if he didn't let it go too far, he could hold her just a little longer.

She kissed him. Her mouth was warm as her tongue tasted his, an intimacy, a joining. This much, he could allow himself. He closed his eyes, kissing her back. Just this, no more. She breathed in against his lips.

"Stop it," she hissed, her mouth an inch from his.

He opened his eyes.

She looked furious, which confused him. *I'm fol-*

lowing the rules, I'm in control, I don't have to set you aside, not yet.

She pushed herself into him. Crazy to think it, but she was like a boxer before a match, intimidating an opponent, chest against chest, trying to back him into a corner. "Stop trying so hard not to kiss me while you're kissing me. You're telling *yourself* no, not me. You're not really kissing me the way you want to."

Her fierce confidence was a turn-on in itself. "If I kiss you the way I want to kiss you, it won't stop there. We'll want more. We'll start pushing clothes out of our way. It won't be enough, and we'll make love."

"Of course we will." She shoved against him, pressing bodies that were already together even more tightly together, breasts pressed to his chest, bare feet between boots. "You can't tell me you don't feel this, too."

He couldn't give in, couldn't back away. "I've got a body, you've got a body—if there's anything a body wants, it's to feel the heat of someone else. Bare skin against bare skin soothes a need." He shifted his stance and pulled her to stand with his thigh pressing between hers. "A body against another body feels better than it can ever feel alone. It's warmer, it's safer, to be with somebody. But that's all it is, Delphinia. Skin wants to feel skin. That's all."

"It's more than that."

"More than sex? It's not."

"I've never wanted anyone the way I want you, and don't you dare say that you have ever, ever fought so hard to resist touching anyone as hard as you're fighting, right this second, to not touch me. You want to kiss me. Me. You want *my* body, my skin, I know it. You know it."

"It wouldn't change anything for me. But you—you'll believe you're in love with me. I seem to have that effect on women between the sheets."

She gasped at his arrogance.

Good. Let her recoil from him. "You'll imagine you're in love with a man who doesn't exist. If you really knew me, you'd be disappointed. You'd be *unhappy*. I don't want you to be unhappy. Ever."

"What am I going to find out that's supposed to horrify me? That you have a criminal record? That you had to fight while you were in prison? That you didn't graduate from high school? I know that already. I know you are that one-in-a-million person who didn't quit when life was unbearable. You won. You just don't realize it, not yet."

Her words evoked some new, unfamiliar emotion, pushing him to the edge of somewhere he hadn't gone before. *Danger. Pay attention.*

"I didn't know you back then, Connor."

"Exactly."

"Think about that. Everything you experienced in prison was already a part of you before I met you. I only know who you are now. I keep seeking you out, because I want to be with the man you are now. I feel happier when I'm with you." In his arms, she softened. The fight was over, or so she believed. "If you take me to bed, it won't make me fall in love with you. I'm already there."

Good *God*—he kissed her. He kissed her hard, up

against the door, like he owned her and her love, like her body was meant for his. She loved him. She'd said it first. *Before* they had sex, not after—but there were rules to the game.

He didn't break rules. If a girl thought she was in love with him before they slept together, then he didn't sleep with her. He wouldn't take advantage of her heart, wouldn't leverage her emotions to get sex. But this was *Delphinia*. His Rembrandt, who had one hand buried in his hair and one hand on his backside, pulling him into her body.

Selfishness overwhelmed him. Who cared that she was naive, what did it matter that she'd end up worse for knowing him?

As he was drowning, losing the will to battle this burning need to carry her to his bed, he slammed his hand against the wall, seeking the jagged edge of his truck keys.

He pressed them into her hand. "Take my truck. Keep it as long as you need it."

He held her against him, shuffled a step back to make room as he opened the door, then he pushed her through, shut it, and saved her.

"Dr. Dee? Hey, hi. Wait up."

Delphinia turned away from the etched-glass door as Bridget came toward her at a jog.

"The pub's closed on Mondays."

"I know."

What could she say? She'd kept Connor's truck parked—hidden—in the detached garage at Dumas

House all weekend, waiting for him to come and get it, to come and see her.

He hadn't come. He'd rather lose his truck than see her again.

I'm here to salvage my pride. I have his car keys and A Mate with Destiny *in this little bag. I'm going to slam them down on the bar dramatically and leave.*

"I came to speak to Connor about…about using his pub for my class. The history of the place is…historic." So much for her professorial vocabulary.

"He's not here. I came to get a ride to see Uncle Murphy, but his truck is gone."

"I just brought it back. He loaned it to me."

"Seriously? So, could you give me a ride to Uncle Murphy's place? It's, like, only halfway to BCC. Kristopher's meeting me there. He's going to read *Othello* with me, since my new professor already gave an assignment on it, and it's due Wednesday."

Bridget said this with a Connor-like, charming wink. Delphinia had walked into the BCC Shakespeare class on Saturday morning to find that Bridget was her student once more.

"Besides, if you want to know the history of the pub, my uncle knows everything. You'd make his day. Please?"

Connor wasn't here. Delphinia would have to wait to do her pride-salvaging thing. In the meantime, she could meet the man who saw Connor the way she saw him. *You sound like Mr. Murphy,* Connor had said under the stars.

"Sure, I'll give you a ride."

* * *

"Shoot. I left *Othello* in the truck. I'll be right back."

Bridget abandoned Delphinia in the pastel hallway of the assisted living facility, not five steps from Mr. Murphy's door. It was open. At least half the apartment doors were open down the hall, as if the apartments were front porches and the hallway was Main Street.

From Mr. Murphy's door, Delphinia heard an unexpected voice. Connor was here, and he was reading *Shakespeare*, and oh—he read with all the right inflection.

"I did tell her the story of my life, from year to year, even from my boyish days. I spoke of most disastrous chances."

Othello, act one, scene three. Connor had once been charmed by her bar trick.

"Her tears, when I did speak of some distressful stroke that my youth suffered…"

Othello, an outsider, had eloped with a nobleman's daughter. Her father claimed she'd been kidnapped. The authorities demanded that Othello explain how it was possible for his sweet, sheltered wife to have fallen in love with a man as battle-hardened as he was. "She loved me for the dangers I had passed, and I loved her, that she did pity them."

"I don't get it." That sounded like Kristopher. "She fell in love with him because he told her how hard his life had been when he was younger?"

"It could be wiser," a man said in an Irish brogue, "to say she loved him because he was a strong, good man despite those hardships, or so I'd be thinking."

Delphinia peeked around the wooden door just far enough to see the man who had to be Mr. Murphy—either a large leprechaun or a small Santa—giving Connor an arch look as he spoke.

Connor. Her heart sped up at the sight of him. So handsome. So…grim. He shut his book.

Kristopher wasn't visible at this angle, but his voice was all smiles. "I'll sound very wise when I help Bridget with her essay."

"Ha. I heard that." Bridget whooshed right past Delphinia. "Hi, everybody. I brought someone to meet you, Uncle Murphy. Where is she?" Bridget spun around and came back out to the hallway. "Come in, come in."

Delphinia had no choice. Cheeks flaming but chin high, she walked into the little studio apartment.

Connor dropped his book.

Bridget made introductions.

"Professor Ray? Ah, my dear, I think you have the look of your parents about you. You must be the daughter of Rhea Ray. Hard to forget such a name, and your father's name? It's slipping my mind."

"Archibald. They remember you, too, Mr. Murphy. Very happy memories."

"You must call me Seamus."

Bridget got a little indignant at that. "Nobody calls you anything but Murphy. I don't even call you Uncle Seamus."

"But not only is Delphinia Ray a beautiful woman, she's a beautiful woman I'm no relation to and one who never worked for me, nor sat at my bar as my customer. We're fresh friends, she and I, and I'd be pleased to have her call me Seamus." He said everything with such a genuine joy and a twinkle in his eye, it was impossible not to feel like a welcome guest in his home.

"I see where Connor gets his charm."

"Well, now." Mr. Murphy gave her hand an extra squeeze and sat back, beaming at her with such approval, Delphinia knew she'd said the right thing.

She looked to Connor, a reflex to share a smile, but he stood at the window, looking out to somewhere far, far away from them all.

As Mr. Murphy told her a few stories about the pub, she caught Kristopher and Bridget sneaking glances at one another. The course of their true love was running smoothly. Delphinia was glad, not green with envy. Not too green.

"Anyway," Bridget said, struggling to look unaffected instead of giddy, "the essay question is 'Who defeated Othello?'"

"Iago." Kristopher sounded certain. "That's the guy who told all the lies and convinced Othello his wife didn't love him. Easy."

"Dr. Dee warned us that 'Iago' wasn't the right answer."

"She's a tough one, that Dr. Dee." Kristopher took Bridget's hand. "Let's go figure it out over a burger."

That was Delphinia's cue to leave, too, but she had Connor's truck.

He remained by the window. She'd made him uncomfortable in his own family.

I don't want you to be unhappy. Ever. When he'd said that, his voice had been rough with emotion, sincere.

She felt the same way toward him. Her will to make any kind of dramatic farewell gesture drained away. "I came here in your truck. Do you want to drive it back?"

"I've got my bike."

"He worked hard to save up for that motorcycle," Mr. Murphy said. "Learned how to do all the maintenance himself, from a book."

Delphinia handed the little bag to Connor. "This is the book I promised you. I'll park your truck in your spot and leave the keys under the floor mat."

And with that, there was no unfinished business between them.

"Goodbye," she said, more to Connor than to Mr. Murphy.

She closed the door behind herself.

Connor went straight for the whiskey and poured two glasses. He barely murmured *"Slainte"* before taking a drink.

"Never have I seen you so at a loss to know where to look or what to say. It's a wonder she described you as charming. You must have made a different impression on her somewhere else."

Connor took a seat. He knew Mr. Murphy had figured everything out.

"But I was more interested in how she looked at you. There's something there, Connor. There's something there."

"I'm leaving it alone. She'd only become another memory. They're all memories."

"I wish I had one like her in my memories. I should have stopped and smelled the roses."

A rose by any other name... Connor set his glass aside. Nothing was right, not even the whiskey.

Mr. Murphy grew somber. "I regret that I never took the time to tend just one rose. It might not have amounted to anything more than a memory, but it might have grown into a whole garden, me and my rose, and a bunch of little roses, besides. I'll never know. A memory would be better than a regret that there is no memory. Regrets are heavy. You can only carry a few, mark my words."

Connor's heart hurt for someone besides himself. "I didn't know you'd wanted a wife and kids. I'm sorry."

"It was my choice not to look for a wife. Don't feel too sorry for me, because I was graced with a son nevertheless, or my father never called me Seamus Murphy."

Connor felt the hair on the back of his neck stand up. "You've never mentioned a child, not once. You have a son?"

"I do, and I call him Connor McClaine. He's carrying on the family business. He takes good care of me in my old age, good care of my grandniece, too. I could not be more proud of him. He's as fine a man as ever walked this green earth."

God. *God.* Connor pinched the bridge of his nose in his fingers, closed his eyes, tried to breathe and not to cry.

"He broke his old da's heart, though, by thinking he wasn't good enough to serve on the council of his own city. Now, my heart is breaking anew, because he thinks he isn't good enough for a woman who looks at him the way he deserves to be looked at. He's letting his past take away his future."

Connor opened his eyes and saw, truly, that there was love for him in his wiser, older friend's face. Not affection, but love. He hadn't let himself see it before. He hadn't let himself see it anywhere, but on a rooftop with Delphinia, he'd had nowhere else to look, no way to pretend he wasn't seeing the truth. She loved him; he was lovable.

Now that he knew it was possible, it was as clear as day that Mr. Murphy loved him. Hell—Hurricane Bridget loved him. And Delphinia...

"Tell her, lad. She looks at you like you hung the moon and the stars. Tell her, and see how she looks at you then."

"I did. I told her everything." *But not that I loved her, too.*

"Well, now." Mr. Murphy spoke more sternly than he ever had. "If you already told her about your past, and she's still looking at you like that, then the devil will laugh for all eternity if you let her become a memory."

Connor did not shake Mr. Murphy's hand before he left. Instead, he pressed his forehead to his friend's and cupped that white-haired head against his a bit harder than he'd intended, a bit longer. "I'll be back Monday."

"I know you will, son. I know you will."

Chapter Twenty-Two

"Don't you look... Isn't that a casual look for you, dear?"

Her parents stood in the kitchen where Delphinia sat, forcing herself to eat a sandwich, forcing herself to read the Shakespeare essays her students had turned in yesterday. Jeans and her burgundy sweater, the one she'd worn the day of the accident, fit her state of mind.

Who defeated Othello? No one had gotten it right yet.

Delphinia flipped the page over. The next essay in the stack was handwritten. Her rubric had specified that the assignment had to be typed. She picked up her red pen and wrote across the top of the paper: *wrong format,-5 points.*

"I thought you might still be dressed nicely after work," her mother said, "at least for dinner."

"There's nothing scheduled." Delphinia waved her red pen toward the wall calendar as she began to read.

The only person who didn't love Othello was Othello.

A bold opening. Delphinia turned the paper over, but there was no name on it, anywhere. The handwriting looked masculine. That didn't narrow it down much.

"I'd like to see one of the new dresses you bought in Austin," her mother said. "Why don't you run upstairs and put one on now?"

Othello testified to the noblemen that his wife fell in love with him after he told her about the ugly hardships he'd survived. He was wrong. She'd already fallen in love with him before then, and he with her. They'd noticed one another from the first, and time after time, she'd returned to him, seeking him out for the pleasure of his company. It was only then that he gave her the details of his youth. If she hadn't already loved the man he was, she would not have cared about the story of the boy he had been. If he had not already loved her, he would not have shared it.

"Your mother is speaking to you." Her father sounded displeased.

"Uh-huh." *Seeking him out?* Hadn't she said those words on a rooftop, seven long days ago?

Othello told the authorities that she loved him because she pitied him, but he was wrong there, too. He expected her pity and even her disgust, so he was unprepared to hear anything else about his youth. When she told him he'd mastered a superhuman task in a dangerous environment, he did not believe her. When she told him he was the one-in-a-million person to beat the odds, he did not believe her.

Connor—oh, Connor—was this—? She flipped the paper over again. It had to be his writing. It must be. Had Bridget picked it up by accident? Had he slipped it into Bridget's papers on purpose?

Iago did the manipulating, the planting of seeds of doubt, but it was Othello who chose to believe them. Othello agreed that it was impossible for his wife to love him, because he refused to believe he was good enough to be loved by her. Who defeated Othello? He defeated himself.

Delphinia clutched a fistful of her sweater. Connor knew…everything. The essay brimmed with hard-won wisdom and obvious regret, but there was no glimmer of hope in it. *Othello* did not end happily ever after. This essay was a dissection of a relationship that was dead. Othello's, or theirs?

"Delphinia Acanthia Beatrix." Her father's angry recitation of her name dimly registered. "People will be stopping by this evening."

"Archibald, not another word."

That got Delphinia's attention. "Another word about what? Please tell me 'people' does not include Vincent Talbot."

Her parents exchanged a worried look.

Delphinia came to her feet. "I don't want him in my house."

"Your house?" Her father let those two words hang in the air.

"I don't want to be in any room in any house with

him. When we broke up, it got physical. He grabbed my wrist and tried to pull me back down. I told you all of this." Her parents had said they were sorry to hear it. She'd thought that was the end of it.

"He wanted you to sit down and talk about it," her father said. "He's a lawyer. Talking is what they do."

"Why don't you believe me?"

"Oh, Delphinia," her mother said. "I do believe he grabbed your wrist, but he couldn't have *meant* to grab too hard. He loves you."

"He does not."

"Then it is up to him to prove to you that he does." Her father had never sounded more decisive. "Give him the chance to do so. If you had a diamond ring on your finger, you'd feel secure about his feelings toward you. You could move on from this misunderstanding and start planning your lives together."

That was the life her parents thought she was destined for.

She was going to take her destiny into her own hands, although those hands shook as she folded up the essay and slipped it into her back pocket. If Vincent was welcome to come in this evening, then she would go out.

Delphinia walked into the Tipsy Musketeer.

Spring break was over, so the Thursday night crowd was large. The cowboy was singing on the stage. The servers with their bouquets of mugs wove their way around the tables. All the snugs were full, overflowing, loud with laughter.

Delphinia had walked straight here, obsessing over the essay in her back pocket with every step. Had it been intended for her eyes? Maybe Connor had been keeping Bridget company so she'd study, and he'd dashed off his own essay as she'd worked on hers, and Bridget had accidentally scooped his up with her papers.

The paperback heroine would boldly ask. But surely, if Connor had wanted Delphinia to read his essay, he would have put his name on it. And if he had never intended for her to read it, then the kindest thing would be to pretend she hadn't seen it. So, maybe she shouldn't ask him.

Her inner wolf paced one way, then the other. Delphinia doggedly worked her way through the crowd toward seat one.

Someone was sitting on her barstool. Someone beautiful, someone who had the confidence to call attention to herself in a short, sequined dress. Someone who was laughing with Connor.

The essay in Delphinia's pocket might be brimming with hard-won wisdom, remorse and regrets, but its author was having a chitchat with a hot chick.

"It hasn't been that many years since you took your diploma and left," Delphinia heard Connor say in an amused tone. "You don't need me to be a tour guide."

"I'm back through the weekend." The woman reached over the mahogany to brush an imaginary spec off his cheek with her fingers. "Three whole nights. That's three whole nights we could spend reminiscing about—"

"Excuse me." Delphinia forced her way in between

the women in seats one and two. She slapped her palm on the bar. "I'd like a drink."

"Hello, Rembrandt." Her heart contracted at the name, at the warmth in Connor's voice as he said it. "It's good to see you."

"Yes," she said. "It's been three whole nights."

The woman in sequins looked at her sharply. Connor bit his cheek as he turned away to take Delphinia's favorite whiskey down from the top shelf.

She remained standing between the two women in their chairs. There wasn't an open seat all the way down the bar. Laughter came from inside the VIP booth, drifting over the open top. There was nowhere private to go.

What could she say to Connor in the middle of his workday? She couldn't unfold the essay, smooth it out on the bar in between these two women, and ask him if he'd intended for her to see it, ask him if it meant goodbye, forever.

He rolled the ball of ice around the glass once before setting it in front of her. "I wish I could join you."

"I do, too." Were they speaking in code? Did he mean he wished he could join her in living the rest of her life, but he wasn't good enough to? Or did he mean he wished he could join her, but the bar was slammed, and it would hurt his employees if he disappeared right this second to take her upstairs to his bed?

There could be more moderate options, she supposed, but professors of Shakespeare didn't think in moderation, and that's what she was. To heck with EN313. She wasn't going to teach it next year.

The woman in sequins folded her arms on the bar

and leaned in, all cozy and all cleavage. "So, Connor, tell me all about—"

"Have you read any good books, Connor? Because I've read some interesting things. Today. At work." Delphinia hoped he understood her code. If he didn't, then he had no idea his essay had erroneously made its way into Bridget's papers.

"Excuse me. Do I know you?" The woman's tone meant *Get out of my space.*

"I don't know. Do you?" Delphinia had never sounded more like a teenager.

Connor rubbed his jaw. Delphinia narrowed her eyes at him. He did that when he was trying not to laugh.

The woman in seat two said, "Can I get a glass of white for my friend?" More people wedged themselves around the barstools.

The sequined woman slid a hotel room key across the bar toward Connor. "You're busy now. Why don't you find me later, and we'll dust off a few memories? Freshen them up."

Connor picked up the key and handed it back to her with a smile that was kind. Only kind. "Those memories are good where they are, but I'm glad to hear you're doing well in Dallas. The drink's on me. It was nice of you to stop by."

You are dismissed.

She took one more sip of her drink, pretended she'd just that second decided to go somewhere else, then squeezed past Delphinia without making eye contact.

Delphinia took the barstool before any of the other people got the chance. Connor handed Seat Two the white wine, then tossed the sequined woman's drink in the sink. It was very busy, and he'd stayed at this end of the bar too long already, but he stood directly across from Delphinia and braced his arms on the mahogany, anchoring himself in place, giving her his full attention.

"Since you asked, I read an interesting book about destiny, three whole nights ago. It had a lot of kissing in it. And wolves."

He'd read her book. It was enough to make her melt.

She picked up her glass and looked at the shades of brown. "Kissing? It had sex."

Seat Two got involved. "Sounds like a good book."

"More than sex," Connor said to Delphinia, a serious statement—followed by his most charming wink. "But the sex was pretty good."

Delphinia took a sip of her whiskey. Emotions were hard to talk about in code. Sex was easy. She let her gaze drop to his shoulders. "Some of those positions would require the man to have a significant amount of upper-body strength."

Connor dropped his head as he laughed. "Ah, Rembrandt. I'm glad you came back."

I seek you out. I'm not alone when I'm with you.

"Did you like the ending?" Delphinia asked. "Together forever. It was hopeful."

"It was unrealistic."

Her heart sank.

Another woman called to Connor from behind Delphinia. "The usual, but only a single. We're going to be drinking champagne shortly. So exciting."

Delphinia recognized the voice of Ruby, Dr. Marsden's assistant. She masked her impatience as best she could and turned in her seat to greet her.

"Dr. Ray! You're here. I didn't see you. I, uh..." Ruby grabbed her drink the second Connor set it down. "Okay, bye."

Delphinia turned back to Connor before he could move on to the next customer. "If it had ended with him choosing to never see her again, even if he thought it was for her own good, *that* would have been unrealistic. He couldn't live without her."

Connor shook off her words. "He was lucky she ever spoke to him again after the way he refused to listen to her."

He served a few more drinks to other people, all friendliness and charm, but his gaze kept returning to something behind Delphinia.

She turned to see the new sheriff standing near the stage. *The sheriff reminded me tonight just how easy it is to call me up in a database.* It made her anxious. It must be worse for Connor.

"It's okay," Connor said to her quietly. Reassuringly. "You don't have to worry about me."

He'd said that last Thursday, too, right before he'd demolished Vincent's scheme. It was downright sexy, the way he did that alpha-male pack-leader thing.

She sighed. "The heroine wanted him just as much as he wanted her, you know. Isn't happily-ever-after a better ending?"

"Better than *Romeo and Juliet*?"

"No. Better than *Othello*."

He stilled.

Her heart beat madly.

He leaned in, close. "When you said you read something interesting at work—"

Kristopher interrupted. "I need the storage room keys. Sorry, but this guy didn't call ahead. He wants a dozen bottles of champagne."

Connor handed him his keys. "Don't uncork anything until I make sure he's aware how much that will cost."

Connor had a business to run. Delphinia needed to be brave and tell him she'd read his essay, and hope he'd agree to meet her after the pub closed. If Seat Two enjoyed the show, so be it. She pulled the folded paper out of her pocket as the crowd chanted, "So good, so good, so good."

But Connor was frowning at the stage behind her. "I need to check on something. People have been coming in the main door and going straight into that first snug for the last ten minutes. Can you stay?"

"Of course." She folded the paper quickly, but he looked back to her just before she stuffed it into her pocket.

"That paper. Is that—? *Rembrandt.* Let me explain. Bridget said they would be read in class this Saturday. I planned to be there. I was going to… Your parents?"

"What?"

"Ladies and gentlemen," the cowboy singer said into the microphone. "Is there a Delphinia Ray in the house? Let's bring her up here, folks. A round of applause."

Her mother and father materialized by her side. Delphinia could not have been more shocked.

Her mother gave her a peck on the cheek, her father put his arm around her, and the crowd closed in as her parents walked her up the stage's single step. The cowboy with the guitar was grinning.

"I don't sing," she said to him urgently.

"You don't have to, ma'am." The cowboy stepped aside, and Vincent took his place and his microphone.

Delphinia thought she might be sick. She wanted to run, but her parents were there, Ruby behind them— and Dr. Marsden?

Delphinia focused on the faces closest to the stage. Dear God, so many of her colleagues were here, half of the English department. One of the city council members from the bridge meeting—no, two—and the *shark* couple were here. Joe Manzetti? She barely knew him— but Vincent wanted to repair his reputation with him. With all of them.

She turned back to Vincent to implore him under her breath. "Don't do this. Please."

Vincent spoke into the microphone. "Ladies and gentlemen, I need your help. Not long ago, right here in this pub, I lost the love of my life."

The crowd murmured in sympathy. Vincent waved away their pity.

"No. I deserved to lose her. I'd spent the evening…" He shook his head like a sad puppy dog. "I'd spent *months* taking her for granted."

He reached for her hand, but she put it behind herself.

He played it off by gesturing to her like she was a new car being given away as a prize. "You can see how beautiful she is, but I'm here to tell you that her heart is beautiful, too. She's devoted to her students. Her family. Everyone who has met her loves her, and I'm no exception. I will never take her for granted again."

"Thank you. That was nice. Good night." Delphinia turned to go, but Vincent made a grab for her hand and caught it this time. The sharks were smirking. Ruby had her hands poised to applaud. Delphinia desperately whispered to Vincent one more time. "Don't. Please."

"This is where I need your help, ladies and gentlemen. I need to impose on your evening so I can make a public apology, so she'll know I'm a changed man. I don't deserve her, but she deserves this." He pulled out a velvet ring box.

The crowd *oohed* and *aahed*. There was a smattering of applause from people who just couldn't wait to cheer.

Vincent dropped to his knee, ring box in one hand, microphone in the other. "Delphinia Acanthia Beatrix Ray, will you marry me?"

Chapter Twenty-Three

There was such a thing as destiny, after all.

Delphinia hadn't been able to escape this proposal, no matter how hard she'd tried. Vincent pointed the microphone toward her, so the crowd wouldn't miss his moment of victory.

"I'm sorry," she said. "But no."

Vincent turned white with shock. Close to the stage, everyone she knew stared at her in silence, appalled, even horrified. *How could she do that to him?*

But beyond them, the crowd began to boo, all the way back to the table by the window. From the loft above, the jeers of disappointment and disapproval rained down on her.

Her parents' faces were the most heartbreaking of all.

Their daughter, their pride and joy, was being booed. They were devastated.

Vincent came to his feet. The private look he sent her was pure, unadulterated hate, before he turned back to the crowd. A hundred people, friends and strangers, were packed tightly around the stage. Delphinia had no way to get off it.

Don't panic. She looked for Connor behind the bar. He was walking away from seat one, but she knew, she *knew*, he was coming out from behind the bar to get her off this awful stage himself.

The boos died out swiftly as the sheriff walked onto the stage from Vincent's end. He nodded at Vincent impatiently, then stood on Delphinia's other side, sandwiching her between them.

Vincent raised the microphone once more and placed his hand and his ring box over his heart. "Please, everyone. No booing. Forgive her. She's shy. I should have known she'd be scared."

Liar.

"It's one more thing I vow to be more sensitive to from now on."

Liar.

"Sheriff, if you'd be so kind to clear the way, I think Delphinia and I need to go somewhere quiet, just the two of us."

He set down the mic, then took her arm with a tender smile and a bruising grip.

Delphinia knew it would be easier just to go along, so she went—but only because it allowed her to get off the stage. The moment the sheriff got them down, she shoved Vincent away.

His arm was around her shoulders; he barely budged.

"I'm not going anywhere with you, Vincent. This is over."

His concerned, loving look remained constant for the public. His murmured words were for her ears alone. "Walk with me around that corner, until we're out of sight of this crowd, and then I'll let you go. It will be less embarrassing for me."

"No. Let go."

"You owe me this. Now walk."

She was pinned to him by his arm, penned in with him by the crowd around them and the sheriff's wide, uniformed back in front of them. Still, she raised her chin. "Make me."

Vincent smiled.

Where did that ass think he was going to go with Delphinia?

Connor stopped halfway down the bar and backed up to the antique mirrors, so he could see which direction they were heading. The sheriff was easy to spot in the crowd. He was making his way toward the employees-only hallway, as if he had the right to go anywhere he liked in Connor's building. Vincent was following him, keeping Delphinia tight against his side.

At first glance, it looked like Vincent had a protective hand on her upper back to guide her along, but her long hair covered his hand, and the angle of his arm didn't look right. Hidden by Rembrandt's brown hair,

Vincent had to be forcing her along with his hand on the back of her neck.

Delphinia started to look Connor's way, but she had turned only a fraction of an inch when she abruptly faced front again—but Connor had seen it, that distinct motion of someone's head being jerked by the hair. Vincent was steering her by pulling her hair, goddammit—couldn't they see?—the crowd was blind—

"Move." With one sweep of his arm, Connor pulled the glassware on the bar toward himself, letting it all crash onto the floor on his side, which was all the warning his guests got to get off their barstools and out of his way. He vaulted over the bar, boots pushing off the mahogany, and was within arm's reach of Delphinia before the customers' shouts and screams added to the sound of shattering glass. He had Vincent's arm in his grip before the music stopped. "Let her go."

Vincent tried to jerk his arm out of Connor's grip, which pulled Delphinia's hair and pulled a yelp of pain from her, *goddammit*.

Connor slid his hand up to Vincent's wrist, trying to avoid catching Delphinia's hair himself. A hair-pull was one of the hardest, most painful grips to break. After his hospitalization in prison, Connor had gotten a buzz cut.

Vincent formed a tighter fist in her hair. Everyone around them was shouting—Delphinia was so clearly trying to hold her head perfectly still—and people could finally see what was really happening. They pointed, they yelled at Vincent, at the sheriff, who didn't move to help.

Of course.

Vincent was a cornered animal, irrational as the crowd turned against him, snarling at Connor. "If you pull my wrist away, I'll take a fistful of her hair with me."

Talking with enemies only worked in movies, not in prison, and not when Delphinia was being hurt.

Vincent kept talking. "There's nothing you can do without getting her hurt. Now back the hell up."

Connor tightened his grip on the man's wrist with one hand and landed a single blow with the other, an uppercut to Vincent's chin that knocked his head back and knocked him out. Vincent went as limp as a dishrag, but Connor held him up by the wrist until Vincent's fingers went slack, releasing Delphinia's hair.

Then he dropped Vincent on the floor where he belonged and swept Delphinia into his arms, where she belonged.

The sheriff stepped over Vincent.

"Connor McClaine, you are under arrest."

The flashing lights of the patrol cars illuminated the scene on the sidewalk.

The sheriff had made a big production of cuffing Connor's hands behind his back while Delphinia's parents held her and wept and apologized. At their feet, Vincent had come to. Nobody had jumped in to help Vincent sit up. Everybody had been more interested in following Connor and the sheriff out the main door. They were still filing out in a steady stream.

Connor leaned against the hood of the sheriff's car and watched. He caught Delphinia's eye as her mother continued to fuss over her. He could tell in a glance that Delphinia's heart was breaking for him, that she was certain he was living his worst nightmare.

He wasn't. The seconds it had taken to get to her while she was being hurt? Those had been far worse.

He'd dreaded these handcuffs for ten long years. Now he could shrug as he wore them, send a genuine smile to Delphinia to put her mind at ease, even wink at her. *I'm fine. Don't worry about me.*

He'd trashed his own bar. He was losing hundreds of dollars by the minute as customers poured out of the pub, thousands of dollars in the future weeks as the Tipsy Musketeer tried to entice them to come back. He'd given the sheriff the opening he'd been waiting for to advance his "tough on crime" agenda.

It didn't matter.

He'd scale a mountain for Delphinia if he had to, because he couldn't live without her. The devil could take everything else he owned—and take the sheriff to hell sideways, while he was at it.

Deputy Grayson arrived as backup, parking his patrol car headlight to headlight with the sheriff's car in front of the pub. While the sheriff and Vincent spoke, Grayson gestured for Connor to walk over to his patrol car, then turned him around and jerked his wrists up by the handcuffs.

"This is a load of bull," he said, as he fit his key into the lock and released one of the handcuffs.

Connor had to laugh. It should have been obvious to him all along: the deputies always spoke to Connor because they trusted him. This particular deputy had sided with him without question against the star foot-ball coach on this same patch of sidewalk.

Connor saw everything more clearly now. He'd been wearing dark sunglasses until Delphinia had come into his life and taken them off. His world was full of more brilliant colors than he'd ever guessed.

The sheriff was red-faced. "Cuff that man, Deputy Grayson, or I will charge you with 'failure to obey.' You know the policy."

"Sure do. You want all participants taken in when an assault takes place in an establishment that serves alcohol. I'm just waiting on you to do it." Grayson looked pointedly at Vincent. "All participants."

The sheriff had no choice, not with fifty witnesses standing on the sidewalk. Vincent's cut lip and un-doubtedly killer headache probably hurt him less than being handcuffed in front of Dr. Marsden and his col-leagues.

"Sorry about this." Grayson put the handcuffs back on Connor, but with his hands in front of his body this time, a far more comfortable way to be restrained. Con-nor could still reach out and grab something dangerous, or he could swing an object like a baseball bat with both hands, so being cuffed with his hands in front of him-self was a statement that the deputy didn't believe he was a threat—and the deputy was betting his life on it. Connor looked for Delphinia, to see if she understood.

He didn't have to look far. She came right up to his side and faced the sheriff across two yards of sidewalk.

"All the participants, Sheriff? Okay, then." Delphinia crossed her wrists and held them out, ready for her handcuffs. "I started it. I shoved Vincent the second we were off that stage. That's why he had to pull me by my hair to get me to follow you."

Damn.

"I'm already in love with you," Connor said. "You don't have to be so spectacular."

There were chuckles and murmurs in the crowd, a few *oohs* from satisfied romantics.

Ernie spoke for the other council members. "What kind of screwed-up policy is this? You're arresting victims, Sheriff?"

"No, I am not. There's an important difference between her and him." The sheriff spoke loudly for the whole crowd to hear. "My policies keep this town safe. McClaine is a repeat offender. He's a *convicted felon.*"

Funny how a crowd could fall so silent, Connor could hear the patrol car's red and blue lights clicking off and on.

"Convicted of *what*?" Manzetti stepped forward, skepticism evident in his tone.

"Joyriding," Delphinia announced. "He was in the back seat of a car that he didn't know was stolen. Ten years ago. Ten."

Fearless, she was. So unashamed of his past that it didn't occur to her to perhaps *not* announce it to half the town. Rembrandt was going to keep him on his toes for the rest of his life.

In the silence, Delphinia's mother came over and stood beside them. "He protected my daughter."

Delphinia's father clapped Connor on the shoulder and stood on his other side.

Manzetti strolled over to Connor, then turned to face the sheriff, too. "Seems safer over here."

"He's the best boss in the world." Gina came out of the crowd.

Kristopher intercepted Bridget as she came running up the sidewalk. He apologized to Connor. "She would have killed me if I hadn't texted her when Dr. Dee got called up on stage."

One by one, people came to stand beside Connor—then behind him, then all around Grayson's patrol car—person after person, until Vincent and the sheriff were left standing by his car, alone.

Everyone in the town of Masterson looked so damned beautiful in the flashing red and blue lights, Connor wished he could paint it to capture it forever.

"Who has a camera?" he asked no one in particular. "We'll go back inside for a proper toast, but someone should take a group photo first. Mr. Murphy will need to see this to believe it."

Everyone had a camera on their phone. In all the laughter as everyone took selfies in the flashing police lights in front of the Tipsy Musketeer, the fact that Connor was still in handcuffs got overlooked.

It didn't matter.

"Come here and kiss me." He reached for Delphinia with his bound wrists, hooking a finger through the belt loop of her jeans and giving her a tug. The crowd was loud, but Connor wouldn't have cared if everyone could hear what he wanted to say to his one and only Delphinia. "It's been a week since I was such a fool on the rooftop. I love you. I think I have from the moment

I first saw you reading your book. I should have told you I loved you when you kissed me in the hallway instead of letting you run out that door, and we should have spent the last two weeks in bed together."

She blinked at him. *"Oh."*

He tugged her even closer. She leaned into him, her body soft and sexy against the backs of his hands.

"You weren't a fool," she murmured for his ears only. "I read the most amazing essay that explained so much. It got a ninety-five-percent A."

"You *graded* it?"

"It would have been a perfect one hundred, but you lost five points because it was supposed to be typed. You say you never break the law, but you broke the school rules." She ran her hands up his arms, over his tattoos—both of them—and tilted his head down so her lips brushed his as she spoke. "But I don't mind. Maybe it's true that good girls love bad boys. I'm not sure if I'm all that good, and I don't believe you're bad, but I do know that I love you."

"Kiss me, Rembrandt. Let's start something good."

It was the best kiss of his life. Delphinia kissed him hard, up against the patrol car. She kissed him like she owned him and his love, because she did. She kissed him as the crowd cheered, and then everyone posed for the most epic group photo ever taken on Athos Avenue.

It made a fantastic first page in their wedding album.

* * * * *

*Look for the next book in the Masterson, Texas
miniseries on shelves June 2020!*

*And for more great opposites attract romances,
check out these other Harlequin Special Editions:*

Her Homecoming Wish
By Jo McNally

Reluctant Hometown Hero
By Heatherly Bell

The Wedding Truce
By Kerri Carpenter

*Availble now wherever Harlequin Special Edition
books and ebooks are sold!*

#2749 A PROMISE TO KEEP
Return to the Double C • by Allison Leigh
When Jed Dalloway started over, ranching a mountain plot for his recluse boss saved him. So when hometown girl April Reed offers a deal to develop the land, to protect his ailing mentor, Jed tells her no sale. But his heart doesn't get the message...

#2750 THE MAYOR'S SECRET FORTUNE
The Fortunes of Texas: Rambling Rose • by Judy Duarte
When Steven Fortune proposes to Ellie Hernandez, the mayor of Rambling Rose, no one is more surprised than Ellie herself. Until recently, Steven was practically her enemy! But his offer of a marriage of convenience arrives at her weakest moment. Can they pull off a united front?

#2751 THE BEST INTENTIONS
Welcome to Starlight • by Michelle Major
A string of bad choices led Kaitlin Carmody to a fresh start in a small town. But Finn Samuelson, her boss's stubborn son, is certain she is taking advantage of his father and ruining his family's bank. When attraction interferes, Finn must decide if Kaitlin is really a threat to his family or its salvation.

#2752 THE MARRIAGE RESCUE
The Stone Gap Inn • by Shirley Jump
When a lost pup reunites Grady Jackson with his high school crush, he doesn't expect to become engaged! Marriage wasn't in dog groomer Beth Cooper's immediate plans, either. But if showing off her brand-new fiancé makes her dying father happy, how can she say, "I don't"?

#2753 A BABY AFFAIR
The Parent Portal • by Tara Taylor Quinn
Amelia Grace has gone through hell, but she's finally ready to be a mom—all by herself. Still, she never expected her sperm donor to appear, let alone spark an attraction like Dr. Craig Harmon does. But can Amelia make room for another person in her already growing family?

#2754 THE RIGHT MOMENT
Wildfire Ridge • by Heatherly Bell
After Joanne Brant is left at the altar, Hudson Decker must convince his best friend that Mr. Right is standing right in front of her! He missed his chance back in the day, but Hudson is sure now is the right moment for their second chance. Except Joanne's done giving people the chance to break her heart.

"Don't look at me like that, April."

She raised her gaze to his. "Like what?"

His fingers tightened in her hair and her mouth ran dry.
She swallowed. Moistened her lips.

She wasn't sure if she moved first. Or if it was him.

But then his mouth was on hers and like everything
else about him, she felt engulfed by an inferno. Or maybe
the burning was coming from inside her.

There was no way to know.

No reason to care.

Her hands slid up the granite chest, behind his neck,
where his skin felt even hotter beneath her fingertips, and
slipped through his thick hair, which was not hot, but
instead felt cool and unexpectedly silky.

His arm around her tightened, his hand pressing her
closer while his kiss deepened. Consuming. Exhilarating.

Her head was whirling, sounds roaring.

It was only a kiss.

But she was melting.

She was flying.

And then she realized the sounds weren't just inside her head.

Someone was laying on a horn.

She jerked back, her gaze skittering over Jed's as they both turned to peer through the curtain of white light shining over them.

"Mind getting at least one of these vehicles out of the way?" The shout was male and obviously amused.

"Oh for cryin'—" She exhaled. "That's my uncle Matthew," she told Jed, pushing him away. "And I'm sorry to say, but we are probably never going to live this down."

Don't miss
A Promise to Keep *by Allison Leigh,*
available March 2020 wherever
Harlequin Special Edition books and ebooks are sold.

Harlequin.com

HSEEXP0220

Love Harlequin romance?

DISCOVER.

Be the first to find out about promotions,
news and exclusive content!

 Facebook.com/HarlequinBooks

Twitter.com/HarlequinBooks

 Instagram.com/HarlequinBooks

Pinterest.com/HarlequinBooks

ReaderService.com

EXPLORE.

Sign up for the Harlequin e-newsletter and
download a free book from any series at
TryHarlequin.com

CONNECT.

Join our Harlequin community to
share your thoughts and connect
with other romance readers!
Facebook.com/groups/HarlequinConnection